A Winter's Secrets

D.S. Broxson

J.L. Broxson

ISBN: 9781670194657

DEDICATION

For my daddy.

CONTENTS

ACKNOWLEDGMENTS

Thank you to Alison Imbriaco, whose editing talents were invaluable.

1 BUD AND ANNIE

Bud quietly closed the door behind him and made his way across the yard toward the thick woods that separated flatland from the river. As he moved through the brush, he settled his pack on his back more comfortably and thought about the trip ahead. He knew he shouldn't be going to get Annie, should just make the trip alone, but he didn't care right then. A man couldn't be expected to live by himself forever, and that's just what it felt like Caroline was forcing him to do. Yes, he felt forced. If he was a stronger man, maybe he wouldn't feel that way, but he wasn't, and a man can only take so much silence. It had been three years since Charlie died…and Caroline along with him. If not for Susan and Ellie, his two oldest girls—and Annie—he didn't know how they'd all have made it this far.

He came through the brush at the edge of the Wilson property and peered at the house. He didn't see her on the porch, but he was a bit early. The dawn was only beginning to break. He stayed where he was. As he waited there, crouched in the damp leaves in the gray morning, his mind drifted to when he first met her in the timber, years ago now. She'd come out to deliver her father's dinner, which he'd left at home, and she stayed to chat with them. He didn't take much notice of her then and only remarked later to her father that she was a real talkative little thing. Her father replied, laughing, "Yeah, she'd talk the hide off a mule." Bud didn't mind chatty people; if anything, he was grateful for them, because it meant he could talk less and get away with it. Over the last year he had come to enjoy Annie's chatter. It took his mind off everything else and reminded him what it was like in those days when Charlie was alive, when everything was alive, and Caroline was up and about and ready to talk to him after a long day in the woods.

Suddenly she was there, taking care to not let the porch door slam, and carrying her shoes in one hand. She smiled when she saw him and lithely stepped across the yard toward the edge of the woods where he waited. Bud stood and smiled, then took her hand as she approached, steadying her while she pulled her shoes on. Her dress was simple, like the dresses Caroline wore, but she was not shaped like Caroline. Where Caroline was tall and slender, Annie was soft and plump, not overweight but pleasant to look at, with warm brown eyes that sparkled when she laughed.

Still holding her hand, Bud turned to walk deeper into the woods, and she let him lead her silently as they made their way toward the river where the raft waited. That was where they would begin their journey to town to get the supplies his family needed to sustain themselves over the next few months. He and Annie had made this trip together several times over the past year, and her ability to gauge just how much sugar and flour to buy had proved invaluable to him when it came to maintaining a household. He couldn't fathom what he'd do without her. The first year without Caroline had been pure unadulterated chaos; there was no other word for it. Since Annie had come, he had found a way forward.

The relationship between Bud and Annie had only recently become physical, and he still struggled with it, cursed himself for it, but was unwilling to bring a stop to it. It was the only thing keeping him sane some days. As they reached the river, he dropped his pack to the sand and turned to kiss her. She smiled, said, "Good morning," and ran her hands through his hair. He put his arms around the small of her back and thought about the blanket he'd brought to keep her warm on the trip down the river. He guessed they could probably shake the sand out of it all right.

As Bud poled the raft downriver and guided it around stumps and submerged logs, Annie sat with her arms around her knees and watched the muscles in Bud's arms bulge and slacken as he maneuvered the pole. She certainly hadn't intended to become a...a *concubine* at the ripe old age of twenty-one. She hadn't intended to become involved with him at all, much less be a stand-in wife. But she had sort of fallen into it, and now she was stuck. Now she loved him, and now she loved his children. And now there was no way she'd leave him.

When she first started working for him, she thought him a statue, barely able to manage a word above a whisper and a nod in her general direction. She'd known him before, of course; she knew practically everyone in this town. She hadn't passed two words to him before he hired her to help out at home. When she had first seen that house…that kitchen… She looked at him now and thought what a difference the last year had made in the man, at least in her eyes. She knew people talked under their breath, knew they shot glances at her in the street. She knew her mama worried, knew her daddy looked at her too long at times, trying to read the answers in her face instead of daring to ask. And they didn't ask, merely watched nervously and judged silently, and she let them.

Bud was not aware of Annie watching him navigate the river, but was lost in his own thoughts, as usual. His gaze alternated between a gray sky shot through with the first pink and orange streaks of sunrise and its reflection in the water as he maneuvered the small raft with the flow of the river. His thoughts turned to the first time he made this trip alone, back when he was a nine-year-old boy with his daddy's scull and a couple of biscuits in a pail waiting for him when he got hungry. That was before he was sent away and before he knew what it meant to really be hungry. He'd piloted the scull down to the village at the behest of his father, who needed a sack of sugar to finish setting the whiskey at the still. Robert had not wanted to send Bud to town alone at that age, but he couldn't be away from the still while it was working. Bud had seen the struggle in his father's eyes as he wrestled with the decision to send him into town on his own.

As an adult Bud could better understand his father's dilemma. How could Robert help wondering if his son would have the sense to ask for the sugar without yapping about what it was for? Could he trust Bud on his own to make the purchase in Bart Golden's general store? Robert would have had no doubts about Bud's honesty, knowing he would spend the money he was sent with for its intended purpose. But could he trust him to not elaborate on the sugar's destination within earshot of the likely five or six regulars who could be counted on to be warming themselves by Golden's stove? Back then, Bud had a habit of talking to anything that would listen, including the cows in the pasture, about anything that came to mind. Robert had tried to impart to the boy that a bit of discretion in certain circumstances would be in his best interest. But he hadn't wanted to stanch the boy's knack for talking to folks; Lord knows, Robert didn't know how to do it himself. A man of virtually no words was Robert; merely a grunt or a nod was the most anybody was likely to get, or a one-word answer if it was a lucky day.

But he'd given Bud permission to go to town that day while he worked the still, with instructions to get the sugar from Golden's but not to stop and chat with any of the men he might see. If he was asked why he came alone for it, he was just to say that Pa was at home. Bud had never asked straight out why they didn't talk about the still; he knew it was there and knew his pa and his uncle worked it, but he didn't give it much thought beyond that. Especially when he was faced with the excitement of piloting the scull all the way into town by himself, who cared what it was for.

Just as he had then, Bud guided the raft along the river as it merged with the rougher waters of the larger Weaver River, although with considerably more skill now and a deft hand. Back then he'd practically wet himself making the curve, scared to death that he'd tip himself over and drown before he'd even gotten good and started. But he'd pulled it out then, getting better each time he went, and now it required no thought, his hands and feet moving of their own accord to the balance his body needed to guide the raft through the channel.

"How're the kids getting along?" Annie asked him, breaking his reverie.

"They're okay," he replied. "Tom and Mac are painting the barn today, and the girls are pickin' the beans, so they're busy. They'll be fine till we get back."

"How's Caroline?"

"The same," he said, not looking at her. It was something they talked about but not often, how Caroline was. It was awkward…the elephant in the room.

After Charlie died, Caroline had slowly and quietly shut down. Understandable at first, for no one had blamed her for not feeling like getting out of bed or not wanting to talk. But as time went on, she still wasn't recovering, and no amount of pleading or cajoling motivated her. She was too ill, she said, though the doctor had been numerous times and said there really was nothing wrong with her. "Humor her," he'd said in the beginning. "She's had quite a shock." But they'd all had quite a shock, and they'd all had to grieve. Yet the days still marched on, with timber to cut and mouths to feed, cows to milk and the garden to tend. Neighbors had come at first, helping with the children and bringing dishes and patting him on the shoulder and looking at him with sympathetic eyes. So much food, at first he despaired of eating it all, but then eventually the dinners stopped coming. Neighbors came by only once a week, then sporadically, and then not at all. As the months passed into seasons, he had hired Annie to come help with the children and the cooking and cleaning. She came from a large family herself, so she knew how to move things along, and she'd been a blessing. More than ten years his junior but capable, sensible, and cheerful in a house that needed waking up. The children had blossomed under her care, and Caroline had allowed it, barely noticing her presence, as she barely noticed anything.

They were coming around the last bend now, and the dock was in sight. She didn't need the blanket now; it was getting warmer, and she folded it and tucked it away. She pulled the list of essentials she'd made the day before out of her pocket. "I think I might need close to five dollars, Bud."

"All right, get what you need together, and I'll come by Mason's in about an hour to settle and help you with it." She was careful not to touch him, not to stand too close. They were in town now, and she felt all eyes were upon her even though no one was even looking in their direction. Milton was a growing town, and several stores were open already, with people going about their business. It had its own post office and a train station, and the streets were starting to get busy. The timber mill had built this town and continued to sustain it, the rivers providing the thoroughfare by which the town prospered. Bud docked the raft and pulled the rope tight. Mason's General (Bart Golden long since in his grave) was one of the largest establishments and carried just about everything. It was there that Annie headed, basket in hand. Bud headed to the timber office to see James Allen, the owner of the mill and the man to whom Bud sold the timber he cut and floated downriver.

"Morning, Bud," Allen said as Bud walked into the front office. Bud took off his hat and nodded.

"Allen," Bud replied. The two shook hands. Allen was nearing sixty now but was still a healthy, barrel-chested man, nearing six foot three and close to two hundred seventy-five pounds. He'd been a brawler in his younger days but always an affable chap who shook hands after he'd beaten his opponent, and he usually did beat them.

"What can I do ya for?" he asked.

"I've got about an acre almost ready," Bud said, "and I want to know what you're payin' right now."

"Well, I can pay about a dollar a log. Is that all right?"

"Dollar and a half?" Bud countered. He knew how to deal with Allen; he'd been doing it half his life.

"Dollar and a quarter's the best I can do."

Bud nodded. He'd hoped for a dollar and a quarter, and he'd known Allen wouldn't part with a penny if his life depended on it, and yet they still had to go through this charade every time Bud sold timber. "Yep, that'd be fine. Start sendin' 'em down day after tomorrow, all right?"

"Sure, just tag 'em and send 'em on," Allen said, pulling a bucket out from under the counter. "Blue for Bud," he said to himself, thunking the bucket on the counter and pulling over his notebook. A blue strip of cloth from the bucket would be tied around each log Bud sent down the river, and the boys on the dock would remove the cloth strips as the logs came to the mill. They would toss the strips in buckets, the girls would sort them, and later Allen would tally them and mark them in his notebook as Bud's. At the end of the timber run, Bud would come collect his payment. Together with what the garden brought in, what he got for the timber had been enough to clothe and shoe the kids and have a little left over to put by. He'd never be rich, not by a long shot, but as long as the timber and his body lasted, he would have an income.

Bud's father had given him eighty acres when he turned twenty-one, and he had pastured about a hundred head of cattle over the years since then. He still had a good number. But timber was where the money was right now, and his herd was bit thinner than he would like, so he'd cut about five acres of timber and sold it to Allen over the past few years. It had sustained him and Caroline for the most part and kept his father fed and out of his business. Bud's brothers Nick and Frank had each gotten fifty acres when they reached twenty, but Frank was just about worthless (as were his acres), and Bud avoided him if he could. It wasn't hard because Frank oscillated between the bar and home and rarely went anywhere else, so their paths seldom crossed.

"How's the family?" Allen inquired, looking up from his notebook when he finished his entry. "School's starting soon, an' we're getting a new master this year, I heard." Jennie Finch had been the school's teacher for the last few years, but she had married last spring, so she wouldn't be back.

"I heard someone from Fall's Church was takin' it on," Bud replied. That was all he knew and really all he cared to know, if he was honest.

"Millie's gonna be in her last year. Gonna sit for her exams in the spring, she says."

"She always was a smart one," Bud said, not really knowing what the exams were for or if Millie was smart or not; it seemed to be the thing to say, and Allen seemed inclined to chat this morning. Bud never had been good at small talk, once he got grown. His ability to talk to a post had vanished with his boyhood. He didn't waste words, and couldn't seem to get the hang of the ebb and flow of chatter that some other folks enjoyed. He didn't mind if others talked, but he didn't like to be held captive. And Allen could talk all day if he got going, so Bud thought it best to get a move on. "I'll be sending those logs down soon and be back in town next week. Sound all right?"

Allen shook Bud's hand. "Sounds fine," he said, a smirk starting to show. He caught it and busied himself with putting away the notebook as Bud turned to go and left the office. *Well, I think he might have used up his allotment on me*, he thought, hiding a smile as he walked from behind the counter and started out to the mill. The quiet but running joke among some of the men in town was that God had given the Braxtons only fifty words apiece when He made them, so they had to use them judiciously. Robert Braxton barely put two words together in public—at least when he was sober—and his boys, Bud, Nick, and Frank, had turned out to be just as closemouthed. It was impossible to carry on a conversation with any of them beyond the barest of facts. None of them were awkward, exactly, just silent, and they couldn't be prevailed upon to hold up their end of a discussion unless they were pointedly asked a question. Frank had turned out to be a drunk, but Bud was dependable enough, if taciturn. And the man had a pretty good head for numbers; Allen would give him that.

Bud walked back to Mason's General Store and found Annie looking through some bolts of cloth near the rear of the store.

"Hey. How'd it go at the mill?" she asked quietly as she noticed him come up the aisle.

"Fine," he replied. "Allen'll take the timber, and I'll come back next week. You almost done here?"

"Almost," she said, holding out some cloth from one of the bolts on the shelf. "Susan has outgrown most of her dresses, Bud. She's got to have some new ones for the winter. Bethy can wear the girls' old ones, but they all will need shoes this winter. They're in awful shape, and they can't be passed on anymore."

"All right. Buy the cloth for the dresses today, and next week when I collect from Allen, we'll bring the whole lot with us and see about shoes." The thought of bringing his brood to town made him physically tired, if not a little sick, and he sighed.

He made his way around her, letting his hand graze her bottom as he moved behind her in the aisle and started back up toward the counter at the front of the store. A little gasp escaped her, and she quickly turned to see if anyone was looking their way. "Bud!" she whispered, smiling. He didn't reply but kept walking to the counter where Alvin Mason stood counting buttons.

"Mason," Bud said, leaning his elbow against the counter. "Need to bring the young'uns in for some boots next week. Have you got some in for the winter?"

"Came in yesterday. What're you needin'?"

"The whole lot of 'em; the baby too. They keep on growin', and I cain't hardly keep up." He didn't elaborate, partly because he didn't have the words and partly because he had no idea what sizes the children wore and couldn't have guessed what to ask for. He was entirely and wholly out of his element. Bud wasn't an especially perceptive man when it came to certain subjects, and cloth and buttons were beyond his wheelhouse.

"I prob'ly got everything you need." Bud nodded and straightened up as Annie joined them at the counter. Alvin smiled at the young woman and took the bolt she placed on the counter. She was pretty, and Alvin didn't begrudge Bud his "help."

"How much you need, there, Miss Annie?"

"Three-and-a-half yards, if you don't mind, sir," Annie said, smiling back.

"Sure thing. Just lemme get Sarah." He turned to walk to the back room, but just then a sharp, thin woman came through the curtain and joined him behind the counter. "Good morning, Mr. Braxton," she said, her eyes completely ignoring Annie and settling directly on Bud. She apparently *did* begrudge Bud his help.

He hooked a thumb at Annie and said nothing. "Need three-and-a-half yards, if you don't mind, Miss Sarah," Annie said, her smile still broad but now undeniably fake. She wasn't stupid, and Sarah's disdain was nothing more than anything else she had encountered in town. Annie, however, was made of stronger stuff, and she could throw just as well as she caught.

"Sure," Sarah replied, accepting the bolt Annie pushed in her direction. "Anything else?" She continued to look at Bud while speaking to Annie. Bud looked pointedly at Annie and avoided Sarah's steel gaze altogether.

"Not for now," Annie said, not the least bit rankled that Sarah still ignored her. That was fine; she could play that game too. "I'll be out in a minute, Bud," she said to Bud, indicating that he should go, and Sarah would be forced to talk to her. Bud was visibly relieved.

"Yep." He tipped his head to Mason. "Mason." And with that he walked out to the raft to wait on Annie and think about the timber.

2 TOM FINDS A TREASURE

Tom kicked the small stones in his path as he dragged the stick in wavy lines behind him. Mac was such a pain. The two were twins but could not have been more different in temperament; where Thomas ran headlong into everything he did without a look back or a thought to consequence, Maclan was reticent and cautious, a yin to Tom's yang. Just that morning Tom had thought of the brilliant idea of hitching Benny the mule to the milk cart so they could have a bully chariot race. And they were having a great time too, right up until Mac got scared when the cart tipped over on top of Tom in the heat of the race and went running in a panic to tell his sister Ellie. Mac told Ellie *everything*. It wasn't his fault the tie broke and Benny kicked the cart over. Just for that, he wasn't going to get any of the pie Ellie was making for supper, and he knew Ellie meant it when she said it.

Well, maybe Susan would sneak him a piece later; she was usually good for that. Susan had a soft spot for her wild little brother; it was she who consoled him when one of his schemes ended badly or he was on the verge of getting switched. Although Mama hadn't switched him in years. She barely got out of bed these days, and she almost never yelled "Please don't kill yourself today!" as he ran out each morning. He wished she *would* yell. That would be something. Anything would be better than the silence that had descended upon the house since Charlie died.

Oh well. He knew where there were some pretty shells down by the bay. Maybe he'd go find some for Ellie and she'd let him have a piece of pie after all. He let the stick fall and took off at a run for the bay, the failed chariot race forgotten and only the next adventure on his mind.

He arrived at the edge of the bay and looked down the beach. The tide was out, which meant he'd be able to search more of the sand away from the felled trees and driftwood that littered the edge of the beach. He made his way down to the water, trousers rolled up to the knees, studiously scouring the sand. He picked up each shell that looked worthy of closer attention, discarding one shell for another more interesting, dismissing those that were not whole. Only a truly beautiful *complete* shell was going to get Ellie to forgive him this time. She was usually annoyed at his mischievous pranks but was not normally as angry as she'd been this morning, mostly because he'd used Benny in his misadventure, and Ellie's tender heart couldn't bear it when any creature was mistreated. Ellie was always bringing home or saving some little thing. It was this maternal nature that served them all so well since Mama wasn't able to get out of bed so much anymore. So it was partly the pie and partly his guilt over wounding her gentle soul that spurred Tom to find the perfect shell for her.

He had never been this far down the beach before; he supposed most people didn't venture this out on their visits to the bay. He couldn't even see back to where he'd come in. Here the downed trees and branches were plentiful, most likely the result of a hurricane years gone by. Usually if the children came to play and swim at the beach they didn't come this far down; with the branches and limbs strewn everywhere, it was too much work to get to the water. He climbed over the trunks and mangled branches, looking carefully at the sand in each little crevice. He didn't really think about the tide being out as he walked, so focused was he on the task at hand. He was mildly surprised to look up and find himself at the entrance to a small cove off the bay not visible to the less-discerning, casual beachgoer, who wouldn't have ventured this far down the beach, not being on a single-minded treasure hunt as Tom was. To get this far one had to climb over driftwood and detritus brought in from the sea, and most beachgoers were not as adventurous. He looked into the cove and saw there on the sand a white thing. As he came closer, he looked—could it be? A whole sand dollar? He'd never been able to find one yet that wasn't broken. The best he'd ever found was three-quarters of a sea biscuit. He found that on a similar shell-searching mission last year with Mac, when they'd been playing at pirates like the ones Mac found in the book Miss Finch had lent him to read. Mac himself had found a sand dollar on that hunt; none of them had ever found a whole one, but Mac had come closest with the one he found that day, just a little over a half and nearly as big as his hand. Even on the rare occasions they could get Sarah and Ellie to come with them, they didn't explore this far, and he knew if he was going to find anything, it was going to be here. He carefully made his way farther into the cove, the water lapping around his ankles as he bent over in studious concentration. No, the white thing wasn't a sand dollar, but he saw a conical shell with ragged edges and then a little coquina, perfectly formed and smooth in his fingers. He slipped it into his pocket and splashed a little farther into the cove, his eyes fixed on the sand beneath the waters before him.

His gaze shifted from the cove floor to the rocks near the wall and some slivers of driftwood that floated in the shallow waves. It was so dim there that he couldn't see exactly what it was. He looked behind him; he couldn't see the beach anymore, but he wasn't worried. He made his way to the rocks where the water was shin deep. He drew closer to inspect what appeared to be some canvas or sailing fabric that had washed up into the cove along with the driftwood. He picked up the edge of the cloth to see... But no, this wasn't canvas or a section of sail; it was just a bunch of torn rags, nothing they could use in the little fort that he and Mac had made in the woods to play in during the days they weren't needed in the field or the timber.

Tom turned the cloth over in his hand but then hurriedly dropped it as though stung. Horrified, he realized that the driftwood wasn't driftwood at all; it was... *bones. Bones.* In the darkened cove this far back, he had mistaken the tangle of rag and bone for driftwood, but he could now see that the jumbled mess was attached to an almost entirely intact rib cage and skull, and an arm bone that reached into a crevice between two rocks behind it and disappeared into the shallow depths of the water. His eyes moved across the rib cage and over the skull in horror, but his horror was mixed with fascination as he took in the enormity of what he was seeing. A skeleton, there in the cove! Near the bay and the beach he'd visited all his life and hidden from hundreds of beachgoers' shell hunts and moonlit beach strolls; children and young lovers had never ventured this far. How long had it been here? How many years had it sat alone, tethered to the rocks and hiding in the cove?

Tom crept closer to the skeleton, his amazement overcoming his initial revulsion at the spectacle. Crouching on his haunches, he reached as far he dared without getting too close to the tangle of rag and bone at his feet to put his fingers on the forehead of the skull. The bone was unyielding to his touch, as he suspected it would be, his knowledge limited as it was to the general structure of the thing as taught to him by the schoolmistress and the diagrams in the science book she showed him. He'd never actually seen a skeleton in person, although he knew one was inside him. He remembered being amazed when Miss Finch told him he had two hundred and six bones in his body; an unbelievable number, he'd thought at the time. Mac was the brain; Tom had barely the patience to sit through a school day, but he'd been fascinated with that discussion.

He looked to the left to where the arm ended in a seam between two rocks near the wall. He stood for a closer look, and the water was up to his knees, soaking his pants. Shells were forgotten as he drew near to the rocks and peered between them. The arm of the skeleton was stuck fast between the rocks, and he moved behind them, nearer to the wall, trying to get a better look. He heaved a rock out of the way, exposing a glimpse of the skeletal hand and a twinkle of something beneath a rock. He was careful not to touch the hand—that was just too much—as he reached beneath the water. He was completely soaked, and in the back of his mind, he knew Ellie would scold him, but he was focused on the treasure literally at hand. His fingers closed around the shiny things, and he brought them out of the water to eye level, falling back onto his bottom in water that was suddenly chest high. In his hand he clutched a silver necklace with a tiny silver cross and a silver circle with something writ on it, unremarkable in its simplicity but a true treasure nonetheless. And this, oh this, would get him out of hock with Ellie for not only that morning's failed chariot race but probably many more misguided ventures to come. And what he held was much better than any shell he could have ever found.

He glanced back at the skeleton and was dismayed at how the water covered the rib cage now and the tangle of rags and bone inched closer to the collarbone with every lapping wave. Suddenly he remembered the tide and knew he had to get out of the cove immediately or risk being this poor fellow's companion for years to come. He scrambled to his feet, clutching the necklace, and splashed back to the entrance of the cove, arms flailing for balance as he struggled to move in the water that was now nearly waist high. How could it have gotten so late? He reached the entrance to the cove and dove headlong into the waves, ignoring his clothes. Any thought of reprimand was gone from his panicked brain as he rounded the edge of the cove and fought the tide coming in. He kicked off the sandy bottom and lunged forward again, taking great strides with his arms as he strained to reduce the distance between himself and the shoreline. Grunting, he lunged again and again, arms outstretched. The panic began to abate as he gained his footing in water now only knee deep. He raised his knees almost to his chest as he tried to run through the water, arms pinwheeling to keep his balance as he gained the safety of the beach. He looked back at the entrance of the cove where he had been minutes before. Huffing and panting, he fell to the beach and sat a minute. The cove entrance was nearly submerged, almost invisible and surely unrecognizable to anyone who hadn't known it was there.

He turned to look down the beach where he had first come in, then looked down at the necklace in his fist as he walked toward the palm fronds and low brush at the bay's edge. He could spread his clothes on the sand there and dry them before he went home, and Ellie would never know he had gotten soaked to the skin. He would be completely dry before it was time to bring the cows back in from pasture, and no one would ever suspect him of any near-drowning experiences or "dare-deviltry," as Annie called it. He shucked out of his trousers and carefully spread them on the sand alongside his shirt as he sat on the beach sand, turning the necklace over and over in his hands and watching it twinkle in the sun.

3 A TRIP TO TOWN

"I'm takin' the children to town today. Annie's buyin' 'em all shoes. Won't be home 'fore dark. You'll have to see to yourself." It was a little more than a week since Bud and Annie's trip to town, and Bud had sent down all the timber he had. It was time to get paid up.

She rolled over to face the wall. "That's fine."

"There's biscuits on the stove if you feel like eatin', and there's coffee, but you'll have to heat it up again. Susan made it strong enough to stand on its own this mornin'."

He sat on the edge of the bed to pull his boots on. He didn't expect her to speak, she rarely had much to say anymore, but he was used to talking to the air, so he kept on. "John Miller'll bring in the cows this evenin' and do all the chores."

It was beyond his ability to understand what to do about Caroline now; she had gotten progressively worse over the last year. No amount of cajoling, pleading, yelling, commanding, or bargaining had moved her in the last year; it was out of sheer desperation that he'd engaged Annie when he had. He didn't know if she was lost to him forever, but he had no idea how to fix the situation. Nothing moved her, stoked her. Not the children, not the promise of a new dress, not a night away in town—even if they could have afforded any of it—he'd tried it all. It wasn't as if his efforts had even been rebuffed; he thought he might have been able to take that. No, it was almost as if his words, his pleadings, were *absorbed* somehow, as if they hit her and just fell into cotton, into the abyss of wherever she was now. It was like talking to an open hole in the ground; not even a dim thud marked his words landing. They just got lost on the journey. He hadn't given up, really, hadn't written her off, but he…he was just tired, that's all. Tired of trying and seeing nothing happen.

With his hands on his knees, he looked over his shoulder at the lump under the covers and sighed. "You want anything from town?"

"No."

"All right," he said and pushed himself off the bed. He took his billfold from the chest of drawers and tucked it into his pocket, then shuffled out of the room, shoulders bent, closing the curtain behind him.

It wasn't as if she *wanted* to feel like this. She'd give anything to feel normal again, to feel anything at all, even if it hurt. But this *nothing*, this emptiness of being—it just sapped everything out of her. She stared at the wooden wall before her. *I'd be perfectly happy to stare at this wall for the rest of my life*, she thought. And maybe she would, if Bud never came home to stop her. Not that he would be able to stop her, that is. It hurt her too, to know how much he wanted to be able to make a dent, make an impression. But how could he? She didn't know how to fix it herself, so how could she possibly explain to him what was so broken inside and what to do to help her? If she'd known how, she would have fixed it herself. And that guilt added to the oppressive nothingness as well, but in a numb, vague way and not in the way guilt might spark one to attention in a valiant effort to change. So she lay there, feeling the nothing, feeling the warm, heavy comfort of the blankets on her, and drifted off to sleep.

Annie was quiet on the trip to town. She was never exactly obnoxious about it, but she was usually a little more chatty than she was today, laughing and joking with the children or describing whatever chaos she'd just left at home. Annie was third oldest in a family of eleven children, and at twenty-one, she was the oldest still living at home. Most of the children were well past being old enough to care for themselves, and her mother was perfectly healthy, so it wasn't as if she was raising her sisters and brothers. But it was such a lively household that she was always regaling Bud and the children with stories of what had happened the day before or of what one of them had said. Just last week she told them about her sister Emma Belle, who refused to wear anything but coveralls and could not be made to wear shoes, even if the family could have afforded to buy them. Her family had tried to get her in shoes during the winters, but Emma Belle would have none of it.

As Annie told it, Emma Belle and her brother Howard had convinced their younger brother Carl to get in the hog pen and try to put salt on the hogs' tails. They'd assured him that by salting their curly backsides, the hogs would become docile, friendly little creatures and he'd be able to pet them and ride them just like Pa rode the red mare pastured in the next field. "And you're sure about this, that he'll let me saddle him and everything?" Carl had asked, with his eye on one large hog and his pockets full of salt from Ma's canister over the stove. At seven Carl was still a little too gullible to recognize the sparkle in Emma Belle's and Howard's eyes for what it really was, and besides, he was much more focused on the idea of riding a hog than he was on the glint in their eyes. How Emma Belle and Howard had howled with laughter at the sight of Carl scrambling out of the hogs' pen! Annie fairly fell over telling Bud and the children about how a hog's tusks tore at Carl's pants as he jumped onto the fence, caterwauling all the way. She had come running out of the house at the commotion and caught them at it, then punished Emma Belle and Howard by making them do Carl's chores for the next week. Secretly she thought Carl ought to have more sense at his age, but with both of them conspiring against him, she guessed he hadn't really ever had a chance.

But this day she was quiet in the wagon next to Bud, the children's chatter a dull roar behind her. She was thinking, preoccupied. Things were questionable right now. She wasn't sure, hesitant to say anything, but suspecting. She didn't know how he'd react, what he'd say. So she kept to herself and was silent on the way to town while he was lost in his own thoughts and the children jabbered away behind them.

"I don't know what they could be playing at, keeping house that way, right under her nose. I've a mind to set her straight, I do, and I don't care what she thinks of me," Mrs. Lundy carped to Mrs. Abraham, as they stood quietly murmuring by the dry goods, stealing furtive glances in Annie's direction. Annie wasn't completely blind to the gossip in town but neither was she terribly distracted by it. Worrying about what other people thought of her or her family had never been her strong point. So she wasn't really paying attention to what they said two aisles over, though she could hear the hushed voices – and even if she *had* heard, she would not have been hobbled by the good ladies' opinions.

"Mac, would you please just *stay still*," Annie pleaded, as she twisted the shoe to get it on his foot. "You could make this a little easier." Mac was having none of it because that shoe was a size too small. Tom was his equal in size and stature, but Mac's feet were a size bigger, and there was zero possibility of it fitting. "Oh, for Pete's sake," she said, as she realized the futility and threw the shoe to the side. "You could have said something." Seizing the correct shoe, she jammed it on his foot and pulled him to his feet. "Walk," she demanded, giving him a gentle push and sending him down the aisle. "How does it feel?"

"I like 'em," he said, coming back to her and staring down at his feet. "They're just like Pa's."

"Yes, and they'll fit you all next year if you'll stop growing so fast," she said. "There's a little room in there."

She gathered the shoes into a pile just as Bud came up the aisle. "We ready?" he asked, picking up some of the shoes from the floor.

"Yes," Annie responded, standing up. "Everybody's got their new ones, except Bethy." She bent down to pick up the remaining shoes and Bethy, who was just getting one of the smaller shoes to her mouth. *So close.* "Two of them were even on sale," she added.

He nodded and walked past her to the front of the store; Annie and the children followed him, eager to get their new shoes. They were like little bulls in a china shop, all eight of them: Susan, Ellie, Sarah, Tom, Mac, Dianna, Robert, and Bethy. She had to get them out of the store immediately, before they pulled the place down around them. "Suze, take them out to the wagon, and get 'em settled while we finish up here," she said, pulling Bethy's dress straight. Annie handed the little girl to Susan. "Yes, ma'am," Susan replied, and ushered the brood out the door before they could do any real damage. "Oh, I forgot one pair," Annie said, dropping the shoes on the counter and turning around. "Back in a minute." She fled back down the aisle, and Bud managed to tumble the shoes he was carrying onto the counter without dropping any. "Mason," he said, as the shopkeeper looked at him, smirking.

"You got 'em all?" he asked, picking up the shoes by tags to make sense of the jumble.

"Mm hmm," Bud mumbled, opening his billfold and taking a few bills out. He had been to see Allen and been paid for the timber, and Mason was going to get a good chunk of it. He watched Mason add up the shoes and write the prices down in his book. Children were Christly expensive, he had come to believe.

Annie got to the end of the aisle and bent down to get the last pair of shoes just as Mrs. Lundy and Mrs. Abraham came around the corner. "You ort to be ashamed of yourself, Anne Wilson," Mrs. Lundy said, puffing herself up to the fullest height of her four-foot-eleven frame. "'Tain't as if Mrs. Braxton's in her grave or anythin'. She's right there at home." Mrs. Abraham sniffed her agreement. "It's an absolute disgrace," she added, frowning at Annie. Their voices were quiet but stern; they were brave enough to confront her but not brave enough to have anyone overhear them.

Annie came up with a huff, raising an eyebrow at the two women. "Excuse me?" she asked, putting one hand on her hip.

"I seen you two, and you ain't foolin' nobody. Mrs. Braxton layin' up there in that bed, and you two goin' around town like you's married. 'S a damn disgrace, I say." Mrs. Lundy clicked her tongue and Mrs. Abraham mm-hmmed. Annie's eyes narrowed and she turned around.

"What I do is none of your business," she threw back over her shoulder, walking to the front. Bud looked at her warily as she flung herself toward the counter. "What's with you?" he asked under his breath. Her anger was making her face red and her eyes spark.

"I'm going outside." She thunked the shoes on the counter and stormed out the door, leaving Mason and Bud to look at each other. Bud sighed and Mason carried on with the purchase, neither of them saying a word.

She swung herself up on the wagon and scowled at Tom and Mac. "Sit still!"

The two boys exchanged a confused glance and sat down in the bed of the wagon, momentarily chastened. Neither of them said anything else, and the chatter in the wagon slackened to a dull roar as Bud came out of the general store, pulled himself up, gathered the reins, and clicked to the horses. He looked at Annie out of the corner of his eye but didn't say anything—her face was still all storm clouds—and the wagon lurched ahead as they headed for home.

4 MAY

Bud opened his eyes carefully and squinted against the sunshine streaming through the window. The boys would take care of the animals this morning, and there was nothing to be done in the field, no more timber to cut or send at the moment, so Bud found himself with the rare situation of having a few days with nothing pressing to do except fill a few jugs at the still. And maybe empty one or two. He was due; he was *allowed*, dammit. It was his own hard work that kept this family, and his father besides, in beans and flour. Ungrateful beast that Robert was. He'd never thank him for it, not if Bud filled a thousand jugs or plowed a thousand fields or sent a thousand logs downriver. But he'd drink the shine in those jugs and eat the cornbread made with the meal the timber bought. Bud didn't go to see his father anymore, but he knew Ellie and Sarah and Susan took care of the old man and that he wanted for nothing. He lay there in the new morning, Caroline sleeping next to him, and his thoughts wandered.

His mind turned back to his childhood, such as it was. He had good memories, it was true, but pitifully few of them that included his mama. Ma had just up and left one day, and she didn't come back. Pa was not what one would call a vibrant sort of man, but by the time he (and everyone else) had finally given up on her ever coming home, Robert had descended into a pit where nothing reached. He hardly talked, never smiled, and seemed to look right through Bud and Nick. Frank, the youngest, Robert outright ignored. Robert had brought the boys together one morning and told them Ma had run off with "that ass" Macon Grundy and wouldn't be coming home. The older boys just looked at each other in disbelief; Frank was too young to even understand. Directly after this revelation, Robert was gone for two days straight, and when he came back; he refused to discuss the matter further. With anyone.

Macon Grundy and Maybelline Jernigan had gone to school with Robert Braxton and his brother Clark, the four of them thick as thieves the year Robert turned sixteen. That's when Grundy had announced plans to ship off on the *Lady Jane*, and while Maybelline had tried to talk him out of it, Robert had not done the same—and was not exactly brokenhearted by his friend's desire to ship out. Friends that they were, by that time May had grown from a scarecrow with pointy elbows to a lovely young woman, and both young men had taken notice. Robert didn't think Grundy had any designs on her, really, but he certainly couldn't develop any from a ship hundreds of miles away.

By the time Macon returned from sea several years later, Robert and Maybelline had become a family of four, and they had been thrilled to see him, Robert now secure in his role as husband and father. They welcomed Grundy with open arms and fell back into their old roles, sitting at the kitchen table while Macon regaled them with his adventures, or laughing about the fun they'd had as adolescents.

In the beginning, that winter was comfortable and pleasant despite the chill weather, with Macon coming over to the house of an evening and playing with Bud and Nick, who was hardly more than a baby. Frank had not yet even been thought of. But as Robert spent more evenings away from home bringing in timber or on a cattle run, Macon and May enjoyed dinners together and evenings without him. Robert's jealousy was palpable, but Maybelline laughed it off. Robert was being ridiculous, and wasn't that just like a man to be thinking something so outlandish about their mutual friend. Robert brooded and wondered if it would be outlandish if the tables were turned and he was having dinner with Fanny Gordon two farms over every other night. When Macon left in the spring, Robert was relieved, and though Macon promised to return the following winter, Robert considered the problem largely resolved.

Macon didn't return that winter, however. When he did return three years later, he found Robert and Maybelline's relationship strained; the bloom was off the rose, and Maybelline fairly glowered at Robert over the table. She was attentive and motherly to the boys, and toddler Frank was the special light of her eye. There had been no more after him, and she had resigned herself to the probability that there would be none; she doted on all of them. Macon joined them in the evenings as he had before and discussed his plans to move to the West. There would be no more sailing for him; he was done with that life and intended to settle down. His parents had moved the previous year, and there was no one there for him; no one anywhere, really. In the spring Maybelline had gone to the station to see him off, leaving Robert cutting timber. Robert had shaken Macon's hand, looking him dead in the eye and wishing him well. That's what made it rankle so—that Macon had returned his gaze with what seemed to be genuine good will and yet had apparently been making plans all the while.

Maybelline had planned to stay a night in Pensacola to do some shopping after she saw Macon off, so it didn't register as an alarm until the end of the second day and there was still no May. She had taken the wagon, so by the morning of the fourth day, Robert was noticeably unglued, imagining all the things that could have gone wrong on the trip home. What if the wagon had sprung a wheel and she lay even now face down on the side of the road—but no, *someone* would have been by and would have noticed. The horse had gotten spooked with the town noises and run off, leaving her stranded with no way home. But she'd have walked to the nearest farm, or someone would have given her a ride by now or sent word. Pensacola was not *that* far away; surely someone would have seen *something*. He left the two younger boys with Bud, with strict instructions to stay near the house. Bud was a relatively responsible child, largely due to his utter lack of imagination, but that suited Robert just fine, especially in times like these when he depended on him to do what he was told.

Robert left on that morning of the fourth day and rode to Pensacola on the family's remaining horse, his brow furrowed in thought. His mind was running every scenario that would have kept her away from home longer than expected. At every farm along the way he stopped to ask after her. No one had seen her, and only Mrs. Lundy had even known she'd gone on a trip. Mrs. Lundy saw everything, knew everything, and it was her God-given responsibility to share everything she saw and knew. He knew as soon as he left she'd be gone to the nearest neighbor so she could discuss the matter in detail with them and cluck over the Braxtons' failed relationship. He focused instead on the matter at hand and settled himself firmly in the saddle. The station master was no help; he didn't remember anyone in particular, and no one at the hotel in town remembered her. Not that she was memorable; she looked like everybody else. There were lots of folks in town by then, and he couldn't have expected them to remember, but still he asked.

Later, on the way home, he took a different route down by the bay. It was longer, but maybe it would turn up something. He spied the horse near the dunes of the beach, wandering in the short grass and grazing happily, still hitched to the wagon and pulling it along behind him as he went. He surveyed the beach; there was no one. He took the horse and wagon home, the suspicion—no, the *knowledge*—growing in him that she wasn't hurt in a ditch somewhere. No, she'd turned the horse loose, and she'd left him for that ass Grundy, and that was a bitter pill to swallow. Bitter that she had done it to him, but more so that she'd done it to the boys, knowing they wouldn't understand, and right under his nose. He hadn't suspected a thing. He had come home to the boys that night with a pit in his stomach that slowly churned inside him, turning from heartache into a pounding throb of anger, convinced that she'd simply abandoned them. After he checked on the boys, he turned right around and left again to spend two days in a drunken stupor at the still in the woods.

Bud remembered how he had watched Robert stumble from the bushes with leaves in his hair and wearing clothes so dirty they could've stood by themselves. Bud had called to him from where he was standing in the yard feeding the chickens, but Robert didn't even look toward him as he fumbled his way into the house and went straight to bed. Bud didn't know where his daddy had been, only that something big was happening and there was no one to explain it. The next day Robert told them that Ma had left, that she wouldn't be coming back, and that it was up to them to take care of themselves. Bud and Nick had just looked at each other in bewilderment; Robert refused to answer questions.

Bud rolled out of bed now and sat up, listening to the girls in the kitchen. He couldn't imagine just walking off and leaving all the children like his mother had. What kind of a person does that? He didn't know, but he guessed it took all kinds in the world. He washed his face in the basin and looked at Caroline, still asleep under the covers. He took his shirt from the back of the chair and pulled the curtain closed behind him. Another day, and she was just going to sleep it away. Whatever.

5 SHARPE REMEMBERS

Bud strolled into the kitchen where the girls were putting breakfast together. Tom and Mac had already carried the wood in for the stove and were sweeping the dirt they'd brought in with it out of the room; Dianna was getting Robert and Bethy settled at the table. Caroline had been a loving and tender mother before Charlie died and was even now, though she seldom made an appearance for more than a few minutes at a time. The children knew their routines and kept them, looking forward to the time when "Mama would feel better" and return to her sunny self. They tended the garden and cleaned the house, fed the chickens, and kept the cows milked and the horses fed, all under Annie's tutelage and Bud's guiding hand. It wasn't idyllic though, as was evidenced when Robert dropped his biscuit onto the floor and dusted it off before he popped it back onto his plate, peeping out under hooded eyes to see if anyone had noticed.

"I gotta go see Uncle Sharpe today, if you want to come with me, Tom," Bud said to his dark-haired son, who was rinsing his hands and face at the basin.

"Sure," Tom replied, always up for an adventure of any kind.

"Mac, you help Ellie and Sarah in the garden and check on Ma ever' once in a while. Annie'll be along later on, I guess." Mac nodded and was already calculating how long it would take him to ditch Ellie and Sarah and find a quiet spot with the book he was currently reading. Mac would have spent all day in a book if he thought he could get away with it. He'd read everything he could get his hands on.

"You want the wagon?" Tom hoped not; it took longer and he preferred to ride.

"Nah, just go tack 'em up, and I'll be out there in a minute."

Tom nodded and headed out, leaving his breakfast half eaten. Ellie nabbed the bacon before anyone else could, and Susan gave Tom the stink eye as he headed out the door. He could have at least taken his plate to the tub to be washed.

Bud finished his breakfast, then went back to the bedroom and leaned in. Caroline was sitting on the edge of the bed looking out the window. "Goin' to Uncle Sharpe's. You wanna come?"

She turned to look at him and sighed. "No, I think I'll stay here with the girls. I might go out to the garden with them."

"Suit yourself." He spied his pocketknife on the chest of drawers and swept it into his pocket, then turned and headed out the door to the barn.

Tom and Bud rode through the woods to Bud's Uncle Sharpe's house, which was about two miles from Bud's homestead. The path was well worn, and the morning was fine; father and son were both lost in their own thoughts as they made their way. Birds twittered in the trees, and the horses' tails made soft swishing sounds as they brushed the occasional fly away.

Tom broke the silence of the morning by asking Bud, "So what're we going over for, again?"

Bud cleared his throat. "Your Uncle Nick run into a cattle buyer in Pensacola, and he said he's going to be in Milton in a few days, and he's buying cows, running a decent price, if there's enough. We're gonna see if Sharpe's got any he wants to take. If you got five or six cows, buyer won't give you much, but if you got fifteen, twenty, thirty, he'll give you about seven dollars a head for 'em. I figgered Uncle Sharpe might have some 'bout ready for the market."

"We gotta dip 'em?" The boys were fascinated last year by the process of dipping the cows for ticks and enjoyed helping Bud round them up and take them; it was a lot of work but fun at the same time.

"No, just get 'em there; hopefully get a good price."

As they approached Uncle Sharpe's home, two dogs ran up to them, barking. They could see the house, and Sharpe came out to the porch. He had never been a handsome man, and after seven decades his face was a landscape of craggy mountains and valleys of wrinkles from years of working in the sun. His beard was grizzled and white, and he moved slowly, but he was able to take care of himself. He held a mason jar in one hand as he sat heavily in the chair on the porch, waiting for them to ride up.

"Uncle," Bud called, dismounting. He handed the reins to Tom. "Go get 'em some water and turn 'em into the field right there." He nodded to the small field by the house. Sharpe no longer kept horses; it was too much work and upkeep for him, but he still had a respectable head of cattle. He lived alone, but his eleven children kept an eye on him and made sure he had plenty to eat and stayed relatively healthy and reasonably sober. The mason jar in his left hand was a rather permanent fixture, and the man's tolerance was legendary.

"Nick tole me there's a cattle buyer in Pensacola that's got a good price," he said, walking up to the porch where Sharpe sat waiting. "Came to see if you want in. We'll take 'em if you want. I got about ten, fifteen head I can round up. I got the timber in."

"When you want 'em?" Sharpe took a long swallow.

"About a week from now I think would be good; give me time to round mine up," Bud replied. Tom, finished with the horses, joined them and sat on the edge of the porch, leaning against the post. Bud continued. "I talked to Willie down there on Boilin' Creek. He's got about eight, and he's gonna throw 'em in."

"How you gonna get 'em across the river?"

"I don't know if you knew it, but Henry, he's got a ferry down there below the mouth of Boilin' Creek, and he'll ferry them across. He can take about ten head at a time." Bud began taking tobacco and a pipe from his pockets, preparing to settle back against a porch post and chat for a while.

"Yeah, okay, I got a few. You come get 'em and take 'em on." Turning to Tom, he looked him up and down. "Boy, you done grown a foot since I last saw you. What you eatin'?"

Tom smiled. "Yes, sir, I guess I'm a bit bigger. I'm nine and a half now."

"You practically a man. Guess you'll be shavin' soon." Sharpe smiled. "My brother Tom was like you; he grew like a weed. Crazy smart too. I bet you're smart."

"Well Maclan's probably smarter than me. But I'm taller. Your brother Tom—he's the one from the war, right?"

"Yeah, he was my little brother." Under his breath he added, "Bastard Yankees."

"Tell me about Tom again, Sharpe," Bud said, sitting down and packing the pipe. "Pa never speaks of him."

"Mm. Well, your pa never speaks a' nothin', that's true."

Bud leaned back against the porch post as he lit the pipe.

Sharpe continued, one gnarled hand reaching up to scratch his bristly cheek. "Well, we lived down in Holmes County, and Pa had a pretty good-sized plantation, with quite a few slaves, and times was pretty good. But the Civil War started, and things got rougher and rougher. Johnny was just a baby. Lydie was gone by then."

Bud puffed silently and waited.

"Well, it was Tom. He was younger'n me, and he was servin' in the Confederate Army." Sharpe took a long draft from the jar, which was almost empty. "Ma'd commenced to go downhill, and it become pretty obvious that she might not make it, so we wrote a letter. Well, we got somebody to write it; none of us could read or write very well. We got somebody to write to Tom to tell him if he wanted to see Ma alive, he better come on back home. Tom went to his commanding officer to ask for leave, but he wouldn't let him go, as it was far enough in the war that they knew their fortunes were goin' downhill and they needed everybody they could get. Well, Tom, he deserted; he left without permission and come home, and shortly after he got there, Ma died and we buried her. A few days later a Confederate troop come through and arrested Tom and hung him, not very far from the house."

Sharpe paused a bit, silent as he remembered that day, and Bud smoked. Tom the younger sat with his back to the post, arms on crooked knees, listening to Sharpe with rapt attention.

"Well, we buried him," Sharpe continued, "and it was gettin' tougher and tougher, without Ma and Lydie, and about a year after that, we was all workin' one day. I was working out in the field, and a Union cavalry came, and they freed our slaves. Just like that, said, 'You're all free. You blacks are free to do whatever you want to. The Confederates have lost the war, and you can go wherever you want.' And they went on at first, but unfortunately, they didn't have anything to eat if Pa didn't feed them. So we stayed around a few days and gathered up what we could, but we couldn't work the cotton without them slaves. We come on up to Santa Rosa County and started cutting timber. 'Bout a month after we'd got there, some of our blacks showed up at the front door. Followed us all the way there. Turns out, they found out the Union Army wasn't going to feed them either, so Pa fed 'em and put 'em to work, built 'em some little ol' houses to live in."

"What was Tom like?" Tom asked. He wondered about his namesake, what kind of a man he was.

"Well now, he was downright bull-headed. Always it was his way. If he took it in his head to do it, then it was done, and weren't nobody gonna tell him different. That's why he got hisself hung, 'cause nobody could tell him not to do somethin'. But he was dependable—if he gave you his word, then it was set in stone. When we wrote him to come see Ma, none of us thought he'd desert to do it."

Bud sighed. "Well I guess he come by his stubbornness honestly; I heard 'is daddy was stubborn too."

Sharpe chuckled. "Yeah, he did," Sharpe smiled. They sat in silence while Bud finished his pipe.

Sharpe's body was old, but his mind was very much present, and he remembered that year very well. His ma had picked up a cough the previous winter and wasn't able to shake it. Having Lydie run off like she did hadn't helped anything, and Tom being in the Confederate Army worried her no end. Sharpe would've been right there next to him, despite the age difference, had he not just been through a bout of scarlet fever. He had been in the army when the war first started but took a bullet in the leg and was sent home to recover. Then he contracted the fever. When he finally began to recover, Ma began to succumb to the pneumonia that would eventually kill her, and as he didn't want to leave her, he wasn't sad about having taken so long in his convalescence. He might have milked it just a bit, knowing what he'd be going back to in the battlefield. The preacher had been by, and they asked him to write the letter to Tom to let him know she was fading. When Tom arrived at the little house, he said he had asked for leave but it was refused, and he took it into his head that he was going anyway. Sharpe understood. By that time Tom had probably seen all the blood and guts he had wanted to see, and leaving wasn't a cowardly move so much as self-preservation against going crazy. Sharpe had seen it himself; boys hardly old enough to shave being blown to bits right next to him. It was enough to make you just want to walk away and never stop.

The day they came for Tom, Sharpe was incensed with the injustice of it. But Tom, he looked so tired. Way too old for his age, for his body. "I don't wanna go back, Sharpe," he told his brother, as they lay in bed talking the night before the Confederates came. "I seen enough; I heard enough. I'm tired of it all. They c'n hang me if they want to, but I don't wanna see no more." The next morning the troop rode up to the house, calling his name and pushing Sharpe and his brothers out of the way as they took hold of Tom by the arms. They hauled him out of the house with his hands tied behind his back and put him on a horse and trotted him out to the big old oak in the back field. Their uniforms were disheveled and dirty, but they were far from giving up, and the officer sat up straight in the saddle as the other soldiers tied a rope around Tom's neck. Tom made no effort to get away or struggle and was as compliant as a man could be.

"This man, Tom Braxton, has been found to be a deserter from the Confederate Army, a violation of protocol, and the sentence will be death by hanging." The soldiers threw the rope over a branch of the oak; the horse stood still. Tom looked at Sharpe and his father, and his little brothers, Clark and Robert. He smiled at them and closed his eyes. Clark stood silently crying as he clung to his father's pants, and Sharpe just seethed, his fists clenched against his thighs. The irony of it all was that the war would be over in just a few short months, and the unjustness of it would seize Sharpe's thoughts all over again each time he thought about this day in the years to come.

Tom arched his neck as though he were just making himself comfortable. His lips moved silently, and he opened his eyes and looked up to the sky, a beautiful cloudless day that was meant for anything but this. A soldier swatted the horse's rump, and Tom dropped, his neck cracking audibly. It was a sick, wet sound, and Sharpe squeezed hot tears from his eyes and looked down at his feet. He peered up at the officer with hate and scorn. The officer was watching Tom with indifference from his mount and wiped his beard with one hand. Clark clutched his father's pants and tried to bury his head in the fabric.

"That's it, then," the officer said, and kicked his horse to a trot away from the hanged man and his decimated family. The soldiers rode away, leaving the remaining Braxton men to bury one more of their dead and mourn alone.

When Bud and Tom arrived back at their own house a few hours later, having agreed with Sharpe that they would come get his cows and take them to town with theirs on Friday, Annie had come, and was out with the girls in the garden; Robert and Bethy were playing in the dirt nearby. Predictably, Mac was leaning against a tree in the yard with a book. Bud and Tom rode to the barn and dismounted, and Bud handed his reins to his son. Kicking a chicken out of his way, Tom led the horses in to untack them. Bud walked out to the garden to see what was going on.

Robert ran to Bud, who picked up his son, kissing his head. "What's all this?" he asked, giving the garden an appraising look as he held Robert on his hip.

"We picked all the beans, and I got a big 'mato!" Dianna ran to him and held up a huge tomato in one grubby hand.

"That's amazing." Bud patted her head and set Robert down. He nodded to Annie, who stood and gingerly made her way out through the row.

Annie took his hand as she stepped away from the leafy greens and tender sprouts and said quietly, "Can I talk to you?"

"You kids keep pullin' weeds and keep an eye on Bethy. Me and Annie are gonna take a little walk." He walked her to the front of the house, steering her by the elbow, and they stood in the shade of the pear tree. She looked down at her dress and wiped her hands on her apron. "What?" he asked her, bluntly.

She wasn't a shy girl, but now she looked down at her shoes. "I've missed my monthlies, Bud," she whispered. "By about three weeks, I guess." She glanced up at him, nervously waiting for his reaction.

At first he didn't reply, only swallowed. He waited a beat before he answered, to get the shock of it out of his voice. "But we were careful," he protested, trying not to show how he felt at her admission and not sure how well he was succeeding.

"I know we were, but I still missed them," she said. "I guess we weren't careful enough." She studied his face, unsure of what she was seeing. "Are you mad?"

Bud took a deep breath. "No, I'm not mad, honey, not at all. Just surprised, that's all." Flabbergasted, was more like it, but he hoped it wasn't showing in his face. "Are you feelin' okay?"

"I'm fine, just sick in the mornings. And during the day. Well, pretty much any time. I guess it'll be like this for a little bit." She had relaxed a bit but still looked at him warily.

"Yeah, Caroline was always sick with hers." The mention of Caroline sobered him. "What d'you wanna do?"

"My daddy's not going to let me stay at home. Oh, Bud, he'll be so mad. Mama'll cry. But I'm happy. I love you."

"I love you too, honey. But I love Caroline too; you know that." Well, this was a pretty pickle.

"Oh, what's she going to say? She'll hate us both." She knew that their marriage was a façade, that they didn't touch or talk. She'd managed to put Caroline out of her mind when she was alone with Bud, despite her pricking conscience, but there was no getting away from it now. Bud was a married man.

"Maybe not. I'll talk to Caroline. You'll come live with us." He grinned as she raised an eyebrow. "Well, you're over here all the time anyway. The kids will understand. It's all going to be okay." Bud hoped he was right and placed his hand over her still-flat stomach. "We know how to raise 'em, I guess."

She smiled and put her smaller, softer hand on top of his calloused one. "I guess so. It'll be a spring baby, I suppose."

"It's not how I'd a had it, if I had my druthers, but it is what it is, and we'll make out okay. I'll talk to your daddy. Go home tonight, and I'll come by tomorrow and talk to him. Tell him I'll come by after dinner."

"All right. I think Mama already knows. She saw me throwing up after breakfast the other morning. I told her I was just feelin' poorly, but Lord knows she's had enough babies to know the difference. She wouldn't have told Daddy, though. What will Caroline say? Will you tell her tonight?" She was apprehensive again, thinking of how Mama and Daddy would react and picturing Caroline's crestfallen face as she heard the news. She was going to hate her.

"Yes, I'll tell her. I don't know *what* she'll say, honestly. Prob'ly slap my face. But I don't know as how she's gonna be able to do anything about it."

Just then Robert came over to them and tugged on Annie's skirt. "Bethy smells bad, Annie," he said.

"Oh, all right, I'm coming," she said, taking Robert's hand in hers. She took Bud's hand with her other hand briefly as she turned to go see to Bethy, and he squeezed it in what he hoped was a reassuring manner.

"It'll be all right," he said. As he watched her walk away to see to the children, he heaved a sigh, then turned to find Caroline, his steps a little less jaunty than they had been when they'd first arrived home. *Well, isn't this a hell of thing? Good Lord.*

Caroline was behind the house on the other side of the yard, boiling clothes over a fire. This was good. This was a step in the right direction. Since Charlie died, she hadn't spent every minute in the bed, but she'd gone through her phases, and there were months where she didn't stir from the house. And then there were days like today when she was up and about and taking care of things. It was unpredictable; it was confusing, and Bud had all but given up, although he tried to take advantage of any good humor. There was a general air of somber melancholy around her; she didn't laugh or smile, but she didn't weep, and she was kind and gentle with the children. He walked over to where she was shaking out a shirt.

"Hey there," he said, and came around to face her as she pinned the shirt to the line.

"Hey, yourself. You back from Sharpe's?"

"Yeah; we're gonna take some cows to a buyer in town next week."

"Oh, is he doin' okay? Is Annie stayin' to supper? When I get done with this, I'll get it started. The girls got a good mess of beans from the garden."

"Yeah, he's good. Old 'n' ornery, same as ever." Thinking of Annie going home to her mama and daddy with her bittersweet news, he winced. "No, she's going home."

"Okay, well, you headed out to bring the cows in?"

"Yep, I'll take Robert and Bethy with me if you want to get 'em out from underfoot."

"No, it's okay, I'll go get them from her. They're fine here. See you when you get back."

"Yep." He turned and went down the path that meandered past the outhouse and toward the gate that led to where the cows were out to pasture. He'd talk to her later, after the kids were in bed. He really didn't know how she'd take it. Caroline was hard to read these days. She loved all her children, but Charlie's death had hit her hard. It had hit him hard too, and they all felt his absence, but Caroline just seemed to fade after his death. He'd gotten sick with a fever in the winter and had never recovered; the doctor had been sent for but there was nothing that could be done, and Bud had cradled his son's limp body the morning of his death, sobbing harder than he'd known he could. His heart had broken that day, and the thought of Charlie could still bring him to tears. It didn't get easier; it just became something he had to live with, this gaping hole in his life. If the preacher was right, Charlie was in heaven now and Bud would see him again, but that was an everlasting time to wait. In the meantime, there were mouths to feed.

He came to the gate and whistled for the cows. There were nearly seventy of them now, with a few calves. He'd lost some last winter; it had been an especially cold one, and he wasn't the only one who had come across a frozen carcass while checking fences. But the calves born in the spring had been healthy, and he was feeling satisfied with the decision to sell a few to the buyer. He hoped Willie was right about how many the buyer was looking for.

He got the last of the cows through and closed the gate again, prodding the herd farther along the path that would wind its way to the rear of the barn, and followed their plodding steps. The late summer sun reminded him of another summer long ago in his young teens, when he'd come back from staying at his Uncle Clark's. Robert had taken his son to Clark's home in Holmes County to attend school with Clark's children. The master in Santa Rosa County that year had quit early on, and there being no replacement, Robert insisted that Bud needed to carry on with his reading and math. So Bud had gone to his Uncle Clark's, and he remembered waving to Nick in the wagon as Robert took him and Frank back home.

Clark had seven children, and while they weren't any better off financially than Bud's family, the boys at school still made fun of Bud's lack of boots and his worn trousers. Bud just scowled and tried to ignore them. School was all right, and it was fun to play with his cousins; Uncle Clark and Aunt Viola were nice to him and fed him plenty, but it wasn't home. He slept in the same room with the other boys on a pallet on the floor and did his sums on a slate. He read by the firelight in the evenings. He had been a chatty little boy, but after his mama left, he became quieter, more thoughtful, and less inclined to idle chatter. The cousins were kind to him but thought he was standoffish because he was quiet. Bud wasn't mad or upset or unkind; he just didn't have much to say. When he did talk, it was about the books he was reading or fishing, which he loved to do. The boys often went out to the bay with a net to catch a mess of mullet for dinner. If they caught more than enough to feed the family, they could sell them in town and buy sweets at the general store; Bud made sure to get a few for his girl cousins.

As much as he enjoyed the year with Uncle Clark, he was ready to go home, and when school was finished in June, he announced that he'd be going back.

"Your pa'll come for you in a few weeks, and you can help us in the field till he comes," Clark said. But no, Bud would have none of it; he'd had enough of being away from home, and he fully intended to leave the next morning.

"No, I'm going home tomorrow," he told Clark, and Aunt Viola made up a few lunches into a pack for the next few days.

"Are you sure you want to do this? It's a long way for a young boy by himself." She worried about him. There was no way she would have let any of her own children make the trip on their own, but Bud wasn't hers and she didn't feel like she could tell him not to go. She knew he missed his family.

"I'll be fine, and I'll be careful," he assured her. He gave her a tight hug and thanked them both for the care they'd shown him. He left early in the morning with his pack of clothes and a few books, her lunches carefully packed on top, and set out for home. It would take him a few days to get there, and it was hot, but he had plenty of water in his canteen and could refill it in the river and walk in the shade. He was proud of himself for his bravery; none of those boys at school would be walking alone for miles, taking care of themselves. He enjoyed the walk, despite the heat, and took a few breaks throughout the morning. On the afternoon of the first day he came across a wagon of corn with a horse hitched to it, and saw a man slumped over on the ground near a back wheel.

"Hey, mister, you need a hand?" he called to the man as he got closer, but he got no answer. He laid down his pack and stepped cautiously nearer, ready to bolt if the man should suddenly rise. He stretched out a hand and nudged the man gently on the shoulder. "Mister?"

The slumping man fell over, sprawling onto the side of the dirt road on his back, eyes staring. Bud jumped back, eyes wide. He'd never seen a dead man before, and this man was *definitely* dead. He toed one foot against the man's thigh once, twice. No response. *Well, okay,* he thought. He looked at the wagon, the bed of it heaped with corn still in the husk. The wheel looked to be in good shape; what had the man been doing? *Oh. I get it.* Another wheel, broken near the hub, lay in the tall grass beyond the man. Apparently, he'd replaced the broken wheel, but then had collapsed with the exertion of it and slumped over dead right on the spot. *I guess I got a wagon of corn now.* He walked around to the front of the wagon and threw his pack up into the seat. He patted the horse's thigh and trailed his hand over the flank as he moved to the front of the horse, who stood patiently. The horse looked in good shape, and Bud stroked his neck, then gathered up the reins. He swung up into the seat, then turned to the dead man. "God bless you, sir," he said, "and thanks for the corn." He clicked to the horse, and the wagon lurched forward down the road toward home.

Toward dusk, Bud stopped for the night and turned the horse out to graze after giving him some water from his canteen and rubbing him down with an old piece of cloth he'd found near the seat. He looked in the bed of the wagon. Pa would be pleased to see him come home with this much corn. He felt sorry for the man who'd lost it and for his family but he tried not to think about it. He found a flour sack tucked just behind the seat, and it contained something wrapped in a towel and a roll of bills that amounted to twenty-five dollars when he counted them out. He hadn't intended on robbing the man. He'd have left the flour sack for his family if he'd known it was there. Well, he couldn't turn back now. He carefully unfolded the towel and found a pistol inside; he spun the chamber and saw it was loaded. He wrapped the gun loosely back in the towel and shoved it back into the flour sack. He lay down under the wagon, tucking the sack under his arm, and slept.

The next day was sunny again and hot, and Bud was sweating through his shirt by ten o'clock. He crossed Weaver River just before lunch and stopped after his crossing to water the horse, eat a bite, and rest. He found a good spot under a tree and reclined against the trunk, eating one of Aunt Viola's lunches while the horse grazed. When he was done, he put his pack away and then filled his canteen from the river. He climbed back into the wagon seat and took the reins loosely in hand, ready to head on his way. The day was hot as blazes, but here in the woods it was shaded, and at least there was a little breeze. It had been a good rest, and he was ready to put some more miles behind him. He clucked to the horse and flicked the reins but then immediately pulled back as a man stumbled out into the road just ahead. He was dirty and disheveled. He hooked his thumbs into the sides of his trousers and gave them a hitch, pulling them higher around his hips as he staggered toward the horse. As he came near, he reached for the bridle to steady himself.

"Boy, what you doin'?" he asked, his voice gruff as he swayed slightly. "You by yerself?" He was clearly drunk.

"I'm headed home, and I'm fine. Move out of the way now, 'fore you get run over," Bud called. He clicked to the horse. "Walk on!" The horse walked forward a few steps, but the man in the dirty shirt and trousers held on to the bridle, and the horse stopped, tossing his head. *Make a decision,* he seemed to say.

The man staggered a few steps forward. He kept his left hand on the horse as he walked to the seat where Bud sat, stiffly, eyes wary. Bud transferred the reins into his left hand and with his right felt for the flour sack at his feet. He tried not to bend or show movement. This man was twice his size, easy, and smelled like he'd crawled out of a bottle of whiskey, even from six feet away. He couldn't let him get a hand on him, or he'd be down in the dirt in a flash. "Git down from there, boy," the man growled. "I b'lieve I'm gonna take this wagon offa you."

"No, sir, I don't think you are." His right hand found the towel, and his fingers pried their way in until they found the butt of the gun. He gripped it tightly. *Oh please, let there be one in the chamber,* he prayed. *Please God, I'll do anything You ever want from now 'til forever more, and I'll never steal nothin' again even from a dead man if You'll just do this one thing for me right now.* He kept his eyes on the man and slowly pulled the pistol from the sack. The man put his foot on the step and began to pull himself up, one hand on the back of the seat, one hand starting to pull back in a fist. Everything seemed to move in slow motion, and Bud felt the pistol catch on something, maybe a loose string, inside the sack. If he couldn't get his hand up in time and shoot, or if there was an empty click, this man was going to hook a left directly into his jaw and send him off into the back of the wagon. He'd never be able to stop him. He took a deep breath in, inhaling the stench of body odor and alcohol and dirt off the man who began to tower over him. Just as the man's fist pistoned out, Bud brought the pistol out of the sack and swung it up to the left, holding the reins tight in his other hand. He pointed at the man's chest, squeezed the trigger, and the gun roared. The man's face contorted and his mouth formed a surprised *O* as he took the bullet. For a moment he just stood there, still hanging on to the seat and staring wildly at Bud, his fist now loosening and reaching toward him. Bud tensed, thinking the man might grab him by the collar and pull him from the wagon with him. Instead the man's eyes rolled back in his head, and he let go of the seat, his fingers stretching out to Bud as he fell back into the soft dirt below.

Bud exhaled in a *whoof* and he pulled back on the reins again; the shot had frightened the horse, and he called, "Easy, easy." He looked down at the man, who stared straight into the sky and didn't move. He looked at the gun in his hand and his white knuckles and just fixated on it, breathing heavily. *Thank You, God; thank You, God; thank You, God.* Over and over in his head, he chanted it, until he managed to get himself under control. He put the pistol back in the flour sack and settled it back at his feet, grateful that it had been there. He took a deep breath, clicked to the horse again, and this time they set off, leaving the bandit behind to stare into the hot sun through the trees.

Bud met no more trouble on his way home, and his father was glad to see him and the horse. They had put the wagon load of corn in the barn and later sold it in town. Robert praised his boy, pleased at his bravery and his presence of mind when he heard the story about the bandit.

It was a good homecoming, and Bud smiled now at the thought of it as he brought the cows into the barn to be milked. He couldn't remember many days when he'd pleased his pa, but that was one of them, and he cherished it.

6 BUD COMES CLEAN

The kids were all in bed, and Bud supposed now was the time, if there ever was going to be a time, when he'd have to tell Caroline about Annie. Oh Lord, this was not going to go well. He looked up from the table as she came out of the girls' room, pulling the curtain behind her. He didn't want to hurt her, and he knew this would hurt; there was no help for it, though.

"Walk a bit with me?" he asked.

"No, not tonight. I'm goin' to bed," she replied, tucking an errant curl behind her ear. She moved to the kitchen and picked up the tub, heading for the door to throw out the water. He got up from the table and took the empty tub from her as she came back in.

"I need to talk to you," he said in a low voice. The children were probably not yet asleep, and they didn't need to hear this conversation.

She sighed. "Oh, all right. Give me a minute."

He walked out the door, pulled it closed behind him, and crossed to the middle of the yard. The moon was not yet full, but it was a bright, clear night, and he could hear the frogs and crickets in the dark. He shoved his hands deep in his pockets and looked down at his boots. *How in the world did this happen?* he thought. He felt shame and dismay at his own betrayal of Caroline, but it was confused with love for Annie and the happiness he felt when he thought of the sweet way she tossed her head when she laughed and how she joked with him. This would not be easy.

Caroline came out of the house, and together they walked to the rail by the barn. One of the horses strolled over, and Bud stroked its nose.

"What's goin' on, Bud?" Caroline turned and leaned against the rail, looking back at the house.

"I need to talk to you about Annie." He paused and took a deep breath. "She's pregnant."

"Oh. Well, that's okay, I guess. I can handle the kids now again without

35

her. I'm doing better right now. Good for her."

"Yeah, I see that you are, and I'm glad of it. I miss you when you're not well." He leaned over and kissed her temple. "But that's not all." He swallowed hard.

"Oh?" Caroline turned to look at him.

"It's…it's *my* baby."

"It's….what?" She stared at him in disbelief.

"It's mine. My baby."

"Your…." The words trailed off. He watched her eyes widen as the realization dawned. "Bud! How dare you!" She straightened up now and looked directly at him, her green eyes blazing.

"I didn't intend it, darlin'. It just happened."

"It didn't just *happen!* I can't believe this! Did you do it in our own *house?*" He could hear the outrage in her voice. "What in the world were you thinking*?*"

"No, never in the house."

"How long? How long has this been going on, Bud? What made you think this was okay?"

"A couple months, maybe. She's only a few weeks gone. Don't look at me like that."

"Look at you like *what?* Like you haven't just gone and got a girl *pregnant?* Because that's what you're telling me! And Annie? *Annie?* She's half your age, Bud!"

"She ain't half my age, she's twenty-one. That ain't exactly robbin' the cradle."

"I don't care what you call it. You're unbelievable."

"Now listen here," Bud shot back, beginning to get annoyed. "You ain't exactly been warming my bed lately."

"Oh, don't you *dare* blame this on me! It's not my fault you can't keep it in your pants!" He could see she was incensed.

"Bethy's a year old, Caroline! And before that, Robert's three! You can't expect a man to just wait forever! I'm not made like that!" He was almost shouting now, hating himself for it, but angry. He'd been patient, damn it. Only twice in the past four years had he lain with her, and he could no longer help himself. He hadn't pressed her, hadn't cajoled or wheedled or guilted her into it. Simply rolled over and gone to sleep, every time. Each time the babies came, he thought it would help ease the pain of losing Charlie, but both times she eventually slipped away again, emerging here and there but never for very long.

She pressed her lips together. "Charlie *died*, Bud! *I* died!" She covered her face with her hands.

He pulled her to his chest, embraced her. At first she pushed against him, but then she fell into him, her hands pressed against her face in his arms. Hot tears burned her cheeks as she sobbed. He held her to him and stroked her hair, the moonlight creating strands of gold in his hand. He kissed her hot forehead. "I know, I know. Shhh."

Slowly she came to herself and wiped the tears away. He looked down at her and brushed her hair from her face. "I love you, but she was there for me when you couldn't be. I didn't plan it, but she's been good for the kids and good for me. Good for you too. She's taken care of all of us." *In more ways than one,* he thought. Maybe he wouldn't say that.

"What do you want to do?" She looked at him bleakly, resignedly. He knew this was hard for her, hard to accept. He hated himself.

He wiped his hand over his chin and let her go. "She's going to come live with us."

"Oh, the *hell* she is," Caroline said, standing back again, fire sparking in her eyes. Caroline never cursed, but this was apparently too much. "I will *not* have her in the house. Ever, ever again."

"She is. She's going to have the baby here, and she's going to come live with us, and you can like it or lump it. That's all there is to it." He was firm. He knew Wilson would turn Annie out the minute he knew she was expecting; he was just that kind of man. And he knew Wilson might come after him with a shotgun too, but that was tomorrow's problem. Tonight, he was dealing with this problem.

Caroline stared at him angrily. She didn't say anything but put her hands on her hips and huffed out a short breath. Finally, she spoke. "You can sleep on the floor tonight." With that she turned on her heel and stalked back to the house. He stayed where he was. The horse had long since gone, and he put his foot up on the bottom rail of the fence and leaned on his arms. That had gone about like he expected. She hadn't slapped him, though she probably had every right to, and he had known she wasn't going to like it when he suggested Annie would come live with them. He wasn't sure exactly how that was going to work, now that he thought about it. There were only three bedrooms and they were all full. But there was nothing for it, he knew, and it was his responsibility. He loved them both. It was just going to have to be.

He closed his eyes. *Lord, I don't know how I managed to get myself in this, but here I am. I'm asking You to help me. I sure don't see how to make it through myself. I know I did wrong, but I'm askin' You to forgive me if You can, and help me figure out a way forward. Amen.* He turned around and looked at the house for a long moment, then started slowly toward the door. *Well, here goes. The journey of a thousand miles begins with a single step, and all that.* The floor was going to be hard tonight, but he guessed he deserved it.

7 ANNIE MOVES IN

"Robert's not sharing the honey!"

Bud walked into the dining room where the children were reaching over each other at the table, and Dianna wailed loudly as she tried to pry the jar from Robert's hands. "You're done! Let me have it now!" Robert hugged the mason jar tightly to his chest.

"Not till you say peese, that's what we're 'posed to say!" Robert stubbornly refused to release the jar until the proper manners had been practiced. Susan had been working on him all summer with his *please* and *thank you*s, and he was becoming a real stickler for it, demanding the words be said whenever he was asked for anything. It was cute at first but was getting out of hand.

"Robert, give Dianna the honey," Bud commanded. "Dianna, say please." He sat down at the table. Caroline came into the dining room with plates and cups.

"Everybody simmer down," she said, putting the plates in front of the children. She did not look at Bud but went around the table settling the children with a pat here and a scoot of a chair there. Normally she'd have served Bud first, but not this morning. It was noted and understood, and he didn't have a problem with it. Likely there were going to be a few daggers to dodge for a while, and he deserved every one of them, he knew, so he sat still and chatted with the children while they fidgeted and annoyed each other.

She brought him a plate, and it clattered on the table, but he didn't say a word. She stomped to her seat and sat down.

"All right, everybody bow your heads," she said and began a short prayer while the children around her bowed their heads over folded hands. Bud peeked at her over his own folded hands and saw Robert peeking back. He winked at his little mischief maker. Robert smiled and closed his eyes, but Bud switched his gaze back to Caroline and watched her as she prayed. This was Prickly Caroline that he was getting this morning. She came out when Bud did anything particularly exasperating or something she didn't agree with; Caroline would never come right out and argue with him to his face, but she sure could make it plenty apparent when she didn't agree with him on something. Usually it would put his own back up, but this morning he took it in stride and didn't let it rankle. He thought she probably had a right to her anger for a while. For a while. At least Prickly Caroline had a personality, and it was a lot different and a little bit refreshing, actually, since he'd had so much of Catatonic Caroline. She finished her prayer, and everyone began eating.

"Tom and Mac, you boys need to put the cows out this morning and then meet me in the field when you're finished up in here," he said to his boys. "Finish your chores first, and you can read after dinner, Mac," he said pointedly, knowing where his son's priorities were liable to be. "And Tom, when you get finished with the cows and the other chores, and you're done in the field with me, you can go fishing this afternoon, if you like."

There were choruses of "Ooh, take me, take me!" around the table, and he saw Caroline smile. "Maybe we'll all go down to the water when we're done here at the house," she said.

"Not me. I'm going to Grandpa's to give him some of the butter Sarah and I made yesterday," Ellie said. "You can go with me if you want, Sarah," she said to her sister. Ellie loved the old man and took good care of him, delivering remnants of breakfasts and dinners and jams or jellies when they were made. Bud himself didn't choose to see the old man, but the children went to see him quite regularly and always told him when they'd been, so he knew his father was in good health and didn't need a thing. Nick took good care of him as well, so he didn't need Bud's company.

Bud was fine with that. He didn't feel hatred for his father, exactly, but neither did he have much use for him; the old man had ignored him most of his life, and Bud bore a certain amount of resentment toward him for that. It was one thing to be left by your mama, but it was another thing to be left by your pa when he was *standing right there*, oblivious to everything you said or did and taking no interest in the world in general. And that's how Bud felt—that Robert had abandoned him too when Ma left. Bud himself had been father to the other boys growing up, showing them attention when Robert didn't. He had been the one to encourage them, admonish them when they got in trouble, and counsel them about girls or anything else they encountered. Together they worked Robert's fields, cut his timber, and tended his livestock. They kept the house, too, and while it might not have been as homey as a woman might have made it, it was clean enough, and they had never gone without.

Bud felt that he had failed Frank utterly, though, and it ate at him. He still had hope that Frank would turn himself around, but Bud no longer sought him out at the saloon in town and helped him sober up, not since the children had started coming and he'd had more to concentrate on. At some point, Frank was going to have be responsible for himself, and if he couldn't be, then so be it. Bud couldn't pick him up out of the dirt every morning at two a.m. when the bar closed. Maybe Nick would, maybe one of his other friends.

The sounds of the breakfast table continued as Bud and Caroline ate without acknowledging one another. The children were in high spirits because Mama was up and about and clearly one of the gang this morning. Their chatter drowned out any heaviness in the air, and Bud ate in relative peace, if peace can be had in the midst of eight hungry and chatty children.

As they started to finish up, he pushed back from the table. "I'll be in the field this morning, but then after dinner, I gotta go see Wilson. Be back for supper, though."

Caroline scowled but said nothing. She picked up some plates and stood, directing the children to follow her and help clear the table. She completely ignored Bud and busied herself with the needs of the day. *Fine, okay,* he thought. So this was Iron Caroline he was also getting this morning, deaf and immune to his presence. Fine. Part of him said, *Pick a mood and stick with it, woman,* and part of him knew she was still entitled to a little bit of petulance. After all, it *was* him who'd knocked up the hired help. And he didn't relish the thought of facing Annie's father later today. Ordinarily they were friendly enough, if not friends, but this was not likely to be a friendly conversation. While he didn't think it was going to come to blows, Wilson was not going to be pleased.

He turned his thoughts to the field, where he and Tom and Mac were headed. It wasn't huge, but it brought in some healthy crops, enough to feed his family and a little extra to sell as well. It was a hot day this late in the summer, but it was clear. Florida rain was predictable and relentless in the summer; you could set your watch by it most weeks. This year hadn't been bad. Some years it seemed to rain every single day, and the fields turned to mud. Bud hoped that it would be a good crop because it was just wet enough to keep the fields watered without drenching them. The fallow field would be in fine shape next year if he could get some fertilizer in it. He would work on that next week after he took the cows to the buyer.

It would be nice to have a few extra dollars, and he kept his money close at hand as well as in the bank. He didn't put as much stock in banks as he used to. He'd tried to get a loan to build the house, just a thirty-five-dollar loan, and the bank had refused. After that he didn't have much use for banks, but he kept an account and made deposits when he was in town. And he kept a few dollars squirreled away at home just to be spiteful. Self-righteous bunch of fools.

Bud and his boys headed off to the fields and left Caroline and the girls in the house with little Robert. He left the problem of Wilson for later. Caroline busied herself in the house with the children and cleaning up after breakfast. She was thoroughly annoyed. She knew she'd been indulgent with herself in the past, and she knew she'd depended on Bud too much, but she honestly could not have done anything different. Having Charlie ripped from her, despite her love for the other children, nearly killed her. She knew families who'd lost children, knew men who'd lost entire families, and she didn't know how they continued to draw breath. Men were different, though, and Bud never talked about Charlie. She knew he grieved too, and she wished she could have helped him through his grief, but hers was too suffocating. She caught glimpses of daylight and hope for stretches at a time, and she participated where she could, but there were some days she didn't get out of bed, and she couldn't remember the last time she'd been to church. She knew Annie and Bud took the kids some Sundays. She should be grateful for Annie and all Annie had done for her, but at that moment, she didn't think she could hit grateful with a ten-foot pole. And she *sure* was not going to have her in the house again. She'd put her foot down about that. She didn't usually go against Bud on much of anything, not that she felt her husband always made the right decision, but because she was basically easygoing and nothing much upset her. *This* decision, however—*this* took the cake. She was damn sure she'd have something to say about *this*.

After dinner, during which Caroline didn't say two words to him, Bud took one of the horses and headed off to Garret Wilson's property. He'd known Garret all his life; they'd cut timber together in one of the camps for several years and occasionally hunted together with some of the other men. They weren't particular friends, as Garret was older than Bud; but they were on good enough terms to pass a conversation in town from time to time. He wondered what he was walking into, exactly, and if Annie had prepped her father at all or if this was going to come as a shock. Regardless, it had to be done, and he felt he was man enough to do it.

He turned into Wilson's gate and dropped from horseback to his feet, taking the reins in his hand. He walked the horse toward the house, and one of Annie's little brothers came running out, calling to him, "I got 'im, Mr. Braxton!" as he came to take the reins from Bud.

"Thanks, make sure you rub him down a little," he said, as he handed the reins over. He looked up and Garret came out to the porch. Bud could tell already that the older man knew. *Oh well, guess it's better to have it out in the open.* At least he didn't have a shotgun in his hand, although Bud couldn't be sure he wouldn't go back in for it before this conversation was over. He saw Mrs. Wilson through the screen door with a dish towel in her hand. She didn't say anything to him, just raised a hand. Her face was drawn. "Becky," he said as he touched his hat. He took it off as he stepped up to the porch. She shot a worried look at the back of Garret's head and then turned back into the house. He could hear the other children in the house, but he didn't see Annie, and he didn't ask to go in.

"I guess you know what I'm here about," he said to Wilson. He propped one foot on the steps but stayed out from under the porch. Garret leaned against one of the posts.

"Bud, you got a lotta nerve comin' over here," Garret growled. He opened and closed his fist, flexing his fingers. "You had no right, no right atall."

"No, but I love her, and I'll take care of her."

"You can't even take care of the one you got!" Garret spat, standing straight. "Annie was seein' that Peterson boy in town before you came around, and they were doin' fine! You done fucked up, boy!"

"That Peterson boy don't know enough to shit or go blind, and you know it. They weren't goin' nowhere." Bud's argument was thin; he knew it, but he also knew the Peterson boy Garret was referring to. The Petersons had money but that was about all; brains did not run as deep as their pockets in that family. Annie had no interest at all in the Peterson boy and never had.

"I'll take care of her," he repeated and stood his ground. "I'll build her a house of her own, and she'll live with me. You can come visit anytime." He'd only just thought of this as it came out of his mouth. That was really the only solution. There wasn't room enough in the house as it was even if Caroline wasn't about to take his head off. He'd have to build something else to settle Annie in. He wasn't going to give her up. It was unorthodox. It was going to be the talk of the town, but he already knew what that was about. The town had had a field day of gossip when his mama had run off, and he'd managed to live through it then. He'd live through this now. His kids might have to put their backs up a little, but he was confident Tom and Mac could take care of themselves. Maclan was a bookworm, but he was no slouch with his fists. He and Tom had had enough scuffles between the two of them; they'd be fine.

"I'd no more step foot in a house a' yours than on the moon itself," Garret said angrily, "nor will any of mine. But you *will* take care of Annie, and you'll do a good job of it too, or I'll beat your damn fool head in." Just then Annie came out of the house onto the porch, followed by two of the Wilsons' younger children. She carried a small valise and looked at her father warily. Bud knew her father would never have hit her, but he could imagine things had gotten loud at their house already. Annie's mother stayed inside.

She touched her father's arm, but Garret didn't move, although he looked at her sternly. "You be good, girl," he told her. She smiled weakly at him. To Bud he merely said, "Don't come back here." Then he turned his back on both of them and stomped inside, leaving them on the porch with the other children. He let the porch door bang shut. She hugged both of the children in turn and told them to be good, then she stepped down from the porch. "You ready?" she asked.

Bud hadn't intended that she'd come home with him *today, right this minute,* but there was nothing for it; he wasn't going to press the issue. The younger Wilson boy brought Bud's horse to him, and Bud helped Annie up into the saddle. He handed her the small case, and she settled herself. Holding the reins, he turned the horse around and walked it toward the gate. He hadn't prepared Caroline, and she'd no doubt raise a fuss, but it was what it was. They'd make it through.

They got back to the house just as the children and Caroline were coming back from fishing and playing in the water. Bud swung Annie down from the horse and handed the reins to Mac. "Go put 'im up, please." Mac took the horse from his father and headed off to the barn. Caroline came over to her husband and Annie, handing off Bethy to Susan.

"Go in the house, please, Susan, and put Bethy down. I'll be along in a few." She turned to Annie, but didn't say anything, merely looked pointedly at her. Nothing could be read on her face.

Annie didn't shrink from Caroline's sharp gaze but clutched her little valise a little more tightly in her hands. Bud put his hand at Annie's elbow and said, "She's going to be staying with us. We'll need to figure out where she can sleep."

Caroline crossed her arms over her body and looked at Bud. "There's no room in the house. She can stay in the barn."

"She's not sleeping in the barn," Bud said, sounding exasperated. "The boys can bunk in the barn, and she can have their room until I can build another place."

Caroline looked at him in disbelief. "You're going to build another house for her? *Here?*"

"Yes, I am, and until then you two are just gonna have to learn to get along. She's here to stay, and she'll be a help with the children, just as she has been. I'm gonna be takin' a few head of cattle down to Henry this week, and you two can settle it out while I'm gone. When I get back I 'spect it to be handled."

"I don't *need* any help," Caroline spat, and she turned on her heel to go inside. Annie followed her quietly, but not meekly. She was going to have tread carefully. She knew she was suddenly an outsider, where two days before she'd been welcome, but she was going to stand her ground. It took two to tango, and Bud would back her up. She had seen that he would. She could stand up for herself too; she was no shrinking violet. She was up to this challenge.

8 A NIGHT IN TOWN

Over the next week or so, Bud and his boys herded fifteen head of Sharpe's cattle and ten of his own into Bud's north field. He and Nick made plans to run them down to Henry's ferry on Friday morning; they planned to stay the night in town and come back on Saturday. Both of the older boys wanted to come, but Bud told them to stay put this trip and they could come next time; the truth was that he was looking forward to a night in town on his own and some peace and quiet.

He had indeed moved the boys into the barn, as he'd suggested to Caroline, and they had been thrilled to go, taking it as an adventure and not in in the least perturbed that they were being evicted from the bed they shared in the house. Robert was practically apoplectic with excitement when Bud had told him they'd be bedding down in the barn. The older boys made comfortable beds for all of them in the hay loft. Bud did not allow them a lantern of their own, which they desperately wanted, but he couldn't take the chance of it overturning and told the boys they'd be fine without. Each night he walked out with them and waited while they settled down and said prayers, talking softly with them about the day. Bud loved his boys and hoped to be a better father to them than his own had been. As a teen and adult, Bud barely put two words together in company, but he remembered what it had been like to be a little boy, full of chatter and energy. He didn't want his boys to lose that exuberance as he had. They wouldn't have to grow up so fast like he did, if he had his say, and he did his best to mix responsibility with freedom as much as the work of the little farm would allow.

He kissed them goodnight and left the barn, hearing their whispers as he made his way back to the house with the lantern. Annie had moved into the boys' room, and she and Caroline had found a tenuous grasp on civility in the confines of the little house as they navigated the shared spaces of the kitchen and dining room. When he got back from the cattle run, he and Nick would work on putting up a small house near this one, and he had already figured out how he was going to do it. The only way to design it was to build a separate kitchen the two women would share; it would be safer for both houses to have the kitchen off to itself, and neither one of the women would be able to call it her own. They'd have to share it equally, and they'd have to work out who was in it when. He remembered hearing his mama say there weren't no kitchen big enough for two women, and he was for sure finding that out.

He planned to talk to Nick about it on the cattle run and see when his brother could make the time to come help. He'd find out how to pay him back in trade—maybe help him build that extra room onto the house he was always talking about or wrap the porch around like Nick's wife, Ellen, wanted. Their house was a little over three miles away, and their only child was a girl Robert's age. They'd had two boys early on in their marriage, but both of them had died as infants and were buried in the church cemetery. Bud could relate; he had one of his own there.

The next morning was busy as he and the boys herded the cattle out of the field and down the road. The boys were going as far as Nick's with him, and Willie and two of Willie's older sons would be waiting at the river with their own small herd. Together they would drive the cattle onto Henry's ferry and move them across the river, ten to fifteen at time, and down to the stocks south of town. The cattle were healthy and fat on late summer grass, and Bud was hoping for a good price.

He had left the house this morning with no goodbye kisses, only a strained hug from Annie as he packed his own lunch. Normally Caroline might have done it for him. Or Annie would, if Caroline was feeling poorly, but Annie tiptoed around the kitchen now, and Caroline refused to do anything for him. The week in the house had been tense but he had been unrelenting, insisting that Annie stay, and Caroline had been forced to accommodate. He had been gentle with her but firm, and he'd tried not to get too close to her but to give her space, as much as the small house would allow. For his efforts he had gotten Prickly Caroline all week. About what he expected and deserved. He had an idea he'd have her for quite a while and had resigned himself to it. That was fine, his skin was thick. He thought Annie's was too.

As they approached Nick's homestead, Bud and the two boys moved the cattle off the dirt road and into his pasture. Tom dismounted and closed the gate behind them. After he remounted, he joined his brother and father in the lane, and together they rode to Nick's house to water the horses and rest them for a few minutes. As they rode up, Nick met them in the yard.

"When you boys finish with them horses, you come on inside; Ellen's got a breakfast waitin'." He held Bud's horse by the bridle while Bud swung down. Bud handed the reins to Mac, and the boys took the horses into the barn. "Come on in, brother, and tell me how it is." Nick clapped Bud on the shoulder, and they turned to go into the house together.

"Well, I'll tell ya', things are a little tense just right at the moment."

Nick smiled and looked at his older brother. "Oh yeah? How so?"

"I'll tell ya' on the ride over; you'll shit your shorts."

"Oh, all right then." They came into the house and were met by a little girl in a dress holding a doll. Nick picked her up and kissed her, and she held her doll out to Bud.

"Why, thank you, Janette." Bud shifted his attention and spoke to the doll. "How are you, little lady?" Janette laughed in her father's arms. She reached out for the doll, and Bud handed it to her, chucking the little girl under the chin and making her laugh again. She was a bright light in the house, and Nick and Ellen were devoted to her. A beautiful little girl with a sweet and gentle disposition, she was treated like a little princess by the cousins, who took special care of her when she came with her parents for a visit. Robert was enamored with her, and for some reason always wanted to brush her hair. She tolerated it well enough, but her patience wore thin after a bit; Robert had followed her around with the hairbrush all afternoon last time they'd been together. The girls treated her as though she were a living doll and fussed over her. Janette, for her part, enjoyed the attention thoroughly, as she was an only child and the cousins were the closest she had to siblings. Today, though, she was happy to be set down by her father, and she ran off with her doll, chattering to her as she went. Bud and Nick came into the large kitchen and washed their hands at the basin, then turned to the table where Ellen was setting down plates. Ellen came over and hugged Bud.

"The boys are coming?" she asked.

"In just a minute; they're finishing up in the barn," he replied as he sat down.

"It's good to see you. How's Caroline and the children?"

"They're all good, healthy, and loud," he replied with a laugh and slid his napkin to his thigh. The boys bustled in with a bang, and Janette ran back into the kitchen and wrapped herself around Tom's leg. He leaned down to pick her up.

"Hey, you," he said, as he tickled her side. She laughed and slid down, then found her seat at the table next to her father. Tom and Mac sat down, and Ellen brought a pan of bacon to the table then sat down herself and folded her hands.

"Daddy?" Ellen asked Nick, and everyone bowed their heads. After Nick said a short prayer, the six of them tucked in to fried eggs and bacon with biscuits and jam. Tom and Mac giggled with Janette while they ate, and Nick, Ellen, and Bud talked about the trip ahead. The men planned to be back Saturday afternoon, and Tom and Mac were planning on coming over again in the morning to help Ellen with the milking after their own chores at home were done. After that they would head to the field again for a few hours, then be allowed to play on their own in the afternoon before the evening chores were due. Ellen thought she might take Janette to see Caroline and the girls in the afternoon, and Bud mentioned that Annie was staying with them. He didn't elaborate; that would be a conversation for later when little ears were not listening.

After breakfast the boys went out to the barn with Nick to get the horses, and Bud and Ellen stood alone on the porch. The day was already warm and humid; it was going to be a hot one. Bud knew he and Nick had plenty of water in their canteens, and they would fill them again at the river, but they'd need every drop today. Bud held his hat in his hand and fiddled with the brim.

"How's Caroline doing, Bud?" Ellen asked him quietly. She knew the trials they'd had with Caroline's melancholia over the years and had seen her at her worst and best; if anyone could understand her depression, it was Ellen.

"She's all right, right now, but she's a little sore at me just at present." He smiled at her without humor. "I done got myself in a bit of a pickle."

"You boys do seem to do that. What'd you manage this time?" she asked, assuming he'd come in drunk one night or lost a few dollars playing cards in town. That was the worst either brother was likely to get up to— minor mischief at best.

"Annie's pregnant," was all he said, and he didn't look at her.

"Oh, really?" The meaning didn't dawn immediately. A moment later her pleasant conversational "Oh," turned to "Ohhh" as she began to get the gist of it. "Oh, Bud. What in the world."

"Yep, I done stepped in it." He looked down at his boots and then off to the barn where Nick and the boys were leading the horses out.

"Well, I'll see them tomorrow and get myself in the middle of it then. Thanks for the warning, I guess." She smiled at him wanly and kissed his cheek as she turned to pick up Janette, who'd come out to cling to her mother's dress. "Come on, let's go say bye to Daddy."

The boys and Bud thanked Ellen for breakfast and then rode to the gate to gather the cows while Nick said his goodbyes. Nick had two good herd dogs that would take the trip with them as far as the river and then turn back home. At the river Nick and Bud would join Willie and his sons, Dewey and Jace, and together they would finish the trip south of town to the cattle buyer. Dewey and Jace were in their late teens and both still lived at home. Jace was seeing a girl and would probably settle down near his parents, but Dewey planned to travel when he got older and didn't stick with any particular girl. He was a pistol, was Dewey; always up for adventure and could never sit still. Already he had broken an arm and a leg in his young life, and his mother was in constant fear of his impending death; if there was something that could be jumped on or swung from, Dewey was liable to do it. He would take any dare. She cautioned him constantly, and he reassured her with the air of invincibility that only a young man could have. Willie was a bit of a wild one himself in his youth, Bud had heard, so he figured the apple probably didn't fall far from the tree. Willie and Sharpe were cousins, although Willie was much younger. The woods were full of Braxtons, and you couldn't throw a stick without hitting one of them, it seemed.

Tom and Mac set off for home, waving their goodbyes, and Bud and Nick herded the cows back down the lane toward the river. As they rode together in the late morning, the dogs kept the cows from straying into the woods, and Bud and Nick found themselves in the back of the herd and able to talk for a few moments. "So what's going on at your house that I'm gonna be so shocked about?" Nick asked Bud, who was prodding a heifer that had stopped to graze.

"You won't believe it," Bud said, as the heifer ambled up to the rest of the herd. He wiped his brow. "Annie's pregnant, and I'm going to be a daddy again."

"You're *what? Christ*, Bud. How in the world did you manage that?" Nick laughed at him. Lord, he was in for it now. Both of them had spent a nickel in the brothel in town from time to time after they were married, and both women knew about it and tended to look the other way, but that was a lot different from knocking up the house help. Nick whistled. "Hoo, boy, you up a creek, ain'tcha?"

"Yeah, I am, I guess, but I intend to stick it out. Annie's moved into the boys' room, and I'm gonna need your help to build her a little place of her own."

"Are you *serious*? What did Caroline say?"

"She's not speaking to me right now, so she ain't sayin' much," Bud admitted. Caroline was still angry when he left, but he knew Annie would stand her ground. Caroline would have to seethe openly as she saw fit.

"I knew she was helpin' out, but I didn't know she was *that* helpful," Nick teased. This was going to be good. He didn't often get a chance to give his brother a hard time, but this was pure gold. He planned to mine this one.

"Oh, shut up. It's not like I planned it," Bud scowled. One of the dogs nipped at the back legs of a cow who'd fallen behind, and she hopped a little as she trotted to catch up with the group. The dog ran off to the side, yipping as it went to move the herd along. They came out of the wooded lane, and green grass grew in tufts between ruts that wagons had cut in a path between fields of high waving grasses. Turkey oaks grew in the distance, and Bud and Nick fanned out to keep the herd from moving off into the meadows.

Eventually they made it down to the river, and the cows joined another herd where Willie and his boys were loading the ferry. Jace tipped his hat to them, taking a brief break from ushering the cows aboard the ferry. Henry tied the rope to the dock to ensure it held fast, then waved to Bud and Nick. Later he would release it and shove off from the dock, and make his way across the river with the cows. The ferry was slow going, but it was a better option than trying to move the herd across the river, where they were as likely to go down the river as across it.

Willie rode over to them and reined in his horse next to Nick. He rested one arm over the horn and leaned on it, tipping his hat back on his head. Sweat ran down in rivulets from his temples. "Gonna be a hot one today, boys," he said. Nick handed him his canteen, and Willie nodded to him, taking it and knocking it back. He emptied it and handed it back to Nick, who capped it and hung it back around his saddle horn. "Better fill that up 'fore we go," Willie said. He took a handkerchief out of his back pocket and mopped his brow with it. "Bud, how goes it, son? You didn't bring them boys? They shavin' yet?"

Bud smiled. "Not yet, but it won't be long. They grow a foot a week, I think. Your boys are shootin' up too, I guess." He nodded toward Dewey, who had dismounted and was filling his own canteen from the river. Dewey looked up and waved.

"Yeah, 'at one especially. He's a good six inches taller'n me now." They continued to chat while Nick rode his mare to the river to fill his canteen then left the river to tap a kidney. The extra cup of coffee this morning was probably not such a great idea in retrospect, but he was glad of this chance to relieve himself before the trip continued. He thought of Ellen back at the house with Janette. Their daughter was the light of their lives, but he envied Bud and Willie their strong sons. His own boys, had they lived, would have been school age now, and he wondered what they would have looked like, what their personalities would have been. Would they be bookworms and thoughtful like Bud's Maclan or daredevils like Dewey? Would they keep him up at night whispering in their beds before sleep took them, as he and his own brothers used to do?

His heart had broken with each small coffin they buried in the churchyard, and he and Ellen had had some rough times, even since the good Lord had seen fit to bless them with Janette. That pain didn't go away just because she'd come. He understood Caroline's spells very well, he thought. But he could understand Bud's pain too and his need for companionship with Annie. There had been many nights that he'd sought out Ellen and she had rebuffed him gently, too wrapped in her own pain to seek comfort in him or offer comfort herself. A night in town here and there had helped him through, and he knew she knew about it and didn't judge him too harshly. She wasn't thrilled about it, but neither was she stupid, and she picked her battles. Overall, they had a good relationship, and he was grateful for a good, dependable woman; he knew plenty of men who complained of a wife who was a nag or a torment, and Ellen was neither.

As Bud and Nick began urging cows onto the deck, Henry came over to talk to Willie, who was swallowing a draft from his canteen.

"How do ye, Will?" Henry called as he came near, wiping his hands on his handkerchief, then poking it into his back pocket. Henry had lost two fingers in a mill accident and had taken on the ferry after Old Man Tolbert had gotten too old to do it. He was deft with his remaining fingers, however, and knew how to tie more kinds of knots than most men knew existed.

Willie smiled at his cousin and wiped his mustache as he capped the canteen. "All good here, Henry; looks like you're keepin' upright." Henry removed his hat and scratched his head.

"It's all right, if that asshat Dixon'd quit sendin' the timber down ever' two minutes. I 'low I can't get the ferry over without knockin' into a fuckin' mess a logs," he complained. "He's cuttin' a set up 'ere in the north forest, and he been sendin' 'em down like to kill me. Puttin' in a railroad or somethin'." Willie knew it wasn't just the logs that irked Henry; it was Pete Dixon himself. He and Dixon had had words in public a few times, and there was no love lost between them. Dixon ran a timber outfit in north Florida and periodically ran camps to clear land; when he sent the logs down the river rather than haul them out and Henry was downriver, you heard about it plenty. The logs made the trip over the river slow going and precarious at times, and Henry wasn't shy about making his opinion known. Two fingers down didn't mean there was anything wrong with his voice.

"I didn't know he'd got a camp up there," Willie said. He didn't want to get Henry started on Dixon, but he was a bit of a captive audience till the ferry got loaded.

"Yeah, he been roundin' up guys for a couple weeks now. Still lookin' for a few, I heard." Just then Nick called to him and he raised his hand to Willie. "Back in a few."

Willie watched him go and noticed a cow meandering down the bank. He'd better get her now before she got too far. With any luck they'd get down to the buyer this evening and have a good rest in town tonight. Good God, it was hot.

Annie hung the sheets on the line and pinned them in place. This was quite possibly the most awkward position she'd ever been in. Caroline refused to talk to her but stalked around the house in stony silence. She was terse with the children, and they looked at Annie in bewilderment. She shooed them out of the house and sent Ellie and Sarah off with Susan to Robert Braxton's with a pail of green peppers from the garden. She didn't know if he liked them or not and didn't care; she just needed the children out from underfoot for a minute. Bethy was napping, and Tom and Mac were back from Nick's and taking care of chores around the barn and field. Caroline was sweeping the house, last Annie saw. At least she was up. Mad as a hornet but out of the bed, so she guessed that was kind of a plus.

Having her daddy so angry at her saddened her. She'd told her parents about the baby the evening before Bud came over, and Garret Wilson had wanted to go over to Bud's house immediately and confront him. The women had talked him out of it but only after a bucketful of tears had been shed. Annie wasn't his only daughter, but she was the only one so far who'd managed to get herself in the family way before marriage. Not that she was the first girl to ever have done it, but he certainly wasn't happy about it. Her mama was disappointed, but she herself had married at sixteen, so she couldn't say much to her twenty-one-year-old daughter.

Caroline came out of the house now with a load of wet shirts in her arms and thunked them into the basket. Without saying a word to Annie, she turned on her heel and walked back into the house. Oh, it was going to be a long day.

Bud stretched out on the mattress and yawned. They'd gotten the herd over the river and down south of town, and throughout the day he'd told Nick about his idea of building Annie a place of her own and a shared kitchen. Nick had agreed to come help him build it after the beans were in from his field. After meeting the buyer in the late afternoon, they'd eaten supper and taken rooms at the Exchange Hotel in town. Then Nick had gone with the boys to the bar. Bud was exhausted and lay down fully clothed in the bed. While Nick might come back in a couple of hours, the boys probably would spend a late night with some female companions. Who even knew where Willie was. Bud was grateful for the peace and quiet. He could hear the noise in the street below, but he drifted off and didn't wake when Nick came in later.

It was three in the morning when Bud was abruptly awakened by a knock on the door. He rolled to his side and watched as Nick opened it to Willie's son Jace, who stumbled into the room. Bud lit a lamp and sat up. He rubbed his eyes wearily as Nick tried to steady a swaying Jace.

"You gotta come help me get 'im, he's sacked out nes' door," Jace said, slurring his words. Nick led Jace to his bed, and he fell into it. Bud assumed Jace meant Dewey; they'd gone for a few drinks after supper.

"Where next door?" Nick asked as Jace's head hit the pillow, his eyes closed.

"Upstairs. Tried to wake him up, but I couldn't. Girl couldn't get him up, after." Nick took Jace's boots off, and Jace rolled over to face the wall. As Bud searched for his own boots underneath the bed, Jace said something else, but it was muffled in the pillow, and neither Bud nor Nick caught it. Bud found his boots, and as he pulled them on, he nodded toward the small trash can beside the bureau.

"Better pull that over here, Nick, case he needs it while we're gone." Nick picked up the can and placed it beside the bed.

"I think he's out, but yeah. I guess let's go find 'im. Where's Willie?"

"I dunno but my guess is he ain't particularly useful right now, anyhow. Either passed out or asleep in his room. Come on, we can handle it."

They left Jace snoring and went downstairs as quietly as they could. It was a small hotel but full, and they tried and failed utterly to avoid the squeaky stairs. As they pulled the front door shut behind them, Nick chuckled. "I remember a few nights when I couldn't get back on my own, myself, a few years ago."

Bud smiled. "Yeah, I can't judge. Think we've all done it a few times."

They crossed the dusty street to Chessie's Saloon, where a pair of women's boots hung on a bent nail beside the door. A busty woman in a satin gown looked up from the bar as they came in, and the bartender, towel in hand, called, "We're closed down now, gentlemen."

Nick raised his hand and gestured toward the stairs. "We're just looking for a friend who mighta overstayed his welcome a bit."

The woman swiveled off the barstool and sauntered toward them, then led them to the stairs. "'Bout time you boys came. I sent that other kid off more 'n half an hour ago." She tromped up the stairs heavily, skirts swishing. Nick and Bud looked at each other and then followed her up the stairs. By the time they reached the landing, she was breathing heavily. She rested a moment and then led them down the hall to a door and pushed it open to a dimly lit room. Two young women were reclining on a sofa near the window, smoking and chatting, and their heads turned toward them as the busty matron led the men into the hazy room. Dewey lay crosswise on the bed on his back, trousers on and shirtless, and a thin line of drool trailed from his mouth onto the sheets underneath his cheek. "Right there," the busty woman said, as she leaned against the open door. "You girls go on now," she said to the women, who gave the men long appraising looks as they sidled past them toward the hall. "They ain't customers," the matron said, and the women quickened their steps as they passed through the door.

"Shame," one of them said, and the other giggled as they continued down the hall. Bud picked up Dewey's boots and socks and started to put them on his feet. Nick kneeled on the bed next to Dewey and slapped him lightly on the cheek.

"Hey, son, you ready to go home?"

Dewey snorted and turned his head but didn't wake. Bud got one sock and boot on and started on the other. The matron handed Nick Dewey's shirt and belt. "Here's his stuff." Nick took them with one hand and felt for Dewey's billfold in the back pocket with his other hand. It was there but no doubt a little lighter than it had been when the evening started. Well, that was Dewey's lookout, not his. Bud shoved the remaining boot onto Dewey's foot and stood.

"All right, you get that arm, I'll get the other." Together they hauled Dewey to his feet, and the young man's eyes opened briefly as they swung him toward the door, his arms draped over the men's shoulders. He alternately stumbled and dragged his feet, and his head lolled forward as they made their way out and down the stairs. The matron called down after them.

"You boys come back again tomorrow, hear?" She laughed and went back into the room as they made their way down.

They didn't reply but focused on getting Dewey down the stairs without falling. As they reached the door, Bud raised a hand to the bartender, who nodded and continued sweeping, the chairs all upturned onto tables now. They half dragged, half walked Dewey down the quiet street toward the hotel, where Bud let Dewey's arm fall from his shoulder as he moved ahead to open the door. Dewey sagged against Nick, and Nick held him around the waist. "Take this," he said to Bud, handing him the shirt and belt as he maneuvered Dewey through the door. Bud closed the door behind them, then followed them as they slowly climbed the stairs to the room where Jace lay. "You got the key?" Nick whispered to Bud, who wriggled past them as he fished it from his front pocket, then tried to slide it home under the doorknob without dropping it. He opened the door, and Nick pulled Dewey in. He sat him on the empty bed, and Dewey slumped over to his side.

"Well, now what? Where are *we* gonna sleep?" Bud closed the door behind him and put the key on the desk near the entry.

"Weren't they going to bunk in Willie's room?" Nick asked, as he arched his back and turned to face Bud.

"Yeah, but I ain't got the key," Bud said, dropping into the chair. "I don't wanna sleep with either one a them, and I ain't sleepin' with you."

"Well I don't zackly wanna sleep with you, either," Nick said, looking at the sleeping boys. "Mebbe he give it to one a' them." He rifled through Dewey's pockets and coming up empty, turned to rifle through Jace's. Jace lay exactly where they'd left him. He found the key in Jace's front pocket and turned to Bud. "Help me get him over a bit, and we'll put Dewey in next to him. Then you can have this bed, and I'll go down to Willie's room and sleep in that one." They moved Jace over to the side of the bed, then together they pulled Dewey up off the other bed and back to his feet again.

"I already paid 'er," Dewey said, as they laid him down next to Jace.

"Yeah, yeah, we know," Bud said, bringing the boy's feet up. He pulled off Dewey's boots. "Go to sleep."

Nick stood up and sighed. It was now after four in the morning, and he was tired. "Don't you be knockin' on my door early," he said. "I'm sleepin' in."

"Nope," Bud agreed. He was eager to get back to bed himself. He sat down on the empty bed and started to take his own boots off. "But we gotta get to the bank tomorrow morning, though, so we can't be here all day." He placed his hand near the lamp, waiting for Nick to exit the room. "Late breakfast downstairs, maybe. Don't expect these two will eat much."

Nick chuckled as he left. "Nope, I doubt it. Night." He closed the door behind him.

Bud blew out the light, rolled to his back, and closed his eyes. The night was quiet outside, and a light breeze gently billowed the curtains as it blew in through the window. He drifted off to a dreamless sleep after a few moments, his soft snores joining those of the boys' across the little room, sleeping off their night on the town.

9 FRANK

Late Saturday morning found the men downstairs in the Exchange Hotel eating breakfast, three of them tucking in to eggs and cornbread, while the other two drank coffee with something less than enthusiastic appetites.

"So what exactly did you *think* was gonna happen when you passed out in a whore's bedroom?" Willie asked his son, wiping scrambled egg from his beard with his napkin.

"Well, I didn't 'spect she'd steal me blind!" Dewey said, holding his head in his hand, his left elbow narrowly missing the butter plate. His head hurt, and the noise of the clattering silverware on plates and chair legs scraping the wooden floor was deafeningly loud. His mouth felt like sandpaper, even though he'd had two cups of coffee already.

"He's right," Nick said, putting his coffee cup on the table. "I believe most of those ladies over there *are* fine, trustworthy individuals," he said, his mouth contorting into a smile as he mopped up egg yolk with a bit of toast. "It was probably an honest mistake."

Bud, Willie, and Nick laughed at the young men as Jace and Dewey struggled to get on top of their hangovers. "How much she get?" Bud asked.

"Five dollars," Dewey mumbled. He looked down at his dusty boots and sighed in resignation. It was his own stupid fault.

"You be glad she didn't get more. Now you know why I told you to leave the rest with me last night, 'fore you boys went on over there," Willie said, leaning back in his chair and picking up his coffee cup. He looked in, saw that it was empty, and moved to set it back on the table, but just then a waitress came by with a fresh pot.

"More coffee, gentlemen?" she asked, taking Willie's cup from him. The coffee was strong and hot, and the men enjoyed having a breakfast in town, though none of them were as finely dressed as some of the diners. Other patrons were in starched collars and coats, but the men were wearing their riding clothes. That was all right, though; the Exchange Hotel wasn't snooty like some of those fancy places up in Savannah and Atlanta Bud had read about in the paper. Caroline had talked about going to Savannah for a vacation one day, just the two of them, but it was just something she dreamed about. They'd never be able to afford it, and who'd take eight children on while they went off gallivanting, anyway?

The waitress filled their coffee cups and moved on to other tables. Bud and Nick finished their breakfasts and Jace absently picked at a biscuit. Willie set down his cup without taking a sip, watching the steam rise. Slowly he tipped the cup until the coffee ran down the side into the saucer, and he let a bit pool there and cool. He picked up the saucer and drank from it. A lady at a nearby table saw him and lifted an eyebrow as she sipped her own coffee; Willie didn't notice and wouldn't have cared had he seen it.

Bud scraped his chair back and drained his cup. "We done?" He needed to get to the bank this morning and then get headed home. The boys would handle most of the chores while he was gone, but there was no need to stick around town any longer, now that he'd seen the buyer.

Nick nodded and began to stand, but Willie demurred and said, "I'm a have one more cup, boys, and then we'll be on our way. But don't let us hold you up. You go on and we' be seein' ya." Jace and Dewey remained slouched in their chairs but shook hands with Bud and Nick as they rose to go.

"Chin up, Dewey, ya still got your health," Nick said, and everyone laughed.

"Yeah, yeah," Dewey said with a sheepish grin, crossing his arms over his chest and slouching down a little further. Five dollars wasn't so much to lose, and his pa was right: it could have been worse. They said their goodbyes, and Bud and Nick each laid half a dollar on the table and nodded to the waitress as they headed out the door. The weather was hot and muggy already, and as they walked down to the stable to get their horses, Bud reminded Nick of his promise to come help put up a small home for Annie to live in.

"I got to get the rest of the beans in, but I can come. Are you sure you know what you're doing?" Nick asked, as they stopped for a moment before they went into the stable.

"No, but I know she can't stay in the house forever, and she's gotta go somewhere. Caroline was right put out with me, but I don't see another way through. If we can cut some cedar outta that back forty acres, we could probably have somethin' up before winter's over." Bud leaned back on his heels. "I'll pay you back somehow, whatever you decide."

"Don't worry about that, just worry about—" he stopped midsentence and looked over Bud's shoulder. "Ahhh...that's *Frank*."

Bud turned and saw a bearded man holding another man's head by the hair, bending him at the waist over a watering trough and dunking his head in the water. As Bud watched, he yanked the man's head out of the trough, sending water flying, and the dunked man staggered back to keep his balance. He spewed water out of his nose and mouth and made a loud *gahh* as the man who had dunked him grabbed him by his shirt and slammed him into one of the posts beside the trough.

"And if I ever see ya again, I'll hold your head down there till ya drown! You got it?" He gave the dripping man a great shove, picked up his hat from the ground, and stormed off. The dripping man stumbled and fell to his knees, then wiped his hair back from his face as he sat on his heels. He raised his hand and waved at the back of the man who'd baptized him in the horses' watering trough.

"You're a sore loser, Buck, an' thass' all!" he called. The bearded man didn't turn but kept on his way, and the soggy drunkard slowly rose, wobbling, to his feet.

Bud frowned and agreed, "Yeah, that's Frank," and began to walk toward the dripping man who was swaying in the morning breeze. Nick sighed and followed him.

"Frank, what'd you do, get caught cheatin' again?" Bud called to him.

Frank looked over when Bud spoke, a smile dawning across his face, and he stretched out his arms as Bud approached. Bud stopped short of accepting a soppy hug and gently pushed Frank away.

"I dint do nothin', Bud, just spendin' a nice day in town. 'E's sore 'cause he lost. Heeyy there, Nick," he said, as Nick dodged a hug from Frank as well. "Whatchoo boys doin'?"

"Bit early to be sloshed, ain't it?" Bud asked, gripping his brother by the elbow to steady him. It was eleven in the morning, and Frank was three sheets to the wind. Likely he'd been at it all night and hadn't slept at all. Unfortunately, this was all too common for his brother, who had had a difficult time staying out of a bottle since he'd discovered it at fourteen. Bud and Nick had spent many an early morning pulling Frank out of the saloon or from a girl's bedroom, only to watch him saunter back in the next night to do it all again. They'd threatened, cajoled, punished, bribed, and pleaded with him to sober up and get hold of himself, and Frank always promised them this was the last time he'd drink his pay for the week. But every time a dollar somehow found its way out of Frank's pocket and onto the bar, sliding over to the bartender or into a barmaid's waiting hand. Eventually his brothers had left him to it, to ruin himself as he pleased.

"You need to get home and get some sleep, Frank. You're an unholy mess," Nick said. "I ain't gonna take you, though; I'm goin' home. Bud, you c'n do it, I ain't got the time nor the patience, and I got 'im last time." He clapped Bud on the shoulder and started walking toward the stable, dodging a horse and wagon in the street. "I'll come see ya next week," he called over his shoulder. Bud watched him go while Frank swayed and bobbed, passersby eyeing him warily as they went about their morning.

"Nice ta see you too!" Frank called after him. The smell of him was overpowering despite his recent bath, and Bud wrinkled his nose as he looked back at him and took in the dirty and wrinkled mess that was his youngest brother.

"You can't be actin' like this, Frank, right in the middle of town on a Saturday morning. It's ridiculous. And you stink."

"A rose by any other name would smell as sweet, Bud," Frank said with a grin. Attempting a sweeping bow, he pitched forward, overcompensated, and crashed into Bud with his hip, knocking him back a step and annoying him further. Bud took Frank by the shoulders and stood him up straight, then grasped him by the collar and spun him around in the opposite direction, toward the stables. Frank weaved alarmingly but stayed on his feet.

"Walk, boy, we're goin' home." He gave him a gentle shove but didn't let go of his collar. Frank ambled forward amiably enough, and Bud steered him through the street. Bud purposefully did not catch the eye of anyone passing by but focused instead on keeping Frank upright and moving through the swish of skirts and clatter of wheels in the bright sunlight. They made their way to the stables just as Nick came out riding his bay roan, and they watched him turn into the street. He saw his brothers, and Bud caught an eye roll and a head shake before he turned away. Nick had undoubtedly done his share of raising Frank, just as Bud had, but his patience with his brother's antics had worn thin, and at that moment he was not inclined to indulge him.

Bud understood how he felt; he himself had all but given up on Frank, but a part of him pitied him as well. At least Bud and Nick had known a mother, however brief it had been; Frank wasn't as fortunate because their mother left when Frank was still a toddler. Their father had done the best he could, Bud supposed, but Bud and Nick had been parents long before they were old enough to be married and off by themselves. Robert had become a broken man after May ran off, and while they had all suffered, sometimes he thought Frank and his father had suffered the most.

He trotted Frank into the stable, narrowly avoiding a small boy who darted around them to catch up with his family. "How'd you get to town? You got a horse? Wagon?"

"Rode with the Lowerys; don't know where they've got off to now," Frank answered, and he looked around as if he expected to see them. "Wednesday, Thursday. What day is it now, Bud?"

"It's Saturday, and they're probably long gone. I'll take you home. Come on." He found a barrel for Frank to rest on while he retrieved his horse from the stable boy and paid the fee for the night's stay. The chestnut Morgan was an all-around good farm horse, reliable and good-natured, and Bud's favorite. His name was Jack. Caroline had named him when Bud bought him eight years ago, and she named the mare Jill. He'd laughed, telling her it probably meant one of them would pitch him off down a hill somewhere, but neither one had done it so far, and both were steady and patient. Together with the older paint he'd had when they married, they helped him do everything he needed around the farm and in the timber. He led Jack out to where Frank slouched on the barrel, eyes closed. "Frank, get up, and get on Jack; we're going home."

Frank opened his eyes and looked up. "Thass' a good-lookin' horse you got there, Bud," he said.

"Yeah, well, get up, and get up on 'im, and let's go." He steadied Frank as he stood and helped him get his foot into the stirrup; no easy task in Frank's inebriated condition. He boosted his brother up and settled his pack behind the saddle. As Frank struggled with the other stirrup, Bud took the reins and waited. Frank sat up and gave a salute that was something less than crisp.

"Ready, sir!" Frank smiled and slouched in the saddle. At least he was upright and hadn't vomited on anything. That was good.

Bud rolled his eyes, turned around, and walked the horse into the street. *Good Lord. This is* **exactly** *how I was gonna spend the day,* he thought. It occurred to him that there'd be no going to the bank now, not with Frank in tow. *Damn.* He thought of the roll of cash in his pocket and sighed. *It'll be fine at home for the time bein'.*

By the time they made it to Frank's sad shack, for that was all it could be called, it was late, and Bud was hot, tired, and hungry. Frank had long since fallen asleep on the horse, and Bud had passed a silent afternoon with his thoughts as he led them to the ramshackle cabin Frank called home. He wondered how the women were getting on without him. The week had been tense, with Caroline giving one-word answers and Annie trying to be helpful without being in the way. He had let them manage the children between them and hadn't said more than absolutely necessary to either one of them.

Lord, he didn't know what he was doing or how he'd gotten himself into this mess. He didn't think of himself as an *adulterer*, exactly, although he supposed that's just what he was. Caroline had just been so absent, listless, and unreachable. He loved her, he knew he did, but their marriage was strained and empty. Annie had brought a light to the house that he hadn't realized was missing until she came, and she was gentle with the children and helpful in ways they had all come to rely on, while Caroline slept days away in the bed or cried silently. Occasionally bits of the old Caroline would come through, and they would enjoy times together, and Bud held out hope each time that the emergence from her self-imposed cocoon would be permanent, but she eventually faded away again into her darkness. He didn't understand it, where she went in her mind, but he empathized. Having Charlie taken away seemed like a cruel trick, and he struggled with the knowledge that a loving God could allow such a thing to happen to a child or his parents to suffer so. That was one thing he was planning to ask God first thing, whenever his day came.

Bud halted the horse, slid Frank from the saddle, and let him slump against his shoulder as he led him to the cabin. He kicked the door, and it gave easily into a two-room house that had once been rather respectable but had fallen into disrepair. Dirty dishes sat on the table and more were piled in a tub nearby. Flies buzzed and crawled over the remnants of suppers past, and Bud wrinkled his nose as he led Frank to the mussed bed in the next room.

"This is disgusting, Frank," he said. "You gotta get a hold of yourself." He sat Frank on the bed and gently pushed him to lie down. He removed his brother's boots and put his feet on the bed, then sat down next to him in the stuffy little cabin. The room had a window with glass, but the glass was cracked, and the air was stagnant and humid. He rested there and looked at Frank.

He loved his little brother but didn't come very often to his house anymore, instead letting him run with the Lowery boys and see to himself. He was no longer a child, and he had to fend for himself the way everyone else did. The Lowerys were nearer Frank's age than Bud's, but he knew who they were and probably more relevantly *what* they were. Robert had had some land to give to his sons, and that had helped them make a living each in their own way, but the Lowerys had never had two nickels to rub together and were constantly in the jail, the saloon, or the still they ran in the woods. Honest work was a foreign concept. The two Lowery brothers Frank hung with were good for a round of cards and a bottle of beer and not much else, and they lived with their siblings and parents in a shabby house down by Weaver River. Bud had been there a few times looking for Frank over the years.

Robert had given his boys his land, and they had built their small houses as they'd grown older. Frank, being the youngest and unmarried, hadn't needed much space and didn't keep livestock. He'd kept to himself as he got grown, taking jobs here and there but never really settling into anything. Bud knew about being a bachelor, as short as his own time had been, and he wasn't the neatest man, but this—this was just nasty, and he hadn't realized it had gotten quite so out of hand. He wondered if Nick knew. He would ask him when he saw him. He stood and began poking into the cabinets in the next room as Frank's snores cut into the quiet late afternoon. He found some dried venison hanging in a cupboard and gnawed on it as he looked around himself. At least Frank had a little food and wasn't starving. He took a couple more strips and closed the cupboard. He spied an empty flour sack hanging over the back of a chair and shook it out, dropping the venison in it. That would keep him till he got home for a late supper.

Clearly they'd have to talk to Frank, but he wasn't going to do it alone, and there was nothing to do for him now but let him sleep it off. He stepped back into the bedroom and opened the window, letting a minimal breeze waft in. At least it wasn't straight up noon, and maybe it would cool off a little when the sun went down. He took a last look at Frank in the bed, saw he was sleeping more heavily, and left him to it. Outside, he led the horse to the pump and filled the bucket to let him drink his fill, then put his head under the water's flow and let it cool him off a bit. He cupped his hands and swallowed, looking around the little clearing in the woods. It was overgrown in some areas but there was bare dirt in others, and small scraggly bushes sprouted around the little cabin. He walked a few steps and saw that a little path led into the brush where it disappeared around a bend and eventually led to a small privy. Jack ambled over to him when he was done drinking, and Bud stroked his head.

"All right, Jack, let's get ourselves home. Won't get there 'fore dark, but I guess that's all right." He kicked the bucket back over to the pump and mounted Jack, pointing him toward Caroline, Annie, and the children, who probably had expected him back from town hours ago. The evening was pleasant, though still humid, and the cicadas and frogs sang as he rode through the woods. The late summer moon emerged from behind a cloud and lit his way through the leaves as he wound through the pines and turkey oak.

The venison was gone now, but it had kept him from thinking about his stomach constantly, although he was looking forward to whatever Caroline had put by for his supper, assuming she'd deign to feed him. As the night wore on, his mind was quiet and untroubled, and he was relaxed in the saddle as Jack plodded patiently on. A sudden bright orange light in the distance made him take notice, however, and he halted Jack as he puzzled out what it was. Not a firefly, the light was too steady for that, and it rose and fell in the night.

He smelled it then, the cigar, and held his breath. He saw only the one small light, and though he didn't know if he'd been heard or seen yet, he hadn't been trying to be quiet and had to assume the smoker was aware of him. Damn Frank! If not for him he wouldn't have this roll of cash on him right now and it'd be sitting in the bank. Now what? He didn't know if Cigar was laying for him, exactly, or just a traveler, but if it was someone just bedding down for the night, wouldn't he have a campfire? His arms rose in gooseflesh, and he reached behind him for his pack. He'd brought a pistol and left his rifle with the boys at home. He couldn't be sure it was just Cigar alone, and while the pistol was handy, if there was a tussle with more than one or two, he wasn't guaranteed to come out on top.

He left the pistol in the pack and instead felt for the flour sack he'd draped in front of the saddle horn after the last piece of venison. He fished the roll of cash out of his pocket and dropped it into the sack, then gently urged Jack forward a few steps to an old oak. He looked around himself, then back at the orange glow. Slowly, and as quietly as he could, he tied the flour sack into a crook of the tree so that it was secure but not entirely hidden; he was going to have to find it again tomorrow, after all. He tried not to make it blatantly obvious, so that anyone passing by would easily overlook it. He examined the tree closely, then looked around again for anything that he could recognize as a landmark. He knew these woods well; knew home was less than a mile away due north. But it wasn't a well-worn path that he was on tonight, and he was damned if he was going to lose a sack full of cash to a bandit or a tree. Just to the left and ahead of his oak was a gnarly old thing that looked like it had been struck by lightning sometime in its unfortunate past, and an entire side of it was blackened and spotted with moss. It was a fairly unique tree, wide at the base and surrounded by lichens and ferns. He thought he could find it again, if he rode straight south from his farm this way tomorrow and kept a sharp eye out.

He studied where he was one more time for good measure, then brought the pistol out and nudged Jack to a walk again toward home, keeping an eye on the orange glow that rose and steadied, then fell again. As he got closer he saw that it was indeed a traveler, and he was not alone; there were two of them crouched in the darkness. He saw packs and bedrolls around them but no campfire and no evidence of a supper. They had no horses but a dog lay between them, silent with ears pricked and alert. They had known he was there, then; there was no way he could have snuck up on them without the dog hearing and smelling Jack as he came near. He only hoped neither of them suspected what he was doing when he stopped to hide the flour sack. He continued forward and thumbed the hammer of the pistol back; at the sound of the click, the dog rose up on all fours and the men stood.

"Evenin'," Cigar said, and Bud could see he had his own pistol tucked into the front of his belt. Bud didn't reply but kept an eye on Cigar's buddy, who wore a dirty felt hat and had a full mustache and beard. He nodded at Bud. Bud pulled Jack to a halt again as the men took a few steps forward. Mustache had a pistol in a holster that rode low on his hips and a sweaty odor mixed with the smell of the cigar in the night air. The dog stepped cautiously forward with the men and stopped when they did, ears twitching with every huff from Jack.

"Nice night, right?" Cigar continued. "You comin' from town? Bit late, ain't it?"

"Spent the day there and heading home. You fellas lost?"

"Nope, we're right where we oughtta be," Mustache said, his hand resting lightly on the pistol grip at his side. He grinned and shot a glance at Cigar, who kept his eyes fixed on Bud.

Bud hadn't missed that glance. He looked from Cigar to Mustache and back to Cigar. "I think you fellas need to get a move on; these woods are no place to spend a night." His palm felt sweaty around the pistol, and he prayed he wouldn't have to shoot. He kept it where it was, cradled near the crotch of his pants in the saddle and hidden by the saddle horn and his hand with the reins. He tightened his grip on it and felt a bead of sweat at his temple.

"I think you need to come down off that horse a minute and show us what you got in town, Mister. That's what I think." Cigar took a step toward Jack and raised his hand to touch the horse's bridle. Bud pulled back on the reins, and Jack stepped back from Cigar, who scowled but didn't follow. Bud raised the pistol where both men could see it, and their eyes immediately darted to the glint of it in the moonlight.

"I don't think I will. Get on, now, both a' ya. Get your packs and get movin'," Bud said, keeping his voice as even as he could. If either of the men had drawn their pistols before Bud had ridden up and had had them ready and waiting, the situation might have been different, and Bud held his breath as each one stood stock still for a long moment, their eyes locked on his. No one moved, and a frog croaked and sang in the distance, as another joined. Finally, Cigar let out a breath, raised his cigar to his mouth, and grinned. He pulled in a deep breath and exhaled slowly. The orange glow brightened and waned in the darkness, then he dropped the stub to the dirt below and ground it out under a boot.

"Rube, I believe we might have to let this one go," he said to Mustache, who didn't reply. Rube only grunted and spat into the dirt. Bud kept the pistol leveled at the men and his eyes fixed on them, breathing shallowly but slowly and calmly. This wasn't his first rodeo, and he wouldn't be letting his guard down until he was safely away from this pair and on his way.

Cigar turned on his heels and bent to retrieve a pack and a bedroll, then shot out a kick to Rube's thigh when he saw that Rube's attention hadn't shifted from Bud. "Get your shit, Rube. Leave it."

Rube took a few steps to keep his balance and then backed up to where Cigar was gathering the other pack and bedroll, keeping his eyes on Bud and the pistol. Sweat dripped into Bud's eye, but he didn't move to wipe it away, and instead kept the pistol trained on the men, thumb still on the hammer and finger on the trigger. Jack snorted and tossed his head, as if to say, *Let's get this show on the road.*

Rube grinned and turned toward Cigar to take his pack, then slung it over his shoulder. "Yeah, I guess we'll keep on movin' a little further on tonight, after all," he said to Bud, and he and Cigar began to move off into the darkness toward the east, away from Bud's house and away from town and the hanging flour sack. "You have a good night now."

Bud watched them go and let out a breath when he thought they were far enough away where they couldn't hear it. He dropped the pistol to his side and pressured Jack with his legs to walk on. He'd get out to the lane in a few minutes and then he'd kick Jack to a trot to put a little more distance between himself and the would-be robbers and get himself home. *Thank You, God, for that. Lord knows that coulda gone a whole lot differently. Now help me get home and to bed 'fore I drop dead of a stopped heart.*

He did indeed come out into the lane shortly but stopped to slide the pistol back into his pack after looking one more time behind him and seeing nothing there. He urged Jack to a trot. *Sorry fella, I know it's late, but I've had all the excitement I can stand for now.* After his late night with Dewey and the hot day of getting Frank home, Bud was exhausted. All he wanted was to fall into bed and sleep, supper forgotten. Before long the little farm came into view, and Bud slowed Jack to a walk, then dismounted as they came to the barn. He rubbed the horse down well, hung up the bridle and saddle, and gave Jack some mash. He made sure the bucket was full of water, tossed some hay into the stall, and finally pulled the gate closed behind him. Sighing heavily, he swung his pack over his shoulder and headed toward the house, not even minding that Caroline was probably going to make him sleep on the floor again. Who even cared. He was dead on his feet.

Inside, he closed the door and pulled in the latch. He slid the pack to the floor and kicked it over to the chair. He'd deal with that tomorrow. Hearing a sound behind him, he turned. Annie was standing at the curtain of her room in her shift, her hair hanging in a braid on her shoulder. She smiled at him and whispered, "Long day?"

He sighed again, a gentle one this time, and toed off his boots. Maybe he wasn't as tired as he thought, and maybe he wouldn't have to sleep on the floor after all.

10 A DAY AT THE RIVER

Caroline lay on her back in the bed, listening to the sound of the children chattering in the next room. Annie was making them breakfast, and from the sound of it, she was also being bombarded with questions from Robert and constant interruptions from baby Bethy. Something must have spilled a few minutes ago, because there had been quite a commotion over it, which was what had woken her up. But she didn't get up to help, just stretched, rolled over, and lay there to listen to the madness. *Fine, let her handle it. She wanted to move in, let her move in. It's fun, isn't it, Annie, when all hell breaks loose first thing in the morning? Some days are just like that; best you get used to it,* she thought. She had been angry and irritable all week with Annie in the house, but now the anger was starting to wear off. She was still annoyed, though. No doubt about it. This whole arrangement was for the birds. What the hell were they thinking, and who did he think he was, just taking up with someone because she happened to be convenient? She liked Annie, and they had had a friendly relationship up until this nonsense. But now....

She sighed and rolled onto her side, looking toward the window where the morning light came in and the gentle breeze stirred the curtains. Late August, and it was going to be another hot day. She longed for the cool evenings of November and December. When it came to seasons, north Florida had about two days of Fall; it was just winter and spring for what felt like three weeks, then hot, humid-hot, rainy-hot, and hurricane. She supposed it was better than snow. She didn't know. Right then she'd take three feet of snow, thank you very much.

She'd heard Bud come in late last night, and she'd heard him talking softly to Annie in the other room. They'd expected him much earlier, and who knows where he'd been. Seeing the cattle buyer didn't take *that* long. She knew he'd slept in Annie's room last night, and it galled her to know that he was with Annie *right in her own house*, even though she wasn't ready to

66

welcome him back into her own bed and the best she was going to offer him was the floor. It saddened her too, however, and then she felt the guilt that ran in a constant undercurrent of her thoughts, day and night. *I drove him to it. It's my own damn fault, and I've got no one to blame but myself.*

She flopped over onto her back and huffed a breath out. *I can't help it, though! It's not like I want to feel like garbage all the time! It's just...just...* Just what, exactly? She didn't know. Just that nothing made her happy anymore. Not even the children, though she loved them and loved to cuddle with them and loved chatting with them and hearing about all their adventures of the day. But there were some days when she walked past the same pile of dirty clothes and just didn't have the energy it took to tote and boil the water and wash and hang them, even though she knew the children were walking around in clothes that were far past dirty. Her mother would roll in her grave if she knew how long it took her to get the sweeping done or how many times she just crawled back into the bed while she was making it. It wasn't all the time. Sometimes she could pull herself out of it, the darkness in her mind, but she didn't seem to have any control over it. And that was the awful thing. She couldn't just perk up because it was time to perk up; she felt empty and numb inside most days. And then some days were okay, and she felt like there was hope again. But there had been many more bad days than good days, and she knew she hadn't been there for Bud like she had been before Charlie died. So maybe she wasn't entirely blameless in all this, but oh, what a strange situation she found herself in now.

She sat up and swung her legs out of bed as Sarah came into the room. "Mama, we want to go to the river today! Can we? Please? *Please?*" Sarah hopped up on the bed and bounded over to her mother, throwing her arms around her neck. "Ellie says she'll teach me how to back float, and we'll all do double chores tomorrow if we can just go today!" At seven Sarah was already a skilled negotiator, and Caroline laughed.

"Of course you will, until tomorrow comes, and then you won't want to do them." She pulled Sarah into her lap and blew a raspberry on her cheek, which made them both laugh.

"I promise, I super-extra promise we'll do 'em all, no complainin' or nothin', and we'll be on our best 'havior, and nobody will argue all day." Sarah's promises sometimes tended toward the impossible for a gaggle of spirited children, but Caroline was sure that at that moment Sarah meant every word she said.

"Do you think that's possible, that all of you could go a whole day without arguing over *anything?* Even when we come home, and we're all tired and worn out, and there's still evening chores to be done?"

"'Course it is. Mrs. Lundy says 'nothing is impossible 'cause even the word says *I'm possible!*' And Mrs. Lundy knows a lot."

"Yes, she does; you're right about that," Caroline agreed, smiling. Mrs.

Lundy knew a great many things because Mrs. Lundy tended to stick her nose into a great many things. She was as old as the hills, but she still got around just fine, and there was nothing whatsoever wrong with her ears or her tongue. She was a tough old bird, Mrs. Lundy. She had a good heart, and she was the first person with a covered plate whenever there was a wedding or a funeral, but she certainly loved to share her opinions, and she had quite a lot of them.

Sarah took her mother's face in her hands, squeezing her cheeks and looking into eyes the same shade of green as her own. "So please can we? Go to the river?"

Caroline sighed. Maybe that's what she needed, a day at the river to cool off and relax and clear her head. Maybe that's what they all needed. "All right. If Pa agrees to take us, then it's okay with me."

"Yay!" Sarah kissed Caroline's cheek and wiggled off her lap. "Thank you, thank you, thank you!" she exclaimed happily as she ran out of the room in search of her father. Pa didn't often take a day off to play, but if Sarah told him that Mama had agreed to go, he might just do it today. Getting Mama to do anything outdoors that wasn't related to laundry, gardening, or chores was a rare occurrence, and she knew Pa might agree to go to the river because it meant Mama was happy. He had tried awfully hard to get Mama to be happy after Charlie died, but it was challenging some days. Today Mama was happy, and it was going to be a good day. 'If Mama ain't happy, ain't nobody happy.' That was another thing Mrs. Lundy had told her, and she agreed with that one.

The wagon bumped and jostled the children as Jack and Jill pulled it through ruts in the lane that were still wet in some places from late afternoon rainstorms. The children obviously didn't mind. They just grasped onto the sides or each other and chattered like little magpies. They were going to the river! Bud knew it was a rare treat for the children when Ma and Pa took off a whole afternoon just to play, and Annie was here, too, so it would be fun. They knew something was wrong between Ma and Annie and Pa although they didn't know just exactly what. Maybe today would put everyone in better spirits and be a nice little send-off to summer before school started up again in a couple of weeks.

Bud felt certain that if he asked the older children if they were looking forward to school, every one of them would answer with a hearty 'No!' He was just as certain that each one secretly was looking forward to seeing friends again and meeting the new teacher. Miss Finch had left after the last year to get married, and frankly the children were happy to see her go. She was an older woman who didn't have much patience with energetic children, and had there been many other options for employment of an unmarried woman of her years, she might have been better off exploring them. Certainly the children would have encouraged her in this; many of them had endured her sharp tongue and piercing glare when a sum was wrong or they were caught whispering too loudly. But there would be no Miss Finch this year, and it was rumored that a pretty young teacher from the next county was being sent over to fill the vacant position. All in all there was reason for hope and laughter among the children, and all of them were looking forward to a pleasant day ahead.

As they neared the river, Bud brought the horses and wagon to a halt beneath the shade of an oak, and the children scrambled out the back like ants out of hill, eager to be first in the water. Caroline climbed down from the seat and went around to the back of the wagon to help Robert down as Annie hovered behind him, making sure he didn't fall in his haste to catch up to the older children. Robert always wanted to be doing what the big boys and girls were doing, but his little legs couldn't always keep up, and it was a frustrating thing when your four-year-old body wouldn't cooperate so you could run as fast and as long as nine- and ten-year-old bodies.

"Hang your shirts on branches. Don't throw them on the ground!" Caroline called after Tom and Mac, who had shed britches and shirts as they ran, with the girls right on their heels. She looked at Bethy on her hip. "Those boys are silly, aren't they? Look at them running like crazy people!" She kissed her and pulled a sheet from the wagon to spread beneath the tree. Annie followed, bringing a basket of food and a pitcher of water from the bed of the wagon.

Bud unhitched the horses, taking his time and leading them away from the wagon, letting them loose to graze in the grass farther up from the bank. They would come when he whistled or called, so he didn't worry about them going too far or running off. While Caroline seemed to be in better spirits today than in the past week and the women had been civil, it was a far cry from their pleasant conversations of months past. Last week Caroline's anger had just about been palpable, and everyone walked on eggshells when she and Annie were in a room together. Bud avoided being alone with either one of them at all costs, preferring instead to spend his days in the barn or the field. He had never before looked forward to herding cattle to town as much as he had this last Friday, so ready was he to get out of the house and avoid any more awkward situations. When Bud woke up in Annie's bed, he thought for sure he was going to hear about it from Caroline, loudly and with feeling. But something had shifted in the air overnight, and the explosion hadn't come; oddly enough her mood actually seemed to have *improved*, which left him perplexed but also a bit hopeful. Thankfully, he'd been up long before any of the children since he'd needed to retrieve his flour sack from the woods, and none of them knew he'd spent the night with Annie. He didn't know how he'd explain himself, and he didn't know what he was going to say when Annie started showing. Probably just the truth. It wasn't pretty, but there was no help for it, and he didn't have the imagination or the energy to concoct a believable lie.

He stroked Jack's neck as he peeped over the horse's back, watching the women spread out the blanket and unpack the basket. Annie said something to Caroline and turned to walk down to the river, leaving Caroline to rest in the shade with Bethy. Caroline removed her hat and placed it on Bethy's head, which earned her a laugh from the toddler. *It looks safe enough*, he thought, and he left the horses to join her under the tree.

"Hey, pretty girl, how'd you get Mama's hat?" Bud sat down at the far edge of the blanket and started taking off his boots. Bethy tottered over to him, hat in hand, babbling her baby language. He picked her up and put her in his lap, looking at Caroline. "You ain't gettin' in the water?"

"No, not right now. Maybe after lunch," she replied.

Okay, this is all right. She was talking to him. This was good. He would tread carefully, though, because these things could turn on a dime, he knew. Years of marriage had taught him a few things, and their current situation was uncharted territory.

"You need help with anything, 'fore I go down there and dunk those boys?"

"No, go ahead. Just make sure everyone hung up their clothes somewhere. They won't like it if they have to put on sandy britches for the ride home."

"Okay." He set Bethy on her feet, then pulled off his own shirt and pants and left them on a heap on the blanket. "Go see Mama; I'll be back in a minute." Bethy waddled back over to Caroline, one chubby hand clutching the hat as she held the other out for balance.

Bud trotted down to the river. Annie had already hung up the children's clothes and was stepping out of her skirt, standing in her shift and keeping an eye on the children while they splashed each other and swam. The current here was slow, and the water was cool and refreshing after the ride in the hot morning sun. The children could play without danger of being swept in the current as long as they stayed where it was relatively shallow and didn't get in over their heads. Bud remembered back to when he was a boy, when he and his good friend T. F. Johnson had gone swimming in another part of the river where the current was swifter and he had gotten in over his head. He had almost drowned, but T. F. had jumped in and saved him, pulling him back to safety. He'd never forgotten that day and how scared he had been. *God looks after children and fools*, he thought and smiled to himself. He supposed that most of his life he'd been one or the other, since he was still six feet above ground and upright.

Bud and Annie played with the children in the river while Caroline and Bethy blew dandelions, chased grasshoppers, picked flowers, and followed butterflies until it was time for lunch and everyone came back to the blanket for sandwiches. They chatted and laughed, enjoying the day and the breeze that blew through the trees. Eventually the older children went back down to the river with Bud while Annie and Caroline cleaned up from lunch and settled Bethy down for a nap under the shade of the tree. Annie took the basket back to the wagon and then arranged herself on a corner of the blanket opposite Caroline, who rested her back on the tree and cradled a sleeping Bethy in her lap.

"I'm sorry about all this, Caroline; truly I am. You have to know it wasn't something I planned. It just happened." Annie's voice was soft, and she spoke with true remorse.

Caroline smiled ruefully and looked down at her sleeping child. "Funny, that's what Bud said."

"It's true. It just sort of...*developed*. It wasn't intentional, and it wasn't done to hurt you. I hope you can understand that." Her voice was gentle, but she persisted, knowing this was difficult for Caroline to hear.

Caroline didn't reply but stroked Bethy's hair back from her sweaty brow and looked up and away, watching the grasses blow in the breeze and the butterflies flit here and there. Eventually she spoke.

"Do you love him?"

Annie held her breath. Should she answer honestly? She didn't know how to proceed. *Better just to admit it*, she thought. "Yes, I do." There. It was out there.

Caroline looked at her now. "So do I. What do we do now?"

Annie let her breath out in relief. She chuckled. "I really don't know. I well, I never expected this."

"I guess not," Caroline agreed. "I'm not happy about it, don't get me wrong. And Bud's not out of the doghouse yet. But I don't suppose it'll do any of us any good to argue over it." She said it with such finality that Annie took that to mean the conversation was over, and she said no more.

Had Bud been there to overhear their conversation, he would have said that Caroline's practical nature was winning out, now that the initial sting and anger were wearing away. It was part of what had attracted Bud to her in the first place, her practical and no-nonsense ways. Some of the other girls Bud had known as a young bachelor were coquettish or teasing, and he hadn't quite known what to do with that and avoided them. But Caroline's frank and sensible manner had appealed to him, and it was that practicality that was now going to be his saving grace in this bend of what had been heretofore his life's very straight and predictable road.

Bud glanced toward the tree as he played with the children in the river and did a double take. Wait. Were they…were they *talking?* They were! Pleasantly, it seemed, and he was cautiously optimistic. Wait, were they talking about *him?* Well, this could go either way, but he chose to see it as a positive development and put it out of his mind as Ellie climbed onto his back. He dunked Thomas under the water, and Ellie laughed.

"Throw me, Pa, throw me!" she begged him, falling into the water. When he picked her up and tossed her into the air, her laughter was cut off as she sank beneath the water with a splash.

"Now me! Me next!" the others clamored, wading over to him in a mad rush to get to him first, and he laughed. His arms would be sore later, but that was okay. Annie and Caroline were talking, and sore arms were a small price to pay for that miracle.

11 ROBERT HAS A VISITOR

Bud sat on the edge of the porch after dinner, oiling a leather bridle and watching the children play tag in the yard. They had finished eating and were focused on getting out whatever wiggles they had before it was time to do the afternoon chores. Annie was putting Bethy down for a nap and Caroline was…well, Bud didn't know what Caroline was doing, only that she was up and about, and that was still good. Since their day at the river, Caroline had continued to be part of the family, not taking to her bed or letting the melancholia overcome her. She was cordial, if not overly friendly, to Annie, and the children had a cautious optimism that whatever storm had blown in was now on its way out. Bud continued to try not to favor either Annie or Caroline and slept on the floor in Caroline's room, not even broaching the possibility of the bed. He did not go back to Annie's bed either, and he didn't offer her any affection when Caroline was present but stole moments alone with her to give her a hug or encouragement when he could. Annie, for her part, was pleasant and mild and worked hard to help where she could. The days had passed in relative calm, and Bud was hopeful that this crazy situation would work itself out somehow.

Nick had told him that he'd be over at some point to talk about raising a little cabin for Annie, so when Bud heard hoofbeats in the distance and looked up, he expected to see Nick riding up. But no, it was Frank. *Frank?* Frank never came over. Mac ran over to Frank as he slowed his horse to a halt. Where did Frank get a horse? Bud laid the bridle to the side and got to his feet, wiping his hands on his thighs. Well, this was interesting.

"Hey, there, Frank," Bud called, walking over as Frank dismounted and handed the reins over to Mac. Mac took them and led the horse to the barn. The other children stopped their play and stared at their Uncle Frank. They didn't often see him; they knew about him, but he wasn't a frequent visitor, and they whispered among themselves as they shot curious looks toward the two men.

Bud and Frank shook hands, and the children lost interest again and went back to their play. "To what do I owe the pleasure?" Bud smiled, and together they walked back to the porch, where they both sat down, and Bud picked up the bridle again. It was oiled and wiped clean, but he fiddled with it in his hands.

"I wanted to thank you for gettin' me home the other day," Frank said. "I know I was a mess."

"You got to do something about your drinkin', Frank. It's gettin' on top a you, and you gonna go under."

"I know," Frank said softly and rested his elbows on his knees. He held his head in one hand, his hat in the other, and Bud reached to put a comforting hand on his neck. "I just...some days I just wanna crawl in a bottle and never come out." He straightened his arms and gripped his knees, looking out into the yard at the children playing. They were hot and tired now and starting to get on each other's nerves.

"Well, you an' Pa, you got that in common," Bud acknowledged. Robert had not been a mean or an abusive drunk but rather an unattentive one, and when he got into a particularly deep bottle he tended to stay there. The boys had all grown up with their father's alcohol addiction, each of them responding to it in different ways. It had made Nick a teetotaler, after a brief love affair with bourbon in his late teens, and while Bud still drank occasionally, he was careful not to go too far. He knew what it could do and felt that it was in his veins, simmering there and just waiting for an opportunity. It would take him under if he allowed it. Frank had succumbed willingly and wholeheartedly to the bottle, but now Bud was hoping he was going to come up for air and stay up. He intended to do whatever he could to help him if it looked like he was serious this time.

"Yeah, I know," Frank said ruefully. He and his father weren't especially close, and Bud knew that was part of the problem. It was why he made an effort to talk to his children each night before they went to bed, even if it was brief and uninspired. Children needed a father just to be there sometimes, even if he wasn't doing anything. Bud remembered how comforting it had been on the occasions that Robert was home and sober—even if he wasn't actively interested in what little schooling they took or which girl they liked. Sometimes it was enough just to have him there. "But I gotta be different from Pa; I know it." Frank sat up straight, and Bud took his hand away, turning to lean against a porch post as Frank continued. He rested his arms on his knees.

"Pete Dixon's got a camp up north o' here, takin' down timber for a railroad. I intend to go work for 'im a while. Get straightened out and make a few bucks."

"Yeah, Henry said somethin' about that, now that you mention it. When me an' Nick took them cattle down. He was hot about it, too, 'cause the logs was gettin' in the way 'a his ferry. 'Course anythin' Pete Dixon does gonna piss 'im off," Bud added.

"You gotta come with me, up the camp."

"I gotta do what?" Bud asked, incredulously. "I damn shore don't," he countered. "What I got is a field a beans to get in 'fore them kids git off t' school an' I lose 'em and a house to build 'fore winter comes. *That's* what I got." He sat up straight and swung his legs over the edge of the porch as Frank had and spat into the dirt between his feet. "I ain't got time t' be cuttin' timber in that camp."

"What you gotta be buildin' a house for, anyhow?" Frank asked. "You got a house, a plenty big one."

Just then they heard the porch door swing shut, and Annie came onto the porch holding a broom. She called to the children, who had given up their games in the heat and were now splashing each other with water from the pump. "Maclan! Thomas! You boys leave off that now and get out to the field! Those beans ain't gonna hop in those buckets all by themselves!" She turned her head and saw Frank and Bud sitting on the porch. "Well, hey, Frank. I didn't know you'd come."

"Just stopped by for a little bit, Annie. How are ya?" he replied. He shaded his eyes with his hand as he looked up at her, the sun blinding him briefly.

"I'm all right, Frank. It's good to see you. I'm just gonna try an' herd these wild animals. Bud, you goin' out to the field with the boys?"

"Yep, send 'em on, and I'll be out there in a bit." He picked up the bridle and held it out to Annie. "Ask them boys to go put that in the barn before they go out to the field, wouldya?"

"Sure," she said, taking it from him and propping the broom up against the house. She stepped down from the porch. "See you, Frank," Annie said over her shoulder, as she walked away toward the children. They had stopped splashing each other and had run over to one of the oak trees to rest in its shade. Rest time was over, however; Annie had a whole list of chores in her head and she was about to dish them out.

"I'm buildin' her a house." Bud nodded at Annie's back, and Frank looked at him, startled.

"You're what?"

"Buildin' a house. Annie's going to stay here a while, and she needs her own space. She's gonna have a baby."

"Well, what for? Let her husband build 'er a house. Why's she livin' here?"

"It's my baby."

"It's your...good Lord, Bud!" Frank started to laugh. "It ain't like you got enough already, now you startin' over on a new one!"

"Shut up. I ain't gonna explain m'self. Least of all to you, ya big alkie." Bud joined in Frank's subsiding laughter, and Frank started up again.

"Well, I guess you don't have to, I c'n figger it all out for myself," Frank replied, and snorted. That set them off again, and as they gradually got hold of themselves, Frank stood and leaned against the porch post, facing Bud. His face took on a more somber look as he spoke. "I'm serious, though, Bud, I need you to come with me up to the camp. I'mma really try this time, try to turn m'self around. I'mma work for Dixon where there ain't no saloons and no girls and no Lowery boys to trip me up. I'm gonna get me some money saved up and start me a little farm. I ain't gonna be like Pa."

"What d'you need me for?" Bud asked. "Go do it then."

"I need you to help me keep straight, just for a little while, just while I get back on my feet. Keep me from crawlin' back into a bottle until I c'n be sure I'll stay out of it m' own self." Frank looked at his feet while he spoke, and Bud knew this must be the truth. He was embarrassed to admit he needed help to do it, but it did appear that he intended to stay dry this time.

"Well, lemme talk to Caroline and Annie about it. If they think they c'n get the beans in themselves before the kids get back in school, I'll go with you. Maybe Dixon'll cut me a break, and I'll use his timber for the house 'stead of my own. When was you plannin' on leavin'?"

"Next week. Any day. Tell me you'll go, an' I'll be ready."

Bud considered carefully. Finally, he said, "If I don't send one a' the boys out to ya before Wednesday to say differn't, you come on Thursday and we'll ride up there together." Bud stood now too, and clapped Frank on the shoulder. "You'll be all right, Frank," he said, encouragingly. "I know it won't be easy, but it's gonna work itself out." He looked over to the barn where Tom and Mac were getting ready to head out to the field. "Mac! Bring your Uncle Frank's horse on over here 'fore you go!"

"Thanks, Bud," Frank said as he clapped his hat on his head.

"Where'd you get that horse, anyway?" Bud asked him, rocking back on his heels, his hands in his back pockets.

"Won 'im in a card game," Frank grinned. "I can't give up all my bad habits at once, y'know." He took the reins from Mac and patted him on the back. Mac smiled and ran back to his brother, who was waiting for him to head to the field. "I'm a pretty good card player when I'm sober."

"I guess you are," Bud chuckled. "That's a good-lookin' horse. Best be careful and hang on to 'im. Don't go losin' "im in another hand."

"Yep." Frank spun the horse around to head back home. "I'll see ya next week. Thanks again, Bud."

"Yeah, go on." Bud waved.

Bud watched Frank go and smiled to himself. Maybe this would work. If Pete Dixon would agree to let Bud keep the timber he cut, he could use it for the house and not cut his own, leaving it to sell another day. Dixon'd have to see the sense in not having to pay a worker to cut it down or pay to haul it to the mill. He couldn't send them all down the river. It might work out for both of them, and he'd keep an eye on Frank until he got his legs under him good and firm. If Caroline and Annie agreed, of course.

He set off for the field himself to work for a while before the afternoon rains set in. *Lord, help me to not keel over in this heat,* he prayed. *Gotta be a hunnerd degrees in the shade.* He realized, gratefully, that Annie would not be heavily pregnant in heat like this. A pregnant woman in late August was nothing for a mortal man to contend with; he knew that for certain. Caroline had been pregnant more than once during the hot summer months, and he remembered well how uncomfortable they all had been. *What if it's twins again?* He pushed that thought from his mind immediately. Nope, he wasn't going there. Best leave that kind of thinking right where it was.

Ellie smiled to herself, swinging her pail merrily, as she made her way through the woods to Papa's house. That was her special name for him; everyone else called him Grandpa. Robert and Bethy, being babies, were afraid of his deep voice and approached him cautiously, but she loved him dearly and was his special pet. She'd never been afraid of him, not even when she was a baby, and laughed when he rubbed his wrinkled, bristly cheek against her soft young one. She came to see him at least once a week, bringing him leftover biscuits from breakfast or a bit of venison from last night's supper. Sometimes Susan, Dianna, or Sarah would come with her, but sometimes she came alone, and she treasured these times. He would tell her stories of when he was a boy, and sometimes he would have a special treat just for her. Last time it had been a Coca-Cola in the bottle, a whole one just for her. She never told anyone of these special treats; it would have made the other children jealous, and she loved this special time between them. They would sit on the porch in hot weather or at his little table inside in the winter, and sometimes she would sift through his treasure box. It was a little box of photos and other mementos that she had found in one of the drawers of the old chifforobe in Papa's bedroom. One morning he sent her after a hanky for his back pocket. She found one in a bottom drawer, and she came back to him with the handkerchief and the little box too. He let her sort through it as she pleased, and though she knew everything in it well, she still liked to bring it out sometimes and ask him questions about what she found there.

She raised her arm and picked off a leaf from a low-hanging bough as she walked under it. She let the pail's handle fall to hang in the crook of her elbow and absent-mindedly began picking the leaf to pieces as she walked. Bright sunlight shone through the trees overhead and made patterns in the leaves of the forest floor, and a startled lizard scampered up a tree as she came up a little rise. Here there was a little clearing of yellow meadow grasses that she loved to walk through, and she knew she was not far from Papa's cabin. Her thoughts turned to school starting, and she was momentarily saddened to think that she wouldn't be able to come over just anytime she wanted but would only be able to come on weekends and only if her chores were done and the weather was fine. *School.*

She liked school but hadn't liked the old teacher, and she was looking forward to meeting the new one. Lisabelle Tucker in Sunday school said the new teacher was young and pretty, and Billy Rollo said it wasn't true, that the new teacher was an old lady who was even meaner than Miss Finch. She didn't believe Billy Rollo and thought he was making it up just to be ornery. He was that sort. Last year she'd accidentally knocked a book off her desk with her elbow, right in the middle of a test, and it had made a big BANG when it hit the floor, which prompted some surprised shrieks from the girls (and maybe a few boys, who would never have owned up to it). She herself jumped in her seat, and her cheeks blushed a hot pink when she realized she was the reason for the noise. Miss Finch frowned at her grumpily and told her not to be so clumsy. Billy Rollo, who sat behind her and was a year older, kicked her chair and laughed at her, taunting, "Nice one, Smelly Ellie!" She turned around and stuck her tongue out at him, but he just crossed his eyes at her. Hubert Johnson, who was also a year older and sat across the aisle from her, only leaned down to retrieve the book and smiled as he gave it back to her. She smiled back, and his gesture made the embarrassment a little easier to bear. She wouldn't mind boys if they were all like Hubert. If they were all going to be like Billy Rollo, then she'd pass, please and thank you.

As she left the sunny little meadow behind her, Papa's cabin came into view, and she skipped a little. School was forgotten as she saw her grandfather emerge from the little barn with a bucket in his hand. He saw her coming and waved, and she waved back. He waited for her at the pump, because he knew she liked to try to draw the water once he got it started. She hugged him when she reached him, and he kissed her on the cheek.

"Well, little Ellie-girl, 's good to see you this mornin'. What you got there?" Ellie turned him loose from her hug, and he began to prime the pump.

"Annie and Susan made blackberry jam, and there's a jar in there for you, and a couple cookies Dianna and I made yesterday. I mighta' ate one on the way," she admitted. It might be okay to steal a cookie, if you were the cook.

He laughed and pushed the bucket under the pump as the water came streaming out. "That's okay; one for you and one for me, right?" He pumped again, and another gush of water flowed into the bucket. "You wanta turn?"

She set the pail down and stepped up to the pump. She pulled the handle down with both hands, but she couldn't budge it more than a few inches. Robert reached up and pushed it down with her, and together they filled up the bucket.

"There now, we got it," he said, bending over to grasp the handle of the bucket. "Lemme just take this to ol' Molly an' you go on t' the house. Pull us up a couple a chairs on the porch, there."

"Okay!"

Robert took the bucket of water to the barn, one arm straining with the weight and the other slightly outstretched for balance. He might be getting on up there, but he was still strong, and years of manual labor had given him sinewy muscles that served him well around his little homestead. He took the bucket to Molly's stall and tossed her a flake of hay. He made sure the back gate to the stall was open so she could come and go as she pleased and left the barn to join Ellie on the porch.

Robert's homestead was small, much smaller than it had been when the boys were young and Maybelline was home, but it was ample for him. He'd given his sons some land of their own as they left home but had kept a respectable twenty acres for himself. He didn't keep much livestock, just a few chickens for eggs and some goats. He had one horse that was nearing thirty years old, but she was a gentle soul, and Robert took good care of her. She had been with him for a long time, and that was saying something. You couldn't count on people, but you could count on a good horse. He kept a small garden, not much, but it kept him busy and fed, with enough to eat in the winter. Nick brought him meat when he hunted and fish in the summer, and he had plenty. He didn't get many visitors, other than the children every once in a while, or Nick, who came by every few weeks to check up on him. That was okay, though; he wasn't much for conversation, and he was content to rock in his chair on the porch and read the Bible or the few books he had. He wasn't a particularly learned man, but he had a few well-worn volumes, and he was easy to please. He hadn't had much schooling himself, and what little he knew was mostly self-taught. He had made sure his boys got a few more years of school than he had, and he was proud that the grandchildren were as clever as they were.

"Papa! Do you want a biscuit with a little jam on it?" Ellie called to him from the little kitchen as he dropped into the old rocker on the porch.

"Uh, yeah, I could have one," he answered, taking his hat off and wiping his forearm across his sweaty brow. Eleven o'clock in the morning, and it had to be close to ninety degrees already. He was glad what little gardening he planned to do today he'd done first thing this morning. He'd picked some beans and dug up a couple of potatoes, and he had already shelled the beans and put them to soak in a bowl.

Ellie came out onto the porch with a plate and a cup of water and gave them to Robert. "Well, look a' that. Thank you, honey."

"Sure." She picked up the small wooden box from the porch floor and plopped herself into the little cane chair next to him, scooching her bottom until it reached the seat back, and crossed her legs underneath her. She placed the box in her lap and opened the lid, which was hinged on one side with strips of leather. Robert smiled as he ate his biscuit. For whatever reason, she was fascinated with that box, and she'd been through it a hundred times if she'd been through it once. He didn't mind. The box contained a few photos and some other little mementos, which might have seemed surprisingly sentimental for someone as gruff as Robert could sometimes be. It certainly would have surprised his sons to know he had it. True, but then it wasn't really his box, after all. He guessed it had become his, and maybe he was getting a little sentimental, anyway, as he got older. He definitely had a soft spot for his granddaughter Ellie. He looked forward to her visits, and since he never really knew which day she was going to come, it helped curb his appetite for alcohol. He never wanted to scare her by being tipsy or appear anything less than coherent when she came to visit.

"Who's this?" she asked, holding up a photo of a young couple. The unsmiling young man in a starched collar was sitting, and a young woman, equally stoic, stood behind him, her hand on his shoulder. Ellie knew perfectly well who they were; she'd asked the question many times before, but neither of them tired of the game, and Robert answered her as though it was the first time for both of them.

"Well, now, that's me, and that's your Grandma Maybelline."

"She's pretty."

"Mm-hmm," he agreed, taking another bite of biscuit. He did agree; he'd always thought Maybelline was one of the most beautiful women he'd ever seen, and years of reflection had not dimmed his memory of her. As angry and bitter as he had been after she left, and as much as he had tried to drink her memory away, it still stuck with him as much as ever, and he missed her. He missed the life he should have had with her. He still had anger, but it had tempered over time, and it was mixed with love and fond memories of their time together, sorrow and regret for words said in haste and thoughtlessness.

She pulled another photo from the box. "And who's this?"

"Well, now, that's your pa."

"Pa's wearing a dress!" She laughed at the photo of the baby, who sat on a dark-colored blanket in a gown of cream and lace, propped up by a hand and arm that extended off the side and out of the frame, presumably Robert's or Maybelline's. The baby's cheeks were chubby, and a fuzz covered his head. Robert hadn't wanted to spend the money on the photos either time, but Maybelline had insisted, and now he was glad she had. There was another one in there of the four of them before Frank was born, but there were no baby pictures of Frank. That was one of his regrets, that there weren't more pictures. They were expensive, and his memory was still good, but he wished the grandchildren could have seen how beautiful their grandmother was or how dirty his boys had gotten the day they'd played in the mud in the north pasture. Maybelline had been livid about that, but he'd just laughed. He supposed that was one of the stories he could tell Ellie, since she liked to hear what it was like when her pa was a boy.

"And what's this?" Ellie asked, pulling a curl of blue ribbon from the box. It was a sky-blue strip of thin grosgrain ribbon, about sixteen inches in length, and as it unfurled in Ellie's fingers, Robert smiled.

"That's one o' your grandma's hair ribbons, I guess." He leaned over to take it from her, feeling the tiny ridges of the ribbon in his hands. He remembered taking this ribbon from May's hair on nights the children had fallen to sleep early, before the young parents had allowed the strain of raising three rambunctious boys to drive them into heated arguments and hurt feelings. He regretted his part in that; he should have been more patient with her. Sixty years knew something that twenty did not.

He gave it back to her. "You c'n take it with you, if you like it."

"Really? It's so pretty!" She held it up between her fingers and let the end pool in the box. "Thank you! I know just what I'll do with it too!"

"Tie it in your hair?"

"No, it's too pretty to just be a hair ribbon. Tom gave me a necklace he found, not long ago, while he was out on the beach. The chain broke, just as soon's he gave it to me, it was so old; but it had two pretty little charms on it, and I can put 'em on this and wear it! They're real silver; I know they are."

"Well, now, that sounds just fine."

The two continued to chat for another hour or so about vitally important things, such as the new shoes for school and what the teacher might be like. Ellie told him about Lisabelle Tucker's puffed sleeves that she was so proud of and showed off in Sunday school and swung her bare feet as she prattled on. Robert didn't mind her cheerful chatter and enjoyed the visit, and when she finally left to go home, the little house seemed awfully quiet and still. He picked up the little box she'd left next to her chair, still open on its old leather hinges. She'd forgotten to take the ribbon with her after all, distracted by their conversation and her own boundless, youthful energy. Well, another day. She'd be back, and he'd try to remember to give it to her again. He closed the box and took it inside to put it away. He thought he just might take a little nap in the heat of the day, instead of sweating it out on that porch rocker.

12 CAMP

Bud and Frank were the last two in a line of men who stood waiting for their turn to sign up for a work detail in a dimly lit wooden camp house. It was a motley queue with various shapes, sizes, and ages. But every man was able bodied and hopeful, each one looking for work in Pete Dixon's timber camp. Men had come from surrounding counties with their axes and hatchets slung over their shoulders, riding and walking, hoping for a place on Dixon's payroll. Dixon's men were clearing a swath from the north Florida woods for a short-line railroad, and Frank intended that he and Bud would be on the next detail sent out. Bud had sent Thomas over to Nick's one afternoon, asking him to pass on the message that Bud and Frank would be cutting timber in the camp for a bit and not to come over, as Bud had asked him to do the day they'd spent in town. That was fine with Nick, who had all he could handle right now with Ellen, who was feeling poorly and couldn't keep anything down.

Frank had ridden his poker pony over to Bud's again later in the week, then spent the night with the boys in the barn, which thrilled them no end. Robert was especially excited that he was allowed to sleep in the hay loft with them, and his little chest bowed with the pride of being able to stay with the "big boys" in the barn. They had lain awake until the wee hours of the morning, laughing and talking, and Frank enjoyed the time with his nephews. He thought maybe he'd come over more often, after they finished at the camp and he'd had some time to make some repairs to his little cabin. He found he quite liked being an uncle.

Annie and Caroline had not disagreed with Bud's suggestion of leaving the boys to finish the work of harvesting the beans and seemed to be forging an amicable, if tentative, way forward between themselves. One couldn't call it a sisterly bond, exactly, but neither was there outright animosity, and Bud took it as a good sign. When he got back from the camp, he'd figure out a way to tell the children about their impending little sister or brother, although he really hoped the women would say something while he was gone and save him from having to do it.

Women knew how to answer tricky questions, and there were liable to be lots of them. Especially from the older children, who knew enough about how babies got born, having been present when the youngest children had arrived. He didn't really want to answer any questions about how the baby got *in*, only how the baby was going to come *out*, and he hoped between Annie and Caroline they'd think of some diplomatic way to cover the relevant information without going into too much detail.

The thought of it made him shudder, actually, and he shifted from one foot to the other as they finally moved up to be the next in line for their turn at the bookkeeper. Men who had already signed up moved off in groups to gather equipment and talk amongst themselves, and the camp house was lively with laughter and conversation as the men began making introductions, joked, or talked with each other about girlfriends or families back home.

"Name?" A young man asked, head bent over a ledger on a desk, where an oil lamp lit pages of names and ages of men who had gone before them.

"Frank Braxton," Frank answered, "and this here's my brother—well hey, now, which one o' them am I s'posed to be lookin' at?"

Bud looked to see what Frank was talking about and saw that the young man, who had raised his head to talk to Frank, had eyes that were going in decidedly opposite directions. One eye looked at Frank in bemusement, but the other veered off to the northeast, and the resulting effect was fairly unsettling. Bud blinked and said under his breath, "Christ, Frank."

"What? He knows his eyes are jacked," Frank gestured to the young man, who seemed to be completely unperturbed by Frank's blunt observation, and in fact sat there smirking, as his wayward eye took a leisurely dip to the southeast. "Wait—you do know your eyes are all jacked up, dontcha?"

The young man laughed and said, "Yes, I know." He smiled at Bud and continued, "It doesn't bother me. It's been this way all my life. I'd rather you asked, actually." His good eye looked at Frank again. "Most people don't want to bring it up, so they don't know where to look." He leaned back in his chair and grinned up at them, pencil and ledger momentarily forgotten.

"See?" Frank said to Bud, wholly oblivious to Bud's discomfort. "He knows." He turned back to the young man, who looked up at him in good humor. "Well, now," Frank continued, "was you born that way, or did you get dropped on your head or somethin' when you was a baby?" Frank was blissfully unconscious of how his complete lack of tact was affecting his brother, who rolled his eyes and turned around, embarrassed.

"Frank! You can't just ask a man if he was dropped on his head as a baby!" Bud hissed, wondering briefly if either he or Nick had ever dropped Frank on *his* head as a baby and if that was the reason why he was as infuriatingly obtuse as he was right now. *Good Lord, save me*, he thought.

The man simply laughed again, however, and answered Frank's question. "I was born like this, and I can't see out of that eye. It goes its own way. The other one's fine, though. Name's Mark Jacobsen," he said, holding a hand out to Frank. As the two shook hands, the men's attention turned to a heavyset man in a jacket and waistcoat, who had appeared behind Jacobsen and was carrying two ledgers in his short arms, both books similar to the open ledger on Jacobsen's desk. This was Pete Dixon, who was the head of the operation, and he had a short temper to match his stature. Jacobsen bent back to his ledger.

"And your brother is...?" he prompted but was interrupted, as Dixon yelled behind him at the men noisily leaving the camp house with their equipment and other belongings. He frowned at the dishes and cups left on the tables.

"Don't leave that there, take it with you! This ain't your mama's house! Nobody's cleanin' up after you fellas!" He dumped the ledgers unceremoniously onto the desk beside Jacobsen, barking at him, "Here, take a look at these when you're done with that." Dixon turned his attention to Bud and Frank. "You boys joining the ranks? The pay's good, if a little hard work don't kill ya." His pudgy stature indicated that he himself might not be too well acquainted with hard work, as the buttons of his waistcoat strained at his stomach, and he rocked back on his heels. He looked Frank and Bud up and down.

Bud answered first. "Yes, sir, and I wanted to ask you a question, if I could."

"Well, get to it, then; I just sent m' other bookkeeper east this mornin', and I've been behind all day. Boy's sick as a dog, and he ain't no good to me if he can't pull his weight around here. Railroad don't build itself, y'know." He raised his bushy eyebrows and looked at Bud expectantly.

"I'm lookin' to build a house on my land, and I need timber for it," Bud explained. "I wanna make you a deal—I'll clear what I need for my house, and you don't have to put me on your payroll. Just lend me a wagon to haul what I need home. You won't have to feed me, neither; I'll take care of myself."

Frank and Mark watched this interchange between Dixon and Bud. Bud hadn't said anything to Frank about this on their ride to the camp, so it was news to both of them.

"Where's my profit in it then? I sell that timber downriver to the mill. I see you savin' me the expense, but I don't see you makin' me a dime," Dixon countered.

"I'll keep your books for you. You said yourself you're down a bookkeeper, and it'll cost you to bring somebody else out and pay 'em a salary, besides. I'm good with numbers, and I'm already here." Bud looked at Dixon levelly, knowing he was making him a good deal. It was also a good deal for himself. He'd get all the wood he needed for Annie's house, and he wouldn't have to give up any of his own timber to get it.

Frank chimed in. "He is good with numbers; I c'n speak to that," he said. "Helped me all through my own schoolin'; couldn'a done it without him." He clapped Bud on the back, making him catch his balance.

Dixon considered this and saw the opportunity. He didn't have another bookkeeper, and he needed one; it was more work than Jacobsen would be able to do on his own. It would take him time and money to find someone and get him down here, and he had other fish to fry. And he did need to get the land cleared, profit or no profit. He'd spent most of yesterday tied up with surveyors and felt like he was spinning his wheels. The damn railroad needed to get built, and it was taking a Christly long time to get started. Men of action like him needed to see results, and so far all he'd seen were impediments and bottlenecks.

"All, right; if Jacobsen here says you can add two and two together, you're hired. You can take two wagons of timber, you use your own horse, and you don't get in the way."

"Yes, sir," Bud said. "Thank you."

Dixon didn't offer to shake his hand and didn't say goodbye to any of them, just jerked his head up as a pile of equipment tumbled to the wooden floor in a cacophony of tin pots and camping supplies. Somebody yelled, "Just put that anywhere!" and the men in the camp house laughed, then resumed their group conversations after the interruption.

"For Pete's sake, clean that up!" Dixon yelled, and left Frank and Bud to Jacobsen, who smiled again at them and resumed his friendly demeanor.

"I guess you know that's Dixon, then," Jacobsen said, his wild eye returning to its northeasterly location in its socket, making Bud a little queasy. He tried to focus on Jacobsen's other eye and found it took a little practice to ignore the wandering eye completely.

"Yeah, I figured. Bud Braxton," he said, shaking Jacobsen's outstretched hand. "And I really am good with numbers; it wasn't a lie."

"That would be great, because he's right, we are behind. Davidson left this morning, and he won't be back. He really was sick as a dog, as Dixon said." Jacobsen stacked the ledgers, having written both Frank and Bud's names in, and rose to his feet. "Come on, and let's get something to eat; we'll go somewhere we can hear ourselves think," he said, leading them toward the back of the camp house and away from the commotion of the other men. Bud and Frank followed, putting their hats on their heads as they exited the camp house, and looked around as they let canvas flaps fall back into place behind them, cutting off some of the noise from within. They could hear saws in the distance and shouts of men, who were still cutting timber and who had not yet come back in for the night. They would be knocking off soon, however, for evening was coming on, and the cooks were beginning to make plates for the first men in line. Mark shoved his ledgers into a bag and slung it over his shoulder, walking toward the growing trail of hungry men. "We better get in there now, or there won't be anything left but beans and bread," he said, leading the way to the chow line.

As the men ate, Bud and Frank learned a bit more about Jacobsen. He was single, thirty, and a chatterbox. He had come from Atlanta, where his family still lived, but he had taken the job with the railroad as a bookkeeper to see other parts of the country. His speech was more clipped than Frank and Bud's, and it was clear that he'd had more education. But he was very personable and friendly—and talkative. He didn't like Dixon, and Bud remembered that Henry didn't either, although Bud guessed Henry probably had more cause, since he'd known him longer. Jacobsen would work for Dixon only until this portion of the railroad was built, and he'd move on, presumably to other parts of the line. Already he had been to several places out West and had all kinds of stories to tell. He was engaging and funny, and both Bud and Frank liked him immediately. He wanted to know, however, if Bud was going to be able to help him catch up with the ledgers, now that Davidson was gone. "Dixon's tight with a dollar; he doesn't pay a dime he doesn't have to," Jacobsen told them. "If he doesn't have to bring a new bookkeeper out here, he won't." He looked pointedly at Bud. "So I hope for my sake, you can add."

Bud nodded, his mouth full.

Jacobsen paused to drink from his cup and continued. "And he'll hire anybody who'll work, no matter who they are or how much trouble they cause. But that'll backfire; I've seen it. Back in Amarillo the rail boss hired this idiot who got loaded one night, and he and another fella argued over who had more meat in their stew." He swallowed. "I'm not kidding!" Jacobsen exclaimed, seeing the doubt on his listeners' faces.

"They went at it over a bowl of stew! An' it wasn't even good meat. It was just some rabbit somebody caught and threw it in there because there wasn't anything else!" Jacobsen paused to chew a mouthful of bread.

"The Amarillo fella, he was too far gone in a bottle, and he was ready to pick a fight. Some men are like that; they just want to fight about everything. Well, this other fella got in his face, and they shot each other right there in the middle of supper. Wasn't anything anybody could do." His face lost its animation at the memory of it, and he looked down into his bowl. "It'd been kinda funny, if it weren't so stupid 'n' sad." He used his last bite of bread to mop up anything he'd left in his bowl, and his spoon clattered out onto the dirt. "Dammit," he cursed, and bent to pick it up. He put it back in his bowl and looked around at the gathering of men who were eating and talking in small groups; some sat on logs or stumps, others sat on the ground or squatted. "There's another one like that here; he came on a little while ago. Came in with some other guy, but then that one left. I swear, when he looks at you, he'd just as soon kill you."

"Well, hopefully we'll steer clear of him, whoever he is," Frank said, and stood. "What do we do with these?" he asked, holding his cup and bowl.

"You wash 'em in that tub over there and stack them on the back of that wagon," he answered, pointing to an empty wagon next to the cooks and the shrinking line of latecomers. He turned to look at Bud as Frank took his and Bud's dishes to the wagon. "Where are you bunking tonight?"

"I don't really know." Bud looked around. "Nobody told us yet."

"There are tents set up back over yonder; just find an empty cot and keep an eye on your stuff. Did you ride in or walk?"

"We rode."

"Keep an eye on your horse too, then. Everybody uses his own in the work, just check on him before you bed down for the night. Some of these guys, when they realize building a railroad is too much like work, they light out but they don't do it walkin'."

"Thanks for the heads up. I've got timber to clear, that's what I'm here for, but I'll help with the books. When do you want me tomorrow?"

"Come see me after supper tomorrow night, and we'll get started. Part of the problem isn't keeping the books; it's keeping up with Dixon's promises." Jacobsen scowled. "He makes deals for supplies we need an' all, but then he forgets to give me the receipts or even tell me what he did. Then when the fella comes to get paid for the horse feed he brought, I don't know nothin' about it. I can't get funds from the company if I don't know what our expenses are. There were a couple weeks I wasn't sure we were gonna make payroll. There's nothing more stressful than three hundred men holding axes, wonderin' why their pay's a day late."

"Yeah, I can see that'd make things a little tense," Bud said, smiling, and stood. He put his hand out, and Jacobsen shook it. "Good to meet ya, and thanks for helpin' us get started. We'll see you tomorrow, I guess."

"Yep, I'll be here. All day long."

Bud left Jacobsen where he sat and went off to find Frank. But first, he thought he might check on his horse.

Annie lay in bed, staring up at the ceiling. She and Caroline had put the children to bed over an hour ago and wished each other a good night, but now she couldn't sleep. She wondered how things were going at home with her parents and her siblings. She didn't miss home, exactly, but wondered how they were all getting on and if they missed her. She hadn't been back since the day she left with Bud. Her daddy was probably over his initial anger, but she thought she'd stay away a little longer just the same and give them time to really get over the sting of it. She and Caroline had not taken the children to church since she'd moved over to Bud's (something she felt guilty about), so she had not seen them there either. Maybe she would go when she started showing a little more, and they could see how well she was doing.

She turned over on her side. Bud had been gone more than a week, and she and Caroline took care of the house and the children and kept up with the chores. There was nothing left in the field right now, until the pumpkins and other fall vegetables were ready. School would start tomorrow, and the children were nervous and excited. Robert had cried when he was told it wasn't his turn to go. He'd go soon enough, she'd promised, but for now his job was to help at home. Caroline had promised him that he could take the cows out in the morning and bring them in each evening, and he perked up with the importance of his new job. He already helped with the milking, but taking over Tom and Mac's job of bringing in the cows filled him with excitement and pride, and he couldn't wait to get started.

She had just come from Ellie's room, where she had watched her fastidiously lay out her school dress and shoes, and Annie had helped her get everything just so. It wasn't often that the children got new boots; usually if they were in decent shape, shoes got handed down to the next one in line. Ellie told her how last year she'd had to wear a pair of Tom's that he'd outgrown, and it had rankled no end that she had to walk to school in boy's boots. Some of the girls in school twittered, and she thought for sure it was about her boots, though no one said anything. Some of the town girls could be snooty, she said. She told Annie how hard it was, when she saw other girls with puffed sleeves and pretty bows in their hair and shiny new boots. Lisabelle Tucker had a rich aunt who lived all the way up in New York, and she sent Lisabelle beautiful things from Paris, which were the envy of every girl in school. The airs Lisabelle put on! She knew there were some children who had no shoes at all, even in the dead of winter when it was forty degrees in the morning, and she herself went without shoes much of the year, she told Annie. But Ellie was especially glad this year that she had new shoes all her own, and happy she couldn't fit into anything passed down.

Annie had understood perfectly about Ellie's mortal shame last year; it worked that way in her own family too. Even though she had been one of the older children who passed down clothes and shoes, she'd still had to wear plenty of hand-me-downs, some of them her brothers', and she knew exactly how Ellie felt.

Annie's thoughts turned to the child in her belly, who would have so many older sisters and brothers and years of hand-me-downs in the future, whether it was boy or girl. As many children as her mama had had after her, she didn't really know much about the actual act of childbirth. Her mama was a very private person, and only her daddy had been present when it was time for each baby to come. She had washed bloody bedsheets, startled at the amount and the bright red stains. She wondered where all that blood came from, but mama didn't explain anything, and she had been too shy to ask. It was like that with sex. She'd never known what it really was until it came time to have it, and then she wondered what all the hullabaloo was about. It felt good, yes, but her first time was with Davy Peterson, and it had been awkward and hurt a little. It wasn't until she met Bud that she truly enjoyed being with a man, and Bud had been patient and gentle with her. She wondered how he was doing, up in the camp with his brother Frank, and said a short prayer to God to keep him safe. Bud had promised to build her a little house, and she hoped that would happen. A little house to call her own, with her little baby in it. She smiled to herself and finally drifted off to sleep.

Ruben lay on his back, staring up at the stars. He'd been at Dixon's camp long enough to figure out how things went around here. The Jacobsen kid was the bookkeeper; he was the only one left, now that the other one'd been carted off. He hadn't been too tough to get rid of. Idiot didn't watch his coffee very well, and it had only taken a second to spike it with something one normally didn't find in a coffeepot. The company sent money for expenses and payroll by train, and in between paydays the money was kept in a safe in Dixon's office. Seemed like there was always somebody in Dixon's office during the day, though, or just outside it; at night Dixon kept it locked and slept outside it on a cot. Too good to sleep with the hired help like most bosses. Ruben hadn't figured out yet how he was going to get in, or when. He knew his getaway plan, though. Plenty of horses for that, so it wouldn't be a problem. He rolled over to his side.

That dimwit Casey had finally left, and he was better off without him. Casey was clumsy, and in Tallahassee they'd almost been caught. He didn't have to work with a partner. Since Gober had been killed, he'd worked with fellas he'd met with here and there, but he preferred to work alone. Gober, he'd trusted. He'd been with him for years, and they'd done time together. A man can really get to know someone when there's nothing to do all day but talk and make plans. He wished Gober was there now, because he'd figure a way in. Gober was good for stuff like that; Ruben was the action man. He made things happen. He'd make this happen, too, and soon. He just had to figure out how to do it.

13 A STORM BLOWS

The fall brought changes to the Braxton household in the form of a new school year and new routines. The garden had given up most of what it had to offer, and nothing would be ready for another few weeks, other than digging some potatoes and carrots. Weeding was a constant chore, but Robert helped Caroline with that and picked off any caterpillars or insects that could damage tender leaves or sprouts. Bud remained at Dixon's camp and would not return home until he had a wagon of good timber cut and ready to bring home, and Caroline had no idea how long that would take. It was still plenty hot and humid. She had spent the morning hanging up the washing, although it looked like it might rain, with the wind blowing the way it was. She had not taken to her bed again with the sadness that had consumed her for so long. Not that she felt cheery, really, but at least she was up. Together with Annie and the children, she took care of the livestock and garden, household chores, and necessary duties that running the small farm required. At least she was functioning.

News of Annie's pregnancy had shaken her up a bit, she guessed; maybe that was it. She couldn't predict what was going to do it, what was going to be the "thing" that brought her out of each episode. There was no way to tell how long a spell would last, how bad it would get, what would finally give her relief, or how long that relief would last. She was grateful for the good days, and prayed through the bad days.

She didn't really want to kill herself, exactly; she was not brave enough for that. But sometimes she found herself imagining things happening to her that would kill her, and the thought of herself dying did not frighten or dismay her. She loved her children and did not want to leave them, but she knew they were capable of caring for themselves, and she wondered if any of them would truly miss her. Children were so resilient. She knew this was morbid, thinking about such things, and chastised herself for being ungrateful—after all, she had healthy children and a husband who provided. There were plenty of women who had neither, and who was she to question what blessings or trials God chose to bring? She'd get the same answer Job had – *Where were you when I laid the earth's foundation?* Nowhere, that's where. *I didn't have anything to do with it, and I don't get a say in what's good or bad. You know what You're doing, God. Forgive me for being ungrateful.*

But the days were relentless, and she supposed it was that, more than anything, that was so trying. When she was younger, it seemed like every new day brought something to look forward to. As a teenager, she had school and boys to whisper to other girls about, and as a young woman, she cherished hope of marriage. Even after marriage, there were babies to look forward to and the excitement of a home of her very own. There was always the next *thing.* But as the years had worn on and the babies had kept coming, there seemed to be only drudgery. Clothes to boil and hang, then iron, that took all day. Suppers to create, sometimes out of nothing but potatoes, for children who wouldn't eat them or a husband who came in tired from a long day in the field and just wanted to eat and fall asleep. Constant cleaning up after. Even as the children got older and more able to help, there was always more work than there were hours in the day. It was this oppression of sameness that was so overwhelming some days that she felt she just couldn't bear up under any more. Tomorrow would look just like today, and the day after that.

But then, of course, something finally *had* changed. It wasn't exactly welcome, but it was something. Bud and Annie had definitely created a little something, who, if she had to estimate based on what she could observe about Annie without directly asking her, would make an appearance sometime early next spring. She thought she'd better talk to Annie about how to broach the subject with the children before Annie started showing more. The older children would understand more than the younger ones, and there might be some awkward questions, ones she didn't relish answering. She supposed Annie didn't look forward to it any more than she did, though, and made a mental note to bring it up to her soon, to figure out how to handle it. *Good grief.*

And what would they say in town when Annie really started showing? Caroline hadn't been to Sunday services in quite some time, although Bud and Annie had taken the children several times over the summer, and everyone knew Annie was working for them. Well, they'd understand *in what capacity* when Annie showed up with a swollen stomach in a few more months. Caroline cringed inwardly at the thought of the wagging tongues and pointed looks she was sure to get. Mrs. Lundy would be all *over* this, and you could be sure it would be quite the scandal for a bit, especially if there was nothing else going on to distract from the sensation. She was going to have to think about how she was going to handle it. Be the angry, betrayed wife or the long-suffering, forgiving wife who stood by her husband in the midst of his very obvious transgressions? She felt like both of those people, frankly. *Ugh, what a pain.* And *dammit, Bud, you idiot.*

The wind that had blown in early with the sunrise now blew stronger, and the skies were gray and cloudy. She came out of the barn with the milking buckets, one in each hand, and began carrying them to the house. The children had gotten off to school late and that had put her behind; Bethy had thrown up breakfast all over the place, and Annie was in the house with her now, trying to get her to take a nap. Robert had gone to take the cows to the pasture, happy in his new job and oblivious to everything else.

The temperature seemed to have dropped a little too, and Caroline knew there was a storm brewing. It was hurricane season, after all, and maybe this was going to be one. Sometimes you just knew that something big was coming. She'd been through hurricanes before, though, and wasn't too worried. They lived far enough from the Gulf that most everything weakened some before it got to them. And they were far enough from the rivers and the bay that the house didn't flood. It was built on a little rise, and they didn't usually have to worry about anything more than some trees down. She'd grown up not far from here, and hurricanes were nothing new. Even with the really strong ones, and there had been a few over her lifetime, they'd been able to rebuild. It was a pain in the butt, more than anything, most times. She supposed maybe she was resilient, too, just like the children. She'd better get ready, just in case this one was a whopper. You never really knew. You just had to go by the wind and the temperature. She thought of Bud in the camp and wondered how they'd fare with all the rail ties and equipment just lying around, waiting to be flung everywhere. She wasn't worried that he wasn't home with her if they did have hurricane; they would handle things just fine, but she wondered how they'd fare at the camp. She guessed they'd figure it out; they were grown men, after all.

Bud and Frank worked together some mornings; some mornings Bud worked alone. He wasn't making ties for the railroad, after all; he was felling trees for his own purposes. The men raised an eyebrow when they found out what he was there for, but no one really bothered him, and most everybody was pleasant enough. He and Jacobsen had been through the ledgers and were almost caught up, but now Bud was understanding what Jacobsen said about Dixon; he was a talker, and he made deals left and right for food and materials, with little thought to how it impacted Jacobsen's job managing income and expenses. Bud thought he might have a solution for that, though.

He sat down on a stump, mopping his forehead with his handkerchief.

He'd gotten used to the clamor and noise of the camp—the sawing, shouts between the men, trees falling, axes thunking, hatchets whacking, horses hauling wagons. Sometimes at night when he lay down, when everything was quiet, he could still hear it all. The days and nights had been clear, although today a wind was kicking up, and Bud wondered if there might be something behind it.

Frank came up to him with supper on a tin plate; he'd gone for weeks now without a drink, and Bud hadn't said anything to him about it. He seemed to be handling it okay; good for him, since town was farther away now and unless he found one of the men who was willing to share his own private stash, he wasn't likely to be able to tie one on way out here.

"How's it goin'?" Bud asked, taking the plate. Frank pulled forks from his back pocket and handed one to Frank as he sat on a fallen tree near Bud's stump. Bud was only taking some of the smaller trees he could fell himself and those that would be good for building the house; the other men were taking out bigger trees and brush, and everything else that would be in the way of the rail line. Some of it went down the river; some of it was piled up near the edge of the woods to be made into rail ties. Frank's stump was just wide enough to hold him, and he balanced the plate on his knees.

"It's all right. There's a guy down there...think I know what Jacobsen was talkin' about. Y'know, the one he said looked at ya like he was gonna kill ya? That one. There's a buncha Irish down there, say he's a 'right dosser.' Guess they picked up on it too. He don't talk much; he just *looks*."

"Well, stay away from him, then, I guess. You gettin' by all right?"

Frank understood the question. "Yeah; last night I coulda give m' left eyeball for a shot, but I did all right. Coupla' guys runnin' cards down by the horses, and they got plenty a whiskey, but I stayed away. I done ya proud." He smirked and stuffed a piece of bread into his mouth.

"Keep it up; you'll be all right," Bud replied, scooping up beans with his bread. "I know I told Dixon I'd feed m'self, but he ain't payin' no mind, and their cook's a real good 'un. I ain't et this good since Mrs. Lundy found us in the barn takin' turns with the calves for the cow's milk."

"What? What're you talkin' about?"

"You don't remember, 'cause you was too small. It was after Ma left, and we didn't have nothin' to eat in the house. Pa'd gone off on a bender, and it was just me an' Nicky an' you. And the cows. I knew enough to milk 'em, and we'd gone fishin' some, but there just wasn't enough to eat. Then one of the horses smashed the milk pail, and we didn't have nothin' to collect the milk in. So me an' Nicky, we pushed the calf outta the way when he went to nurse and took turns at the cow, right there in the barn, and Mrs. Lundy found us there. She was 'bout damn *horrified*, that's what she was, and she stayed with us till Pa came home. And boy, she lit inta him like you got no idea. She brought us all kinds a food, an' so did a bunch of other folks. She taught us how to take care of the house, an' how to cook for ourselves, an' how to take care a you. When she saw you walkin' around nekkid as a jaybird, I thought she was gonna fall over dead right there," he laughed, thinking back to the look on her face when Frank had come waddling over to her in a dirty shirt and no diaper.

Bud and Nick knew about diapering; they'd watched Ma do it. But keeping up with cleaning them proved too much for two young boys who were also trying to feed themselves and take care of the barn animals when Robert was on a drunk. It was just easier to let Frank run around without a diaper. Mrs. Lundy had indeed "lit into" Robert when he'd come home after a weekend of drinking and had raked him up, down, and sideways for the state of the house and for not taking better care of his boys. She helped them, though, despite her anger, and while Robert was more than annoyed at the interference, he grudgingly accepted her kindness and that of Mr. Lundy, who came over to help with the livestock and to make repairs around the farm. Robert gradually began to get hold of himself, although he still went on short benders every once in a while. But Mrs. Lundy checked in, and the boys grew older and more capable, and they had made a way forward. That first year, though, Bud remembered with clarity, because it had been rough. It was good that Frank didn't remember, because *he* did, and it was nothing he wanted to talk about.

As the day wore on, the wind picked up and the sky clouded more ominously. Some of the older men insisted it was "gonna blow a 'hairc'n'," and Bud agreed it did look like there might be a hurricane coming. He looked around at the field of tents and wagons, horses, and felled trees. It was a nightmare scenario for a hurricane; they couldn't possibly secure everything, and the sturdiest structure they had was the camp house. At four o'clock Jacobsen came around and told everyone to knock off and start pulling down tents and doing what they could to strap down anything that could fly.

Bud thought of Annie and Caroline at home and hoped they would be all right. They knew what to do; they had both grown up in the area, and hurricanes were nothing new. They were both fine, capable women, and he had a moment of pride in that. Despite his mistakes, he'd managed to be surrounded by women he loved who were no shrinking violets—very much the opposite, in fact. After he got through this, he'd take his Sunday leave and go check on them. Maybe take Frank with him, in case there was anything they needed to take care of before coming back to work.

By midnight, every man was crowded into the camp house. Tents had been taken down and stowed as securely as possible, some tied to pines that would bend in the wind and some held down with heavy rocks and rolled stumps. It was the best they could do in such circumstances. Equipment that could be picked up was brought into the camp house, as well as pots, pans, and buckets; anything that could be kept safe from the gathering winds was brought inside. The horses, who had no barn anyway but were fenced off, were left where they were, and they whinnied and snorted as the rain began and the winds howled. Dixon locked himself in his office, where he slept on a cot in solitude. Everyone else found a spot to recline or lie down, and they were packed in like sardines, arm to arm. There were no fires tonight, and the cooks brought around cold beans and salted pork. Rainwater collected in barrels outside, and the dishes were washed and rinsed hurriedly after the men ate.

By two in the morning, the hurricane-force winds were at their strongest. Bud and Frank lay awake, whispering quietly over the snores. Every so often he heard a bang against a wall as some untethered item flew against it, but the walls were sturdy, and even though the walls and ceiling were canvas in spots, the leaks were relatively well contained. About six, Bud could stand it no longer and picked his way through the throng of legs and outstretched arms, pots and pans catching rainwater, packs and bedrolls, to the door of the camp house and let himself out to relieve his aching bladder. There was a lull in the rain and the wind, and he supposed that either they were in the eye of the storm or it was much worse for someone else out there and what they were getting was only one of the outer bands. The sun had not yet risen fully, but already he could see tents and limbs strewn everywhere, as if some giant child had become distracted and left his toys in a jumble on the floor, running off to some other game. They would be all day cleaning this up when the rain subsided. Huge puddles of water were everywhere, and one wagon lay on its side almost submerged in a low-lying area that was now a small lake. He sighed. What a glorious mess.

He came back into the camp house as quietly as he could and stood with his back against the closed door, trying to let his eyes become accustomed to the darkness again. He once again concentrated on his feet, picking his way carefully through arms and legs, trying not to step on anyone. He paused as someone moved underneath him, and swayed, catching his balance as he tried desperately not to fall on the slumbering man beneath. He sighed in relief, then looked up again to continue on his way. He caught the eye of a man reclining against the wall, just under a window, and momentarily stopped breathing. The man had a bushy mustache and a crop of dark hair that curled over his forehead. Bud recognized him immediately and saw that recognition mirrored in Mustache's face as their eyes met. For an eternally long moment, Bud did not move, only stared at the man, who then slowly smiled at him. Bud's lungs suddenly remembered their purpose, and his paralysis broke. He looked down at his feet and concentrated on moving forward once more to the corner of the camp house he shared with Frank. He did not look again at the man, the one whom he had felt sure had planned to rob him in the woods on his way back from town not too long ago, but he seemed to feel the man's stare burning into his back.

He slid down onto his bedroll next to Frank; from this angle and in the darkness, he could not see Mustache. He knew instantly that this was the man Jacobsen and Frank had described, the man whom they felt would "kill 'em soon as look at 'em." He already knew that look, and it chilled him. He did not fall back to sleep.

Caroline and Annie had surmised by early afternoon that there was going to be more to this storm than just a little rain cloud, and they put the children to work just as soon as they got home from school that day. Clothes were taken in from the line, everything that could be lifted was put into the barn, and the horses were turned into the pasture. Caroline wasn't sure if it was safer for them in or out; if the barn fell, it would kill them all, and if they were hit by a flying tree it would do the same. She figured they'd just have to take their chances, same as everyone else. *Lord, please protect us and all we have, all our friends and family far and near,* she prayed quickly, as she shut the barn door. It would have to do. They ate together at the table, and it was rather a subdued affair for the normally garrulous children. They shot nervous glances at each other and spoke in low tones, since for some of them, this was the first time a storm of this strength had come through. Annie and Caroline tried to keep their voices cheery and pleasant as they attempted to distract the children from the thunder and pounding rain outside. Something pounded against the wall, and Dianna let out a shriek. Robert was trying his very hardest not to cry; he was a big boy. He would not tear up like one of the girls. Susan sat with her arm around him and stroked his hair; he clung to her tightly but made no sound. Tom and Mac tried to act brave but both were nervous, and they sat close together on the bench at the table. No one had much appetite. Realizing supper was over whether anyone had eaten enough or not, Annie rose to begin cleaning up, after giving Bethy to Caroline.

"If you want to take them down to the root cellar, I'll clean up here and join you after. I'll bring a book and we'll read. There's oil in the lamp," Annie said, as she gathered up the dishes and the uneaten food.

"All right," Caroline said, and felt Bethy's forehead. If anything, it was hotter than it had been this afternoon, and Bethy had refused to eat anything at supper. She sipped a little water, but that was all. She was cranky and tired, and Caroline was worried. There was no chance for a doctor in the middle of a hurricane, and her mind turned to Charlie. She pushed the thought of him away, and rose from the table, cradling Bethy's sweaty head in the crook of her neck. She would not think of Charlie right now, could not think of Charlie right now. She didn't even know that this was the same thing Charlie had; it could be just a late summer bug like the children came down with occasionally. Even Bud had gotten a sick stomach last fall. It lasted only a day, but he had lain in bed with a fever as though he were on his last legs. Men were babies when they were sick. Let them try childbirth just once, she thought, and they'd know what suffering really was.

"Come with me, everyone; we're going to go down to the root cellar and wait out the storm down there."

"We're going to sleep in the root cellar?" Robert asked, taking Caroline's hand. That was kind of exciting, but scary, too. He did not like the root cellar and tried very hard to avoid going down into it. If Annie or Mama sent him after something and one of the big girls was nearby, he'd pass the request on to her and have her do it. It was dark in there, with all kinds of earthy and pungent smells, and his imagination ran wild with what might be lurking in the shadows.

"Yes, just for tonight, and we're all going together. It'll be an adventure," Caroline replied. She hoped her voice did not give any hint of the trepidation she felt right now, with the worry over Bethy's fever, the fate of the horses, and the storm in general. They had done the best they could to batten down the hatches, and now they just had to ride it out. She did not think anything would flood, and the root cellar itself was very well built, but she knew there would be a mess in the morning, regardless. She led them to the door of the root cellar and gave Bethy to Susan. Bethy cried and stretched out her arms to Caroline, but Susan pushed the child's head to rest on her shoulder, and Bethy acquiesced and clung to her instead, whimpering. Caroline pulled the door of the root cellar open and stepped into the hole in the floor. Bud had built it first before he had even put up the walls of the house around it. He had been convinced that it was the best way to do it, and she was grateful for his insistence on it now. The cellar was not a big room, and with all the hanging vegetables and milk buckets and the butter churn, they would practically be on top of each other, but it would be much better for the children, all snuggled down here and out of earshot of the screaming wind and torrents of rain. She felt stair after stair with her feet, bringing the oil lamp down with her and then setting it on a shelf. The lamp cast a pale orange glow in the cellar, and the air was cool. She looked back up the stairs at the pairs of wide, worried eyes.

"Ellie, you and Sarah go get the blankets off the beds and gather up the pillows. Maclan, you go back to the kitchen and get the big stockpot; we'll have to use it as a chamber pot. Susan, come on down here with Bethy, and we'll try to make us a comfy little spot for the night."

Susan carefully made her way down the stairs holding Bethy, and Caroline steadied her daughters as they came down. She took Bethy, and Susan joined her at the bottom of the cellar.

"Let's move all these things to the sides, and make as much room as we can," Caroline said, shifting Bethy to the other hip. Goodness, she was so hot. *Please Lord, don't take Bethy from me too*, she prayed. *I gave You Charlie. Can't that be enough?* She knew in her heart it was blasphemy to question what God chose to do, but she asked anyway. It couldn't hurt to ask. Even Abraham had asked, and Isaac was spared. She was going to keep asking, all night long.

The children were back now with their scavenged items, and as they carefully descended into the cellar, Caroline helped each one of them down—one-handed, since the other hand was supporting Bethy's behind. They made little pallets of blankets and pillows, and as they organized and moved baskets and buckets aside in the little room, stacking things on shelves and making a homey space, their spirits seemed to rise. The clamorous noise of the storm was muffled, and they chattered with each other and even laughed. Caroline smiled. They would be fine, and as long as Bethy got better instead of worse, they would all have something exciting to talk about tomorrow at breakfast.

Annie came to the door of the cellar and handed a bucket of water down to Caroline. "Here, I'll be back in a minute." Caroline found a spot for the bucket of water and waited for Annie, hearing her footsteps above her. Little puffs of dirt fell from the ceiling as Annie walked over the cellar, but the floor had been made strong and firm, and there was no danger of anything caving in. Bud had known what he was doing, and she had another moment of worry for him at the camp. *Lord, please keep him safe, she prayed. I'm still pissed at him for the moment, but I need him to come home in one piece.* He was a good father and a good provider and had always been gentle with her. She knew some men who talked with their fists and was grateful Bud was not one of them. This craziness with Annie would work itself out; just exactly how, she had no earthly idea, but onward and upward, as the nuns in the orphanage had always said. There was no sense dwelling over things that were done and couldn't be changed. She thought she'd gotten her practicality from her mother, as little as she could remember of her, and for the most part it had served her well all her life. She certainly was depending on it now.

Annie's feet appeared again at the stairs, and she handed down another bucket of water to Caroline, then a few cups. She climbed up again, but this time just to pull the door of the root cellar closed.

"How's Bethy?" Annie asked, catching her breath. She came down the last few stairs and looked at Caroline as she sat on one of the lower rungs, her feet on the bottom of the wooden staircase. Caroline's face was sweaty and tendrils of her hair stuck to it. She brushed it back with her hand. "Still feverish; she's so hot," Caroline touched her daughter's forehead again with the back of her hand.

"Well, let's get these cloths into the water; we'll cool her off a little,"

Annie replied, taking two dishcloths from her apron pocket. From the other pocket, she drew a small book and, handing it to Susan, said, "Here, Susan, read the children a story, and we'll get settled down to sleep."

Caroline dunked the dishcloths into one of the water buckets and started to wring them out with one hand. Annie took Bethy from her and laid her down on one of the blankets in the corner where there was space for her to stretch her little legs out. She kneeled down next to her and pulled the blanket up over her shoulder. Taking the damp cloth from Caroline, she laid it on Bethy's forehead.

"She'll be all right, Caroline; I know she will," Annie said encouragingly, as she brushed Bethy's hair back from her hot forehead.

Caroline rested her hands on her knees. She didn't reply, and Annie was about to speak again, when she heard a muffled sob. She looked behind her to see if the children had heard it, but Susan was still reading to them from the book Annie had brought. Annie put her arms around Caroline and pulled her head to her chest; she felt tears soak into her dress.

"I can't lose her too, Annie, I can't," Caroline whispered, her chest hitching with the words. Annie rubbed her back soothingly.

"You won't; I know you won't," she promised, hoping she was right. "She'll be just fine; it's just a little fever, and it'll be gone by morning. We're just going to keep her comfortable, and she'll be right as rain." Caroline continued to sob quietly for a few moments; grief, mixed with worry and exhaustion, overwhelmed her practicality for the time being.

After a bit, Caroline wiped her face with her hands and sat up. She sniffed and gradually managed to get herself under control. She took Annie's hand and looked at her. "Thank you," she said, and Annie smiled.

"We'll make it through," Annie said. "It'll be all right."

Dianna came over to Caroline and put her arms around her neck. "The story's over, Mama, but we're not tired. We don't have to go to sleep just yet, do we?"

Caroline uttered a short laugh and wiped her eyes. "You're never tired when it's time to go to bed, have you ever noticed that?" She smiled at her little fair-haired daughter, who giggled and plopped herself in her mama's lap. Caroline turned her smile to Annie and said, "Why don't we sing a few songs together before we go to sleep, and maybe that will settle us down a bit." Annie smiled back and took the cloth from Bethy's head, dunking it back in the bucket.

"That sounds like a great idea," Annie said, and wrung some of the water from the cloth. She blotted Bethy's head and neck with it, as Caroline moved to sit with the group of children and gathered them around her. *It's gonna be a long night*, Annie thought. *Please Lord, heal Bethy, and keep us safe. Don't let us blow away. Keep Bud and Frank safe at the camp, and Mama and Daddy and the kids at home. Thank you for the root cellar. Amen.*

14 AFTER THE STORM

Annie and Caroline spent the night trading off with Bethy, trying to keep her forehead cool and watching her fitful sleep. The other children slept in heaps on the floor of the cellar, undisturbed by the howling wind and driving rain above. Caroline woke from a doze and looked at Annie questioningly. Annie sat on the cellar floor, cradling Bethy in her lap, her back to the wall.

"Still the same," Annie whispered, stroking Bethy's forehead.

Caroline looked at her forlornly. "I don't know what else to do," she confessed. "I don't have anything to give her, and I don't know how to help her." She looked ready to dissolve into tears again. Caroline was not a woman given to tears, generally; it took a great deal to rattle her. She was not an unemotional person, in fact she felt things very deeply, but she tended to keep her emotions to herself. She'd actually had years of training in not giving herself away, and it had served her very well. It did, however, give others the impression that she was unfeeling, which was far from true. The fact that she was close to tears again was testament to how truly undone she felt over Bethy's sickness.

Annie looked up at the ceiling. "Do you hear anything?" she asked quietly. She suddenly realized how quiet it was. She had gotten used to the sound of the rain, muffled though it was down here in the cellar, but suddenly realized she wasn't hearing it. She wondered if the storm had spared them or if she'd see the sky when she opened the cellar doors. There was no telling what to expect.

Caroline looked up, too, realizing the absence of the pounding rain. "I didn't even notice," she whispered. "I think it might be over."

"Here, take her. I'll go up and check. If it's really over, we could go get the doctor." Annie shifted Bethy in her arms, and Caroline took her, kissing her forehead. It was still hot. How long could the fever last? She thought back to Charlie, who had never regained consciousness after his fever had set in. When had Bethy last been really awake? It must have been yesterday, after they had eaten and Bethy had thrown up all over everything. It had only been a day, but what an eternally long day.

"Please be careful," Caroline said to Annie, who had begun to climb the cellar stairs.

"I will."

"See if the horses are okay, if it looks safe to go out."

"Okay." Annie lifted the cellar door and tried to keep it from banging back onto the floor and waking the children. She cautiously stepped out into the pantry and into the kitchen. She heard nothing outside, not the howling of the wind, not the rain, not any sound at all. It was quiet, and by the light streaming in the windows, it looked to be early morning. She went to the mantle clock, but it had stopped at one o'clock. They hadn't wound it last night, of course. She opened the front door cautiously, looked out into the dooryard and beyond, gauging the damage, and gingerly stepped outside. Branches were strewn all over the dooryard and puddles were everywhere. She closed the door behind her, walked out to the middle of the yard, and turned full circle. The pear tree was still standing, but the garden was completely underwater. Branches lay intertwined with broken sprouts, and mud was splashed up against the walls of the house. The fences of the pasture looked all right, and she could see the horses grazing between puddles of standing water.

She looked toward the barn and saw several shingles torn from the roof, but the structure itself was still intact. She walked over to it, picking her way through the puddles and holding her skirts up so they wouldn't drag in the mud, and stopped where the chicken coop should have been. There was no sign of it anywhere. Gone entirely, and there was no trace of wood or wire. Chickens meandered around the yard and pecked the sodden ground in vain; mud was everywhere. Annie had no time to run around and count chickens, but she knew this wasn't all of them; she hoped they'd survived. If they'd gone flying with their house, she supposed they weren't in such great shape. Oh well—if all they lost in this hurricane were a few shingles and a chicken coop (and a few chickens along with it), she supposed that wasn't the worst thing.

There were no fallen trees on the house or the barn, although she could see several trees down in the woods nearby. Some had come up by the roots, and some trees were just broken clean in half. Someone would have to ride the fences to make sure trees had not fallen on them and look for any cows who might have escaped through broken fence rails. They would be picking up branches for days, and it would take a while for the puddles to dry up, but overall, they appeared to have come through the hurricane relatively unscathed, all things considered. Annie sent up a silent prayer of thanks and went into the house to tell Caroline.

Bud and Frank joined the mass of men to get breakfast. Dixon had routed the men at seven, and they all trundled out of the camp house to see what the hurricane had left in its wake. Wagons were overturned; one lay half-submerged in a giant puddle of water and mud. Trees had fallen on the fences that penned in the horses, and Bud could see horse legs underneath the branches of a fallen tree. The camp house itself had lost some roof shingles and would need to be repaired, but overall it seemed to have come through the storm structurally sound. The rail ties that they had gathered and piled in the woods lay scattered, and branches covered the clearing they had forged through the pines and oaks. Standing water filled every crevice and valley, and even the trees that had not fallen had a definite lean to them, whereas before the storm they had stood tall and straight. The root systems of the trees that had fallen were thrust into the sunlight, and earthy gnarls of roots were exposed; the ground from which they had been wrenched was torn and gouged. The roots, when splayed into the air, stood as tall as a man and even taller. The sight of the fallen trees and branches, puddles, and detritus of the storm made the men somber as they took in their changed surroundings. Those who had left families behind to work on the rail line were undoubtedly wondering how their homes had fared in the storm.

Groups of men gathered around the fallen wagons and digging their heels into the muddy soil, righted them; the cooks went about cobbling together a breakfast for the horde of workers, doing what they could to get food and hot coffee out to the men in preparation for a day of cleaning up. Bud had not told anyone about his revelation of the morning, that he had recognized the man he had met in the woods. Rube, his friend had called him. Short for Ruben, maybe? He didn't know. He also didn't know if the man had any ill intentions here at the camp, but Bud thought he bore watching, all the same. As he stood in the line to receive whatever the cooks had been able to round up, he thought back to the night he'd encountered the man and his friend lying in wait for him and his impulsive decision to leave his cash in the flour sack in the tree. The next morning he'd ridden back to the spot and had managed to find it, still hidden, and counted himself lucky to have avoided what could have been a premature ending to his short life had the night gone differently. But here the man was again, and he wondered if he'd manage to skate by a second time. There was definitely something off about him, whether he had done anything yet or not.

But what could he say, and to whom? You couldn't exactly lock a man up based on what you thought he might do. Besides, Frank and Mark had already remarked that they'd noticed him, and maybe that's all that needed to be done for now. Frank, who was ahead of Bud in line, turned to him now and relayed to him what he'd learned from his conversation with the men who were ahead of him in line.

"Hey, Bud, listen—they say Dixon's gonna let us go for a week, say he's gonna let us go back home and check on our families, that it's too wet to do anything here anyway. Thinks we'll kill ourselves if we try to haul anything through the middle of all this water. They're sayin' we'll have a better time of it if we let it dry out a bit."

"Well, I don't know that he's wrong, but it's gotta piss him off no end that we'll be a week behind. Don't mind goin' home to check on the girls, though; I'm grateful for that, if it's true."

Soon it was their turn to receive breakfast, which was salt pork and hardtack. Hardly fine fare, but the coffee was hot and all Bud really wanted anyway. They found Mark sitting with a group of men in a wagon; everything was wet, but at least the wagon was out of the mud and water. Mark moved over to allow them room, and Bud and Frank sat to eat.

"Is it true, what I heard from them over there, that Dixon's lettin' us go?" Frank asked Mark, around a bite of pork.

"That's what he said," Mark replied. "Unless he changes his mind, I guess. It's such a boggy mess right now, we can't make any headway with the line. He's better off saving a week of payroll until it all dries out. Doesn't help folks like me that need the work and have nowhere to go, though."

"Damn straight," one of the other men on the wagon agreed. "I come too fur t' be goin' home now. What'm I s'posed t' do for a damn week, no pay? That's a crocka shit, that's what it is."

"Well, I got five kids and a woman at home, and I don't know if my home's standin' or six feet under water, so I'm goin'," said another. The other men in the wagon assented or disagreed, as their situations dictated, with Dixon's plans. They were all still arguing about it when a shrill whistle pierced their conversation, and they turned to see Dixon in the center of the camp, standing in the bed of a wagon. His normally shined shoes were caked with mud, and his tie hung askew at his neck. Bud thought he looked like one of the street peddlers who came through town occasionally, selling liver pills or hair tonic, and his disheveled appearance and the tufts of wild hair that blew in the breeze about his head suggested a slight insanity. It was a marked departure from the primly attired man Bud had first encountered, but then a hurricane *had* just blown through, after all. The man looked like he'd been directly in its path.

"Listen here!" Dixon yelled now, from his perch in the wagon. "Any man that has a mind to, can take a few days' furlough to check on his family or his land, and his job will be waitin' for him when he comes back! Any man what wants to stay, and clean up, will get paid for the work! We start back on the line Monday week, an' if you ain't here, you ain't got a job!"

"Well, that's all right, I guess," said the man who'd said he'd come too far to go home. "Least we'll get paid; guess I don't care whether it's buildin' a rail line or haulin' trees. Don't make no differ'nce to me." The others agreed; work was work, no matter what the end result. If it brought pay at the end of the week, then it was worthwhile.

Bud hopped off the end of the wagon and wiped his hands on his pants, turning back to look at Mark and Frank. They were polishing off the last of their breakfast. He cocked his head to the side and spoke in a low voice. "You done? Lemme tell you somethin'."

The two looked at each other, and Mark shrugged, hopping off the wagon. Frank followed suit, and Bud led them over to a nearby tree, close enough that he felt wouldn't be too suspicious but hopefully out of earshot of the groups of men chatting and eating.

"I think I know that fella you two were talkin' about, the one you said had a look in 'is eye," Bud said quietly. He leaned back against the tree trunk, scanning the gatherings of men, searching for the one he still thought of as Mustache. Rube, his mind corrected. He gave Frank and Mark an abbreviated account of the night he'd met the two men in the woods and how he'd been sure of their intent to rob him.

"You're sure it's the same one? What'd the other one look like?" Mark asked.

Bud described him, as much as he could remember, and Mark nodded in recognition. "Sounds like the fella he came in with, all right. He lit out just a few days after they came, but he stole a horse 'fore he went. Dixon liked to choked, he was so mad."

"He send anybody after him?" Frank asked.

"He sent two fellas the next mornin', just as soon as we realized what happened, but they came back that night. Couldn't track him. Wasn't worth losin' two more men over, Dixon said. I told you, hirin' just anybody comes back to bite ya." Bud smiled to himself. He was sure Mark didn't hear it, but he had started dropping his gs. His clipped "town" accent was slowly being consumed by the southern drawl he heard all day from the men who worked around him, and he was subconsciously picking up the twang. Before long, he wouldn't sound like a city slicker at all.

"Well, I don't know if he's up to anything or not, but I'm just sayin', if he stays and half the camp is gone, you better be on your guard. It'd be a good time to get inta somethin'," Bud cautioned.

"All right. Dixon keeps a pretty good eye on things, and it's likely the train'll be delayed with the roads bein' like they are. But I'll keep an eye out, and I appreciate the warning." Mark was scanning the crowds of men now too. "Are you two planning on going back home, or are you gonna stay here?"

Frank looked at Bud. "Do you want me to come with you? I will, if you think you'll need a hand."

"No, if I need anything, Nick can help me. You c'n stay here, if you want." He looked at Mark again and stood up. "I wanna show you somethin', though, 'fore I go. Somethin' I think'll help us get those receipts outta Dixon, maybe solve that problem."

"Lead on, then. I'm all for that," Mark said, and the three of them went back to the wagon and gathered up cups and plates. They dropped them off to be washed and headed to Frank and Bud's tent.

"Tom and Mac, go see to the horses, and get them fed and watered. Tack up Jill and get her ready for me," Annie directed, wiping off the table. They had brought up all the blankets and pillows, eaten breakfast, and now everyone needed to tackle what they could to start setting things to rights after the hurricane – the work of picking up branches, checking fences, corralling the chickens, and cleaning up. They had brought Bethy up from the root cellar and put her to bed, still feverish, and Annie planned to go to town to fetch the doctor. Caroline and Annie had given the children a list of tasks to get started on, and the house was bustling with everyone preparing for their appointed assignments.

"But you don't know what the roads are going to be like, and you don't know if you can even get down the road," Caroline said to Annie, putting the broom away.

"No, but I'll just waste time going over to Nick's and asking him to go, and he'll run into the same obstacles I will anyway," Annie countered, firm in her decision to ride to town.

"But he's not *pregnant!*"

"It'll be fine, I promise. Mary rode a donkey, remember, and she was nine months gone." She smiled at Caroline.

"I don't think it's the same thing," said Caroline, laughing, "but I suppose you're right. Just be careful. Maybe Mac or Tom should ride with you. You don't know what you're getting into. A woman shouldn't be riding that far alone, anyway, pregnant or not." She was still skeptical about it.

"I'll be fine," Annie repeated. "I've ridden to town plenty of times on my own, and this time will be no different. I might have to go around some fallen trees or through some puddles or something, but I'm sure I'll figure it out. You need to stay here and take care of Bethy, and the boys have plenty to do in the barn and with the cows and all. Just let me pack a little food, and when Tom gets Jill tacked up, I'll be off."

Caroline sighed, resigned. "All right." There was no use arguing about it anymore; Bethy was no better, and she really had no idea what else to do. She couldn't count on Bud coming home from the camp, even with the storm, and she didn't know when she'd see him again. She didn't even know if he was safe.

Annie finished cleaning up around the stove, took off her apron, and found her hat. She wrapped a heel of bread in muslin and placed it in her pack with a cup and few other things she could snack on if she got hungry, and drew the pack closed. "There now; I'll be back with the doctor just as soon as I can, but don't you be carryin' on if it takes longer than you think it should. I'll go as fast as I can, but I don't know what I'll run into."

"I'll be fine," Caroline said tersely. She resented the implication that she might be fragile in a crisis. Admittedly, she'd cried on Annie's shoulder last night when she'd been worried about Bethy, but surely anyone with a sick child in a hurricane could be expected to be a little overwhelmed? "We'll just wait till you return and keep her comfortable. We've plenty to keep us busy. Don't we, little boy?" She smiled as Robert came into the room, holding three big carrots and some potatoes in his shirt.

"What? Mama, lookit these carrots! They was floatin' in the garden! There's so much water they just came right up!" He was a filthy, sodden mess, and Caroline sighed. So much for the swept floor.

"My goodness! Well, it's a good thing you found them. Let me have them, and we'll clean them up for supper. Go see what else you can find in the garden that needs to come up, and just leave them at the door. I'll come get them." She took the vegetables from Robert and shooed him back out the door before he could touch anything.

"Okay, see you in a bit," Annie said, following Robert out and heading to the barn. Caroline waved and shut the door, then rested her back against it for a moment before going to check on Bethy again. *Lord, it's been a long night, and it's going to be a long day too. Give me strength,* she prayed.

Mark and Bud were in the camp house talking quietly, waiting for Dixon to come back from the privy. Since Bud had arrived at the camp, he and Mark had gone over each ledger in detail, making sure that Davidson's entries were correct and that nothing was missing or out of order. They'd found a few mistakes but nothing major, and the only concern that remained was Mark's suspicion that Dixon had receipts that he'd not passed on or had made deals that hadn't been accounted for. Mark had already been surprised more than once by suppliers who'd been angry about late payments after Dixon had placed orders he'd failed to mention. The rail lines were being funded by some very wealthy, very particular investors, and word got back when payments were late or suppliers were disgruntled.

"All right, what's the problem?" Dixon barked, coming into the camp house. Mark and Bud looked up from the ledger they were discussing as Dixon trundled in, digging his key from his waistcoat to unlock his office. It was the only room with a door in the camp house, and Dixon guarded it protectively. Whenever he left it, unfailingly and without question, he locked it, and just outside the office were his cot and trunk. A folding screen with Chinese characters separated this small living space from the greater expanse of the camp house where the men periodically gathered for meetings, during rainstorms, or to receive their pay each week. Dixon seldom left the camp house, preferring instead to use runners who gave him constant updates on the line and on the conduct of the men as well. This, of course, earned him no end of rather undesirable nicknames; most of the men had little respect for a boss who was too important to dwell among the common man. In truth, Dixon was an excellent manager who wasn't afraid to dicker for the right price with his suppliers and brought the hammer down hard on those who failed to deliver on time. He was equally hard on his men and expected a solid day's work for good wages. Not one to suffer fools gladly, he had no patience for any who would complain or grumble about their lot. He did, however, tend to treat the office as his private kingdom, and lorded it over those who reported to him. He was a capable and important man, but unfortunately he knew it.

Mark and Bud followed Dixon into his office, where he hung up his waistcoat and dropped into his chair with a loud *Hrumph!*. Mark nodded to Bud, who opened his ledger and spread it out on the desk in front of Dixon. Pulling on a pair of spectacles, Dixon sat upright in the chair and stared down at the open pages. "What'm I lookin' at?" he demanded.

"Mark and I've been goin' over the ledgers and just want to draw your 'tention to somethin' you should be aware of, bein' as how you're 'countable to the comp'ny, and all," Bud began. Dixon's tendency to self-importance had not gone unnoticed by Bud. He took a quick look at Mark, who gave another imperceptible nod, and continued. "Looks like we're gonna be a little low on funds unless you got some other receipts we can send back to the comp'ny, so they can see that we got expenses to pay. We ain't gonna make payroll next week, based on what we got in the till." Bud put on his most concerned face, and Mark looked somber as well. The railroad funded the portion of the line that Dixon managed, and he had a lot of investors to keep happy. Not paying his bills on time might get back to the suits, and he'd be out of a job. Dixon had no intention of having that happen.

"Unfortunately we weren't able to pay for the flour Cook just got, but we convinced Mr. Albertson to give us one more week before he sent a letter to the company," Mark said, his face still serious. "He's willing to work with us." In fact no such thing had happened, but Mark thought a little prodding might be necessary to get Dixon moving in the right direction.

"What?! How'd we get this low? Mark, han't you been keepin' up with the receipts I give you, boy?" He flipped back a page in the ledger and scanned over the numbers. Mark held his breath. If he flipped one more page back...but no, he turned the page forward again and scanned over the lines as Bud had first put it in front of him. He looked back up at Bud and Frank. "Well?"

"I think if you just look through your desk there, maybe look at your appointment book, and see if you can find any receipts you might've forgotten to give me, or think of anyone you've met with that you've not told me about, we can send word to the company tomorrow and have them increase the payout on the next train. Then we'll be back on track, so to speak." Mark smirked a little at his unintended pun, but it was lost on Dixon. "The company need never know that our funds were a little low."

Dixon grunted and immediately pulled out every drawer of his desk, sifting through papers. Bud stepped back to allow him room to rummage, hiding a smile. It had been his idea to cook the books a little, and Mark had agreed wholeheartedly. In past weeks he'd found receipts by checking Dixon's waistcoat pockets and by harping on him incessantly, but he couldn't babysit the man forever. By rewriting a few of the last ledger pages and dropping a few zeroes here and there, they'd made their accounting outlook a touch more dire than it actually was. If Dixon had the presence of mind to open the safe and actually compare the books to the cash on hand, they'd have been found out immediately and had a lot of explaining to do besides. Or if he'd flipped back one more page... But Mark was counting on Dixon's tendency to go off half-cocked whenever he met with the slightest inconvenience or challenge, and he was rewarded handsomely with immediate action. Dixon was fully committed to a complete search.

"We'll just step out for a bit, Mr. Dixon, so we're not in your way. I'll be back a little later," Mark said, picking up the ledger and tucking it under his arm. Bud followed him out the door.

"Yeah, yeah, give me a minute," Dixon muttered, his head and arms practically buried in a drawer.

Bud and Mark made a quick exit from the office, shutting the door on Dixon's slamming drawers and ruffling papers. They walked to the front of the camp house. "Well, see what he comes up with. We might have to just keep a few 'Dixon' pages going each week to make sure we stay ahead of him," Bud said. Mark smiled. He was no stranger to managing up, but he might not have been brave enough to actually go through with the ruse alone. It was always nice to have a partner in crime.

"You headin' out?"

"Yeah, just gonna go say goodbye to Frank, then I'm gonna tack up and be off. Gonna take a while," Bud replied. "I'll be back in a week. Mind what

I said 'bout that shady fella."

"I'll keep an eye out," Mark said, laughing.

The two shook hands and left the camp house with the sounds of slamming drawers behind them. Bud headed to the tent to finish packing and turned his thoughts toward home.

15 A STORM BLOWS

Annie had been in the saddle most of the day and she was beat. Between the swollen river and the fallen trees, it had taken much longer to get to town as it usually did on horseback. It was well past midnight before she'd even come close to the outskirts of town, and by that time she was muddy and worn out. She'd had to dismount several times and pull Jill over fallen trees and through enormous puddles. Once they both had to wade through waist-deep water where there should have been a road. She'd dried out, been soaked, and dried out again before making town, and both she and the horse were exhausted. She went straight for the doctor's house, despite the late hour, and dismounted at the gate, throwing the reins haphazardly around the post. Jill wasn't going anywhere, and Annie didn't care if she did. She rapped upon the door, then sank to the step. A young woman came to the door, took one look at Annie, and called to someone behind her for help. She sat down next to Annie.

"Are you all right? What's wrong?" She started to put her arm around Annie, tentatively, as she realized how dirty she was.

"I'm fine, it's not me... It's... Is the doctor here?" Annie looked up at the nurse who had come to the door at the young woman's call. She knew she probably looked like she'd been through...well, a hurricane. "I need the doctor to go to the Braxtons'. Their daughter's sick; she's got a fever...all the children...they need someone...right now."

"Well, honey, you look like you need someone too. You're a fright," the nurse said. "You come on in here—"

"No, I can't," Annie cut her off and stood up. "I have to get..." her words trailed off. She'd stood up too quickly, and the exertion of the long day without much food was too much for her. The world went black, and she fell back down to the steps, where the ladies caught her and pulled her across the threshold.

"Goodness! I didn't want to sleep tonight, anyway, did you?" the nurse said to the young woman, as she hooked her hands underneath Annie's arms. With a chuckle and a heavy sigh, the young woman grasped Annie's dirty ankles.

"I had no intention of it," she replied, and together they managed to get Annie into the doctor's hallway and into a chair.

While the nurse attended to Annie and tried to bring her back around, the young woman who had first opened the door, Maggie, went to fetch the doctor, who was catching an hour's sleep after a long day. Being the only game in town meant he was in high demand when major events like this hurricane occurred, and despite Maggie and Verna's help, there were some things only he could do. Most towns Milton's size did not have the luxury of a doctor and a nurse, but Verna had made good use of herself, having had some experience in the war and a contempt of idle hands. Her clear head and patient ministrations had proved useful in the last seventy-two hours: Tom Cochran had been out hunting when the winds came, far away from home and unable to get to shelter before the big gusts hit. His brother had dragged him into the doctor's house half-dead and half-crazy. Vincent Barnard had been kicked in the head by a frantic mule, and Mrs. Grant had gone into labor just after the first rains had started. Verna, Maggie, and Dr. Joseph Matthews had been running almost nonstop since the first winds came. And now here was Annie Wilson at their door, herself a mess and raving about illness at the Braxtons'...? This was quite the week. Verna found Annie's pulse and counted under her breath, watching the clock in the hallway.

Dr. Matthews, roused by Maggie and somewhat alert but shedding the last vestiges of sleep, came around the corner to find Verna still trying to bring Annie around. Annie's eyelids fluttered, and her lips moved silently, but no sound came out. "She doesn't seem to be physically injured, Doctor, not nears I can tell, anyway," Verna said, as he kneeled down beside them and took one of Annie's hands. She'd had a few minutes to examine her patient while Maggie went to fetch the doctor from his stolen sleep, and as far as she could tell, there were no major physical injuries, but the lady was certainly filthy. She thought she knew who this was—one of the Wilson girls—Anne, or maybe it was Alice or something. The one the Braxtons had brought on after the loss of one of their boys.

"Let's get her into one of the beds; we'll look her over," Matthews said, picking up Annie and taking her to one of the rooms. Maggie followed, but Verna stayed where she was a minute. One in the morning, and it looked like it was going to be a while again before any of them got any sleep. She sighed deeply, then gathered herself and made it to her feet, before plodding off to start a pot of coffee.

While Annie trekked to town through the detritus of the storm, Bud was making his own way through the chaos the hurricane had made of the roads back to his house. Along the way, he met several people dragging fallen boughs out of the road and was grateful for their work; he had to stop enough times to move trees on his own or navigate around boggy areas. He'd brought the wagon of trees he'd felled working for Dixon and more than once regretted it, as it was just one more thing he had to maneuver through the wreckage the storm had left behind. It would take forever to get home at this rate. Oh well. At least he'd get the load there, and that was the first step. He'd figure out the building part later, talk to Nick about it. He wondered how his brother had fared through the storm. He supposed he'd need to go check on him after he got home; his father, too. *Hmph.* His father.

He wondered if Robert even knew there'd been a storm, or whether he'd been too far into a bottle to be aware. He hadn't always been a drunk. Bud had memories of his mother and father sitting at the table together, eating dinner, talking. He had memories of his mama at the stove, cooking while he played on the floor. He had been old enough to miss her after she left. He had tried to talk to Nick about her, but Nick didn't really remember a lot, and Frank certainly didn't. She used to sing to him, he remembered that, and the feel of her dress against his cheek. She was warm, and she smelled like flowers. He remembered rocking with her in the rocking chair by the fire at night, and she would tell him stories from the Bible.

"Joseph's brothers threw him in a pit, to get rid of him." Her voice, quiet and soft by the firelight. "They were jealous of him because they thought their daddy loved him the best." Rock, rock. "They weren't bad brothers; they were just frustrated, and they made a bad choice. That's what happens sometimes when you get a bunch of boys together: they just lose their minds. They make decisions they wouldn't make if they were all on their own. But they did, and they threw him into a dark, deep pit, all by himself. They were gonna kill him."

Rock, rock. He inhaled her flowery smell. This was a scary story, but he wasn't scared. "But then some Egyptians came by, and they sold Joseph to the Egyptians. They told his daddy he died, and his daddy was really sad. The Egyptians took Joseph away, and he grew up far away from his daddy and his brothers, and he became an important man there." Her skin was like velvet, and his fingers traced the lace on her nightgown. "He was in charge of all the food for the Egyptians, and when there was a famine in the land, everybody came to him to get something to eat."

"What's a famine?" he asked.

"A famine is when nobody has anything to eat. When the fields are bare, and there's nothing in the root cellar."

"Are we going to have a famine?"

"No, baby, we have plenty to eat."

"Oh."

Rock, rock. "So then the brothers all came to Egypt looking for food 'cause they were starving. And guess what? Joseph was there! And he recognized those bad brothers, and guess what he did?"

"He said, 'Go home!'"

She laughed, and he smiled, his cheek against the soft cotton nightgown, his drowsy head nestled on her breast. His fingers traced a button. Rock, rock. "No, he didn't say that, though he could've. No, he gave them more'n they could eat, and sent 'em home with extra!"

Bud smiled to himself now, thinking about that memory. He didn't have much in the way of riches of this world, but he remembered being loved by his mama, and he guessed that was more than some folks had. More than Frank had, anyway. His thoughts turned to Frank as he held the reins in his hands, his elbows resting on his knees. Jack was doing fine right now; the road was good and actually pretty dry in this stretch. He could afford to let his mind wander as the horse plodded his course in the humid morning air. Frank was going to be alone with no one to watch him for a bit, and Bud wondered how long it would take until he fell into a bottle. Maybe Mark would keep him from getting too far gone. Who knew. Maybe he'd have enough to keep him busy. Lord knows he had enough to keep himself busy. Good Lord, what the hell was he thinking?! Two women, a houseful of children, fields that had to be plowed, cows that had to be milked, houses built... Madness. He shook his head abruptly, as if he could shake off the weight of it all, and huffed. He refused to think about it anymore. It could break a man, it could, thinking about all his responsibilities. Best just to get on with it and get going.

"Hep, Jack!" he called, as he slapped the reins on Jack's backside. Jack woke up a little and quickened his step. "Best be gettin' home."

Caroline was beside herself. Annie was still not back from town. Even if the roads were bad, she knew how well Annie could ride, but she worried. Her mind was a whirlwind, and she hadn't slept in...who knew. She leaned in the doorway of the little room and tried to calm herself, hearing the children play outside in the yard. Bethy was much better; her fever had finally broken, and she slept peacefully in the little bedroom. Caroline kept a watchful eye on her, however, and she took nothing for granted. Not anymore. Things could change on a dime, she knew, and she wanted to be ready for anything. She heard the children calling out to her; someone was here. *Annie! Finally!* She rushed to the front door and expected to see Annie, but instead it was a horse and rider she didn't recognize. A large, hefty woman with a straw hat perched atop a great fuzz of gray hair was dismounting from her grateful horse and straightening her skirts. As Caroline came to the porch, the woman greeted the children, who stared a little wide eyed at her appearance.

"My land, ain't you a one!" she said to Mac, who took the horse's reins from her and blinked at her in reply. "You're just as helpful as you c'n be, and I'm sure glad to see ya!" She patted her behind. "I'm a little worn out, I think. Yes, sir, I sure am." Mac took the horse to be watered in the shade of the barn.

Ellie and Sarah stared at her in expectation and quite forgot their manners. They didn't get many visitors, and those they did, they knew. They'd never seen a personage quite like this before, and in their defense, there weren't many women just like Verna Dade in the world.

"Good day, Miz Braxton; I understand you've got a little girl who's not feelin' too well. I come to see about her. I'm Verna Dade," she said to Caroline, who came out on the porch as Verna dusted off her hands, then wrangled an overstuffed bag over her shoulder.

"I'm so glad you came, but my daughter's feeling better now," Caroline said, offering her hand to Verna, who harrumphed as she came up the porch steps to meet her. "She certainly was ill, but I believe she's come through it all right. Didn't Annie come with you?"

"No, ma'am, Annie had to stay with the doctor in town, as she was feelin' poorly after her ride." Verna mopped her neck with a handkerchief. "But she'll be all right, and I came to look in on you'ins. I'da been here sooner, but with the storm 'n' all, we just been chasin' ourselves." The three steps up to the porch seemed to have taken the wind out of Verna, and she stopped to catch her breath. "Well now," she said, after a few moments of heavy breathing and taking in the lay of the little farmhouse and yard around her, "let's see what we're about, shall we?"

Caroline blinked at her. She really wasn't sure what to make of Verna and her giant bag, and she wasn't a person who was easily unsettled. But Verna was just so very large and...*present*. "Through here, honey? Yes, that's just the thing, let's go see..." She trailed off as she let herself into the house, and Caroline stared after her, still mesmerized by this hurricane of a woman who had just descended upon them. She trailed after Verna a moment later, collecting herself and giving herself a little shake.

Verna bustled into the house, quickly making a note of things as she went, somehow discerning just where her patient lay, despite never having been in the place before. She bundled herself and her enormous bag into the little room where Bethy lay peacefully sleeping, her little hand curled up under her chin, blankets awry and tangled at her feet. Verna placed her bag on the floor and took off her hat. "How about you put us a pot a water on t' boil? That'll get us started, now," she said to Caroline, then turned her attention to her patient. Verna always started off with a pot of boiling water, whether she needed it or not. She found sometimes it was needed, and best to be started right away, but mostly it gave people something to do and kept them out of the way and feeling useful in those first few critical moments that she had with her patients. If nothing else, it usually made way for a cup of coffee before she left, and Verna Dade was nothing without coffee.

Leaving Verna with her patient, Caroline turned to the task at hand, glad for a single purpose. Of course there was nothing for a fire; everything was out of sorts just now. She called to the boys to bring in some firewood, then started sweeping the ashes out of the stove.

"Yes, thank you, that'll do, just right there. Mac, Tom, after you get done there, you all go down to the bay and see if you can catch us a mess a fish for supper." Caroline began to lay out the tinder for the fire, as Mac dumped the rest of the load of wood into the bin.

"Absolutely, yes, ma'am," Tom grinned at Mac. Fishing! It had been nonstop work since the hurricane had blown through, and they were thrilled at the prospect of a few hours of goofing off. The boys bustled off to the barn to find nails they could bend into fishhooks and buckets to catch crickets and worms in.

Caroline began to tend the fire, brushing her hair out of her face. She was exhausted, mentally and physically, and worried about Annie. Why hadn't she come back with Verna? Didn't she know they'd need her? She sat down at the table while the little fire in the stove grew. She looked at her hands, which were filthy with ash and dirt from the wood.

"*Phuah.*" She blew her hair out of her eyes. No rest for the weary; she needed water for the pot. Sighing heavily, she got to her feet, picked up a pot and a bar of soap, and headed for the pump in the yard. One foot in front of the other, she thought. That's how we'll get through this.

Annie stared at the wall, her hands curled under her chin and her knees drawn up to her chest. Soon—oh, too soon—she'd get back on the horse and ride home. Maggie and the doctor had been very good to her, and she knew Verna would take good care of Bethy, so her mind was at ease about that. In fact, her mind was very empty, and she took care to keep it so, lest it be drawn to other matters more disturbing. The last of the blood had finally ceased, and with it had gone Annie's hopes for a future. Annie closed her eyes and slept.

16 JOY AND SORROW

Verna and Caroline sat at the table in the lamplight, each with a cup of coffee before her. The children had long since gone to bed, and the women had finished all the chores the little farm required and now sat quietly sipping in the dim light of the evening. Order had not yet been fully restored after the hurricane had blustered through, but it was at least on its way there, and Verna wanted to stay for a little while to be of what help she could to the family. Annie had ridden in this afternoon, tired but heartily welcomed by the children, and Caroline had put her to bed just after supper. She felt no animosity toward her now, only sorrow and understanding.

After the first night of Verna's stay, once she had been sure that Bethy was safely out of any danger and Caroline had been able to catch up on her missed rest, Verna had been able to fill in the missing details of Annie's trip to town and subsequent stay. Once they had been able to bring Annie around, the nurses had bathed her and washed her clothes, taking care of her in the little infirmary at Dr. Matthews's house. At first Annie had insisted that she ride right back home as soon as she was awake and able to stand, but the nurses would hear none of it, having become aware of her maternal condition as they took care of her in the first few hours of her stay. Dr. Matthews himself had prevailed upon her to remain at the house, especially after hearing how she had been on and off the horse, hauling tree branches out of her way, and fording swollen streams to get to town in her haste to send the doctor home to Bethy and Caroline.

Indeed, her efforts had taken their toll, and so in the early morning hours when she had woken to find blood in her bedsheets, she'd been horrified, scared, and grieved at the results of all her good intentions. For days afterward, Annie had remained in bed, reluctant to go anywhere or take interest in anything around her. She knew she could not stay, however; Verna had gone to the Braxtons' to take care of Bethy, Dr. Matthews and Maggie had patients to see and a practice to run, and she could not remain in the infirmary forever.

When Annie and Jill arrived back at the Braxtons', despite her joy at hearing Bethy was well and on the mend, a cloud had descended over her, and she had been only too willing to go to bed when Caroline suggested it. Now Verna and Caroline sat together at the table, sipping their coffees by the light of the lamp and thinking about the day. Verna was planning to go back to town in the morning, and Caroline was grateful to her for her help and tenderness with Bethy.

"I sure do appreciate everything you've done for us, Verna. Both with Annie there in town and here with my little girl. I don't know how we'll ever repay you."

"You go on, now, and don't worry about that. That's what us old nurses are here for, you know, and that's all we'll say about that. I'm sure sorry about Miss Annie, I am, but she's young, and she'll be all right. Just takes time, that's all."

Caroline knew all about time and what it could and could not do, but she did not contradict Verna. She supposed everyone had their own burdens to bear.

A dog barked in the yard suddenly, startling the women, and they both sat upright.

"You got a rifle, Miss Caroline? If you do, you might best see to it," Verna said, standing up and making her way to the door.

"It's probably Mr. Braxton come home from the camp," Caroline said, hoping her voice sounded more confident than she felt; she tried to keep any tremor from creeping in. She sat bolt upright, her hands on the table, torn between running for the rifle and her need to remain calm and retain her composure. "He's been up at the timber camp for some time, and he's just home to check on us after the storm, I suspect." She hoped. The dog had ceased its barking, but her nerves were still on alert, anticipating any new noise.

A knock on the door made her jump. "Miss Caroline? It's Nick. I come to see after you and the children."

Caroline's shoulders relaxed, and she rose with relief, motioning for Verna to release the latch and open the door.

"Nick! What brings you here so late?" she asked, relief and concern struggling to assert themselves while Verna closed the door behind their guest.

"I'm sorry to haunt your doorstep so late, Caroline. Hope I didn't cause ya a fright." Nick came in, taking off his hat, and nodded to Verna. "Ma'am."

"Not at all! We just didn't expect you. Is everything all right?" Caroline hoped her voice sounded steady and belied her fear of just a few moments before.

"I'd planned to be here earlier, but I got waylaid by a few trees in m' path. Ellen insisted I come check on ya, knowin' Bud was up to the camp and all. Wanted to make sure you folks made out okay after the storm."

"Oh, Nick, I appreciate that! Here, give me your hat and sit down. Verna, would you mind getting Mr. Braxton a cup of coffee and something to eat? There's biscuits and jam from supper and some dried pork in there. This is Verna Dade; she's a nurse from town come to check on Bethy. Here now, Nick," Caroline said, as she guided him to the table and pulled out a chair.

"Thank ya' ma'am." Nick took the coffee from Verna and took a sip. "Hoo, that's good. Took me a sight longern I thought it would to get over here, with all the mess that storm made. Bethy okay?"

"Oh yes, she's fine," Verna replied, placing a jar of jam and a plate of biscuits and pork in front of Nick. She pulled out a chair and dropped her considerable bulk into it, the wood giving a little creak in protest at the test of its ability to bear its burden. "She was a little feverish, but she's just right as rain now."

Caroline nodded. "We're all good; we got through it all right, I guess, though the chickens may say differ'nt. How'd you all make out? Everythin' all right with Ellen and Janette?"

Nick nodded and swallowed a mouthful of biscuit and jam. He hadn't realized how hungry he was until he got started, and this was good jam. "We did all right. Ellen'd been a little poorly right afore the storm, and I's worried I wouldn't get everythin' tightened up fore she hit, but we just got a few shingles loose and one of the barn doors to fix. And just a mess in the yard. Thankfully nothin' major."

"That's good, then, and glad to hear it," Caroline said. "How's Ellen doing now? She better after the storm?"

"Don't quite know what to make of it, actually," Nick said, sipping his coffee. "She's been sick off an' on fer quite some time now. Some days she's good, some days not. Don't seem perdictable. When I left she was doin' all right, and she and Janette send their best. I told her I'd get right back to her once't I'd seen to you and the children. There anything I c'n do for you? Anythin' needin' attention?"

"It's mighty kind of you, Nick, but the boys and I've been able to get everything mostly back into shape, and we're all doin' all right. I hope Bud'll be here 'fore too long to check on us; I actually thought you might be him comin' in."

"You ain't heard from him yet from camp? I guess they been keepin' busy up there."

"No, but I didn't expect to. He and Frank were going to stay for a while until this storm hit. I 'sume it'll change things up a bit up there."

"I 'magine it's a frightful mess." Frank mopped up the last of the jam on his plate with his last bite of biscuit and drained the coffee from his cup.

"Let me get you another cup," Verna said, and rose to take Nick's cup from him.

"No, no, best be gettin' off t' bed, and lettin' you ladies do the same, though I sure do appreciate the offer. Caroline, I'll bed down in the barn with the boys, if that's all right, and leave in the mornin', if you're sure there's nothin' I can do for you."

"No, we're fine here, Nick, but I sure am glad to see you and thankful you came to see about us."

"I'm headed back to town in the mornin' myself, Mr. Braxton, and I'm glad to come see about your wife 'fore I go, if you're a mind," Verna offered.

Nick gathered his hat and rested his hand on the door. "Well, now, I might just take you up on that, if it don't put ya out none. It sure would put m' mind to rest to have her looked to."

"Not at all; happy to do it," Verna assured him. "I'll be glad to take a look at her and see if there's anything she needs, and then I'll just be on my way back to town."

"Well then, I'll come for ya at breakfast then," Nick said, and started out the door. "Caroline."

Caroline nodded and drew the latch in behind him. "That's wonderful of you, Verna, to go check on Ellen. I know it'll be a blessing to her. I'll send you with some things in the morning for your ride."

"Well, don't be goin' to no trouble now. Best we be gettin' to bed; it's late. You go on now and check on Bethy and put yourself to bed. I'll see to these dishes and put out the lamp."

"Thank you, Verna; I'll see you in the morning." Caroline left to do as she was bid, and Verna surveyed the remnants of Nick's late supper.

"Well now, there's a biscuit and some jam that won't be good in the morning, there is. Best we take care of that 'fore we head off to bed, why don't we?" Verna slathered the jam on the remaining biscuit and plumped herself into the rocking chair. In the next room, Caroline drew the covers up to her chin, and drifted off to the rhythmic sound of the rocking chair against the wooden floor and slept a tired, dreamless sleep.

They had buried their pa two days ago, after he'd drawn his last shaky breath. It had taken most of the day to bury the body and a day to recover from the exertions of it. The five children, all under thirteen years of age but feeling much older than that, rested in the shade of the tall oak, whose branches watched over the final resting place of their father. It was there that Bud came upon them, guiding Jack to a halt near a wagon with a broken axle. He himself would ordinarily have stopped to rest and turn Jack out by now, but it had taken so long to get the few miles he'd managed to come that he just wanted to put a few more miles behind him before he stopped for the night. The road back home to Caroline and Annie seemed much longer this time than when he and Frank had set off for the camp weeks before; back then they had made good time and the trip had been easy. But today had been rough, with felled trees in the road, swollen streams and swampy branches, and mosquitoes that nearly drove him mad. The wagon got bogged down more than once, and at times Bud despaired of ever getting it out, it stuck so fast. But each time he and Jack had managed to move a little bit farther ahead, and they were both ready to pack it in when they spied the wagon with the small group huddled around it.

Bud tipped his hat at a tall boy who stood as the horse and wagon drew closer. At first taking the boy for a Negro, he realized his mistake as he came nearer and saw that the boy, as well as his companions, was caked in mud and dirt.

"Here now, everything all right?" Bud called to the boy, who was holding his hat and watching Bud as they rode up.

"No, sir, not really. Our wagon's took an awful turn, and our pa…well, our pa weren't able to fix it." The boy looked like he wanted to say something else, decided against it, and stood still. The other children were quiet. A small girl clung to an older girl's legs, while two boys stood under the tree in silence, warily eyeing Bud and his horse.

"Where's your pa now? Mebbe I can help him get it back on the road," Bud said, climbing down from the wagon. He tied the reins, then looked around at the children and back at the boy.

"He's over there, sir." The boy pointed to a mound at the farthest reaches of the low branches of the oak, where a cross of sticks stood erect at one end.

"Oh," Bud said quietly. "I see." The boy's pa was beyond needing help with the wagon, it seemed. "Why don't you tell me what happened, son?"

The boy swallowed, and gripped his hat tightly in his hands. He looked back at the older girl, who nodded to him in encouragement. "Our pa, he was tryin' to fix the wagon, see. The axle got banged up when we crossed a river a few miles back, and it finally give out. Pa was tryin' t' get the axle set when he slipped and fell underneath, and the wagon rolled over him." Bud could see in the boy's face that he had had a front-row seat when it happened; the boy looked ill and offered no more explanation of the events. Bud could surmise enough and did not press the boy further. He had no desire to ask for details; it hardly mattered at this point, and he could tell just by looking at the children that they had undergone a terrible loss.

"Your ma?"

"Been gone a few years now. It was just our pa and us. We 'as headin' over to Tallahassee."

"You got people there?"

"Pa said ma had a sister there. We was goin' to be closer to her. We ain't never been there before, though. We don't know which way to go now."

"Well, now, you can't be takin' on a trip like that in this condition. Lemme take you home with me, then, and we'll see what we're about. It ain't too fur, and likely you're all hungry. We'll get this all settled out."

Bud helped the children gather what they needed from their wagon and managed to find them places to sit, tucked in with the timber. Perhaps they'd come across the horses as they continued on their way. He had been ready to camp, but he thought one more night here probably wasn't the best idea. Even a half mile would be enough, just to get the children away from what had apparently been tragic circumstances.

They camped near a small stream later that night, and Bud learned more about the little band of newly made orphans. Harper Bohannon was the oldest at thirteen; June, the oldest girl, was eleven years old. Little Claire was four, and Elijah and Levi Bohannon were seven and nine. Their mother had died the winter before, and their father was moving the family to Tallahassee, where an aunt supposedly lived. None of them had ever met the aunt nor heard anything about her until they were told they were going to see her.

The children had come all the way from Mississippi, and it was clear they were tired of traveling and worn out. They were all thin, and the buck Bud shot one morning probably had been the first real food they had eaten in quite some time. He knew Annie and Caroline weren't expecting him home, and they certainly weren't expecting him home with five more mouths to feed, but there wasn't another option, and they would all have to make the best of it. He remembered what it was to be hungry and without a mother, and he could no more have left them to fend for themselves than he could have left his own children. They would have to manage somehow until the aunt could be contacted and the situation explained. He wondered what Caroline would have to say about this—he certainly was upsetting her applecart lately. Bud sighed. In for a penny, in for a pound, I guess.

While Bud pondered his sanity and questionable reception when he arrived home with another entire family for Caroline to house and feed, Mark and Frank were busy at the camp with problems of a different kind. Many of the men had taken Dixon up on the offer to go check on their families after the storm; some lived only a few days' ride away from the camp, and they were concerned not only for wives and children, but also for livestock and homes after the heavy winds and rain. Others, however, had come much farther looking for work and resented their neighbors' absence, leaving fewer men to contend with the unholy wreckage the storm had caused in the camp and farther down the rail line. Ties were broken; rails were twisted. The cuts made for the line were sodden, boggy mud pits, and there was absolutely nothing that could be done about that; it would take eons to dry out in this humidity. Land that had taken weeks to clear for the rail line was now cluttered again; not with pines and turkey oak, scrub oak, and palmetto fronds waiting to be felled in orderly fashion, but with a mishmash of strewn limbs, ties, fallen trees, dead cows, and horse carcasses. While Bud would be relieved when he eventually made it home to see that his own little farm had managed to scrape by relatively unscathed by the storm, the same could not be said for the camp.

It was as though a giant child had left his Tinkertoys scattered as far as the eye could see. Mosquitoes and blowflies thrived in the heat and moist richness of decay; the men were at their mercy from morning till night. Needed supplies were slow to arrive or did not appear at all. Tempers were short and flared white hot when bellies were empty; fists flew at the slightest provocation, and Mark spent more time keeping the peace than keeping the books. The water-logged conditions made trench foot a new and formidable opponent. Since all the tents had had to come down before the storm hit, the men found precious little dry land upon which to re-pitch them. They toiled, trudged, slept, ate, and fought their meager battles in filthy mud and water with little relief.

One man in particular, whose fuse was unnaturally short even on a fine spring day and thus was virtually nonexistent at present, took his resentment at current events out on what was closest, which happened to be a tree that had had the audacity to fall in arm's reach of his ax. Ruben hacked out his aggression on the hardwood and contemplated his situation. Getting rid of Davidson had been his first move, but he had not been able to follow up this bold advance with a second maneuver swiftly enough to ensure that he could gain access to the safe in Dixon's office. Indeed, his every effort seemed to be taking him further from his goal, rather than closer to it. Having Braxton so easily step into Davidson's shoes had been an unlucky break and not one he could have anticipated; Braxton was in the camp house nearly as often as Davidson had been, and Ruben had seen no opportunity to go near the office, much less inside. The hurricane had complicated matters more, and now the payroll would not be delivered for another three weeks or so, according to the latest telegram from Atlanta.

Ruben roared with indignation at the injustice of it, and with his next strike into the tree's flesh, he left his ax embedded in the wood and thrust himself down onto the oak he was trying to dismember. *Dammit, it shouldn't have been this hard*, he thought. When he and Casey first arrived at camp, it seemed clear enough, and their plan had been formulated with ease and confidence. But nothing had gone according to plan, and his patience was at its breaking point. He was going to have to do something reckless, he knew. He'd have to get that payroll in transit, and that was easier said than done. He had to find out how it was coming into the camp and how far away it was. He got up from the oak and brushed off his hands, then worked the ax handle free. The payroll was out there, and it was waiting for him. It was on a train somewhere further up the line, and he knew just the man who could give him what he needed to know. And he would do it, too…or perhaps Ruben would just take that remaining eye from the man in trade. Either way.

17 SUSPICION, AND ANNIE STAYS

Caroline was indeed shocked to see Bud in a wagon with so many children, but she rose to the challenge and had them all off the wagon and into the little house before they knew it. The children were worn out and exhausted from their grief and their travels and so weren't very talkative, but Caroline put them all at ease right away and paired them up with one of her own children to help them get clean clothes and feel settled. Once Bud explained the situation, her heart went out to the forlorn little flock; she knew what it was like to not have any parents, and she wanted to draw them all near to her and take care of them right away. She controlled herself, however; they didn't know her, and she didn't want to frighten them or make them uncomfortable. So she allowed the children to help each other and just guided them gently from table to bath to bed. By the time everyone was asleep, it was well past midnight. Bud had unloaded the wagon and taken care of the horses and cows when he arrived, and he sat at the table now, resting his feet before he went out to the barn with the other boys for the night. He thought that might be best; to not favor Caroline over Annie or the other way around. He was bound to do something wrong if he stayed in the house.

"How long you plannin' on stayin', Bud?" Caroline asked him, as she sat down at the table across from him.

"Well, I just wanted to see how you were all gettin' on after the storm and make sure everything was okay. Didn't really know what to expect when I come, but it looks like we made out all right. I guess I'll go on back in a day or so; won't get under your feet. 'Less you need me to go to town fer anything. I c'n do that, you know. Guess I just laid a mess a' children on ya."

"It's okay, really. We had a fright with Bethy while you were gone. She caught fever, and I was worried to death she'd go the same way as Charlie, but she pulled through, and we made it somehow." She did not relate Annie's trip to town or Annie's miscarriage. That was for Annie to tell, and she wouldn't get in the middle of it. "We'll manage with the children. I'd much rather you brought them here than left them all alone out there by themselves. We'll see if we can't get word to their people and let them know they're safe."

"All right, I'll see ya in the mornin', then," Bud said, and taking his hat, he stood to go. He paused at the door and looked back at her. Her face was soft in the lamplight, but she didn't smile, and she looked off to the far wall as though she was deep in thought. "You still hate me?"

She smiled now, a small, tired smile, and looked at him kindly. "I don't hate you, Bud. I never have. I guess I just don't have anything to say to you anymore, though."

He looked down at his hat and nodded, then shut the door behind him. He supposed not.

Later as he squirmed against the hay that tickled his back, he decided there wasn't really a way to get comfortable. The boys were asleep downstairs; he had said his goodnights to them a few hours ago, but he lay looking up at the moon through the barn window, wide awake. He heard light footsteps come across the barn and stop at the ladder and wondered which one of the boys he'd see poking his head above the hay in a minute. He was surprised to see not a little boy but Annie, barefoot and in her shift, climb over the ladder and sit down next to him. He folded her into his arms, and they lay down together in the prickly hay, which was suddenly not quite so annoying. Her soft skin shone in the moonlight, and he remembered what he'd missed over the last few months of being in the camp.

Mark was exhausted, frustrated, and ready to fall apart. He had been out all day helping the men move rail ties and timber, and that work was not his forte. He was there to keep the books; manual labor had never been his strong suit. Not that he wasn't willing to help— it was just that with his one good eye, he'd never been very good at gauging distance or periphery, and he wasn't skilled at carpentry or building. When he was younger, everything he'd tried to turn a hand to fell apart. Numbers were his skill. Give him a math problem to solve, he was your man; but give him a house to build, or any structure to construct, and he was practically useless. Tomorrow would be better; he would be back in the office and in more familiar surroundings. He lay down on his bunk and sighed.

He had left Atlanta with hopes and expectations of adventure. Although he had not been entirely sure what he might encounter, he had felt certain it had to be better than working for his father at one of his businesses. That was so dull and boring—seeing the same folks day after day and doing the same thing over and over. Mark wanted to see what there was in this country, and he had thought that signing onto the railroad was the best way to do it. But working with men like Dixon would try the patience of a saint. Dixon talked, and Dixon promised; he assured and he cajoled, but Mark was learning that he very rarely had the substance to back up his claims. Just before the hurricane came through, the payroll was delivered, but instead of putting it into the safe for later distribution to the men, Dixon packed it in a box, then was gone all day to Brooksville. When he came back to the camp later that night, he instructed Mark to tell the men that the payroll hadn't come on the train as it had been expected to and that it would be a little later than normal. He had brought kegs of beer back with him from Brooksville, and they made the announcement easier to swallow, but Mark knew the truth, and it rankled within him. Something was going on. Managing up was one thing, and carelessness with retaining receipts was frustrating, but it was entirely another if there was some kind of criminal activity going on.

Mark swung his legs from the bunk and pulled his boots back on. As tired as he was, he intended to find out what Dixon was up to. He pulled a few tools from a leather bag he kept under his pillow and slid the bag back underneath, then patted the pillow and smoothed it over. He crept out of his tent and looked around in the moonlight; there was nothing to be seen but trees and the silent camp. The horses nickered to each other and swished flies away with their tails. Snores from the tents came intermittently, and bunks squeaked as men rolled over in their sleep. Mark made his way in the moonlight to the camp house and carefully squeezed through the heavy canvas at the back; the walls inside were wooden but having canvas around the outside allowed for airflow when a breeze came through in a hot and humid environment. Dixon slept outside the office on a bunk behind a partition. Mark knew that during the day he couldn't hold his water for more than an hour at a time, so he felt reasonably certain it wouldn't be long before he would need to visit the outhouse at night. He would just have to wait him out. He crouched in the darkness behind some boxes of rice and waited for his opportunity.

It finally came about an hour later, just when Mark's ankles were screaming for a different position. Dixon stumbled out of the camp house in search of the privy, and Mark made his move. Quickly he darted over to the office door; his ankles and knees stung with the sudden movement after having been motionless for so long. He tried to stretch them and massage the needles out of his limbs with one hand as he took the tools out of his pocket with the other. Swiftly he picked the lock, then closed the door behind him. The canvas ceiling would not keep his movements quiet; he would have to be extra careful to not be heard. He went straight to the safe and opened it quickly; the safe was where the ledgers were stored when he was not using them. If Dixon had anything to hide, he would put it in here; there was no other place in the camp that was as secure. Dixon had had it specially brought from New York; he claimed it was impregnable, and only he and Mark knew the combination. Even Davidson had not been given access; Dixon kept few people close in business.

Mark always placed his ledgers in a leather satchel and rarely looked at anything else Dixon kept in the safe; he had been taught at an early age to mind his own business, and he scrupulously tried to give others privacy at all times. Now, however, he sifted through the safe's contents and tried to quickly discern what was what in the fading matchlight. Deeds. A small bag of coins. He picked up the bag and tried to transfer it to his other hand, but in the process dropped it. It didn't fall far, but it was far enough to make a sound in the quiet of the little room. Mark sat stock still, holding his breath. He hadn't heard Dixon come back in, but he was probably on his way back, and how close was he? Had he heard that? Mark waited in fear, his heart pounding in his chest. He listened and heard nothing. Dixon was still not back from the privy, and he'd not heard the coins fall but there was something odd about the sound the coins made when they fell from his hand. The sound should have been flatter…should have been less… *hollow.* That's what it was. It had made a hollow sort of sound, and the muffling of the bag against the clink of the coin wouldn't have changed what his ear insisted it should have heard. He felt around the bottom of the safe with his fingers, and discovered a bit of a gap between the bottom and the side of the safe. *There shouldn't be a gap here…a…a false bottom? What?* He pried up the bottom of the safe, and sure enough, it was a platform. Underneath the platform were ledgers similar to those that Mark used in his bookkeeping for the railroad. He pulled them from under the false bottom and let the platform fall back. Then he replaced the coins and papers where he'd found them before closing the safe door.

When Dixon come into the camp house, Mark sat silently with his back to the safe and clutched the ledgers to his chest. Then he heard the protestation of the bunk as it bore Dixon's weight. He was careful to breathe quietly, and he moved not a muscle. Soon Dixon's breathing gave way to sonorous snores, and Mark felt brave enough to leave the little office, step by careful step, the ledgers held close to his chest. He slipped back through the canvas and crept in the darkness back to his tent, where he lit a lamp to look over his find.

"If I'm Mary I'm going to wear my blue calico dress," Ellie said, as though there were many dresses to choose from in the old chifforobe and one could not be expected to know just *which* blue dress she could have been speaking of, were she not careful to be specific about its design.

"You'll wear the one you've got on, same's always, and maybe Ma'll let you wear the frilled apron Annie made for you last Christmas," Susan said, pulling the brush through Ellie's hair—and not being especially gentle about it, either—as she prepared to braid it before school one morning.

Ellie scowled as her head was pulled back with the brush, and she grabbed the edge of the bed to keep from toppling back with it. "I will not. I'll wear my blue dress. Ma'll let me; it's special and this is a special occasion," Ellie insisted.

"If you're Mary I bet you drop Jesus right there on the floor in front o' God and everybody," Tom said, as he came into the little bedroom to interrupt the morning's discussion, dropping a schoolbook on the floor in the process. "He'll roll right off the stage and land in Mrs. Lundy's lap."

Ellie whirled around, pulling her hair out of Susan's hands and frowning in indignation. "I will not, either, Thomas Braxton. You take that back!" Ellie fumed.

"Then you'll go to hell because you dropped Jesus on His head, and everybody'll know you're the reason Jesus has a goose egg on his noggin," Tom continued, grinning. Teasing Ellie was one of life's finer pursuits.

"Thomas, get out of here!" Susan said angrily, grabbing Ellie's hair. "Now I've got to start over!"

"Fine," Tom said, as he bent to pick up the book, "but we're gonna be late if you girls don't get a move on. Annie says she's comin' in here next if you don't get goin', and you won't like it if she does," he said, his warning not exactly a motivation to the girls, who knew Annie threatened more than she actually delivered.

"I would not drop Jesus," Ellie insisted, as her head was jerked back violently with the brush again, and Susan started the braid.

"No, you wouldn't," Susan assured. "And you don't know that you'll get to be Mary, so don't be disappointed if you're not, okay? It's just as important to be a sheep or a wise man. They were both there too, you know."

"I know," Ellie said, not agreeing at all. It would not be just the same to be a sheep, and who wanted to be a wise man? The play that the little school was planning for Christmas was all the talk right now, and all the girls wanted to be Mary. All the girls except Barbara Jameson, that is, and there was no accounting for Barbara Jameson's taste in any matter of things, in Ellie's humble opinion.

The nativity play was the most important production the little school put on, in the young thespians' opinions, next to the May Day celebration they had before school let out for the summer. This year was going to be especially interesting, because Mrs. Beaufort was expecting twins this fall.

Each of the girls hoped that Mrs. Beaufort would deliver in time for the play, because it would be so much more interesting to be Mary holding a real live baby Jesus, rather than Lisabelle Tucker's old doll with the singed hair wrapped in a blanket, like last year. Mrs. Beaufort had four children already, and Ellie knew she would let the girls hold her babies, not like that grouchy Mrs. Preston and her precious toddler John Barfield, whom none of the girls had been allowed to hardly be near, much less hold, when he was born. John Barfield was Mrs. Preston's one and only son, and Mrs. Preston was especially particular about who and what encountered John Barfield and under what circumstances. For one, she insisted that he be called his full and proper name by anyone who referred to him, and she was quick to correct anyone who referred to her darling as "John" or the even more blasphemous "Johnny." Mrs. Preston was especially careful that no dirt should foul John Barfield's frilled collars or Sunday shoes, and it was indeed rare that John Barfield's little shoes ever touched the ground when Mrs. Preston was present. It would not have pleased her in the least to know that the children referred to her beloved John Barfield Preston as "Barfy" out of her earshot, nor would it have pleased her to know what they thought of her fastidiousness in his regard.

Ellie was especially nervous this year about the play, not only because she was finally old enough to be selected as Mary and there was a possibility of there being a real live baby in the play and not just a boring old doll, but also because she had invited Papa to the play. Papa never came to anything, but he had assured her that he would come this year, whether she was selected to play Mary or not, and she was sure he would keep his promise. Robert had succumbed to her relentless wheedling, her animated pleading each time she visited him, more out of exasperation and his desire that she leave off her begging than because of any real aspiration to see thirty young people mumble and stumble over their lines or stand frigid and wide eyed on a stage. Each time she came to visit him, she regaled him with the latest in the development of the play, and he listened with good humor, although not necessarily to every detail. He enjoyed her company. She brightened the otherwise stale days he spent in his little cabin, and he looked forward to each one of her visits.

Ellie prayed with all her might that the teacher would choose her to play Mary and tried to sit patiently while Susan finished the last of her braid. It would be a wonderful Christmas, indeed, if everything worked out according to her plans.

Caroline sat at the table with a heavy sigh. All the children, save the three youngest, had gotten off to school, the dishes had been washed and set to dry, the cows had been milked and set out to pasture, Bud had been seen off back to the camp, and water had been set to boil over the fire for the wash. The five Bohannons had added an extra layer of chaos to the busy morning, though she did not begrudge their presence. They had enlivened the household, actually, despite their recent grief, and had made fast friends with the other children, as Caroline had hoped they would. She had been able to find clean clothes for all of them, and they were polite and did as they were bid, for the most part. Harper had found a fellow adventurer in Tom, and the two spent as much time as possible in the fields and meadows around their home. One day they were Indians, and the next day they were formidable explorers searching out new routes to be mapped and logged. Elijah and Levi had been delighted with Mac's army men, and they had raged bloody battles throughout the house, under chairs and tables and over the floors, and not even the girls' room was safe from the thunderous marches of their mighty hordes. June and Susan had become fast friends. Annie was just now settling Bethy on the floor with Claire and some paper dolls, and it was the first real moment of rest that either one of them had had in quite a while.

"My word, I thought I might never sit down again," Annie remarked, as she sank onto a chair at the table, where Caroline sat with a cup of coffee before her, now lukewarm after the morning's bustling activity and exertions.

"They certainly are a handful, as Mrs. Lundy would say," Caroline agreed. She didn't mind the chatter and busyness, and having five more children in the house had certainly taken the decibel level up a notch. She sent them outside as much as possible, and she was sure there was an extra pound of dirt that she swept up each evening before she went to bed. Having them there was not an unbearable burden, exactly, but they certainly had made the household louder.

Annie sat quietly and watched the children playing on the floor before her. She supposed there was really no reason for her to stay anymore, now that there was no impending little stranger to make a debut. She hadn't told Bud about the miscarriage; there hadn't seemed to be a good time for it, and she hadn't wanted to spoil their time together with talk of her lost hopes. So she had stayed silent, and they had spent a wonderful night in the hayloft, hot and prickly though it had been, and altogether too short. When he came home from the camp later, she presumed they would speak, and by then it would be evident that there was no reason for her to remain among them.

"I guess I'll be going back home, then, now that everything's settled with the children. They seem to be getting along very nicely, and that's a blessing," Annie said, crossing her legs beneath her and settling back in her chair.

"Oh no, you won't," Caroline countered, setting her coffee cup on the table. "You absolutely will not be leaving me with this passel of children to manage all by myself and all the washing and cleaning and cooking besides. Annie Wilson, I swear if you leave me now, I'll go curl up in the corner and pull a blanket over my head and just let them run ragged around me." She laughed. "It's all hands on deck with these ruffians, and I need you more now than I ever did before," she affirmed.

Annie laughed with her and looked fondly on the children playing with their dolls on the wooden floor. "I suppose you're right; I guess I wouldn't let you leave me here alone with all of them, either." She rested her chin in her hand. "They're an unholy mess, but I guess they're all right. You're sure about that, Caroline? That you do want me here?"

"Yes," Caroline repeated, this time more confidently. "There was a time that I didn't want you here, and I admit that. There's no denying it. But yes, I need you here. I want you here." She reached over and placed her hand over Annie's on the table. "No foolin', as Robert says," she said.

Truth be told, Caroline had come to accept having Annie around—enjoyed it, even, if she had to admit it. She'd never really known what it was like to have a sister, despite growing up surrounded by children. Caroline had been bereft of parents from a young age and had grown up in an orphanage many miles from her current home. Indeed, she'd dreamed of having a home such as this one day and a family to call her own, having had nothing of the sort as a basis of comparison throughout her formative years. Many young lives had surrounded her and many she could call a friend; however, none had been close enough to feel like a sister. Only her friend Ben had come near to that feeling of family, and when he left at fourteen, it had been only one more loss in her young life, one of several more yet to come.

Having another adult in the house, one who understood her frustrations or just the sheer enormity of the mental focus it took to keep a busy household and little farm like this running, was comforting. Bud certainly couldn't relate. That took someone who could comprehend what it was like to have a million little questions thrown at you a day, from "Where does the moon go during the day" to "Why CAN'T I bring live lizards into the house and keep them as pets?" or any number of other things that were required of her during an average twenty-four-hour period. The mitigation of numerous arguments or ruffled feathers required her attention at intervals throughout the day, as well as small worries and general concerns that befell the brood around her, and it all came with regularity and without end. It was just part of being a mother, and she loved it, but it was wearing, and it was nice to have someone who appreciated the nature of the matriarchy, such as it was, in her little kingdom.

'If you're sure you want me to stay, I'd like to," Annie said, relieved that Caroline had said out loud what she dared not ask for. Even if she wasn't to be a mother herself, and even though the situation was an odd one, she very much wished to stay with the Braxtons rather than return to her mother's home, or worse, be turned out into the wide world to make of it what she would. She was not prepared for that. She didn't necessarily think they would turn her away at home should she be found on their doorstep, but neither was she eager to test that theory. She enjoyed being a mother to the children, and somehow, though she knew not how, she and Caroline had forged a sort of comfortable communion between them with Bud away.

She didn't quite know how that might change once he came home for good, although if the night they had spent in the barn was any indication, perhaps Caroline had given him his answer about how he might be expected to be received back into her bed. She decided she wouldn't read too much into that for now, however, but be thankful for the day set before her. There was no use worrying about what might come to pass, anyway, she thought, for how could she ever have predicted she'd be in the situation she was currently in, even a few months ago? There was no way. No, she was just going to have to take it as it came just like everybody else did in this world.

18 MARK'S SECRET

October found Bud back at the timber camp felling trees for the railroad once again. On his way back to the camp, he had stopped at Nick's to spend a night, and it was there that he was greeted with the happy news that Ellen was expecting. The sickness that she had had wasn't the flu after all, but morning sickness, and none were more surprised at the development than Ellen herself, who had given up all hope of ever having another child after Janette. But Verna Dade had confirmed it during her visit, and Nick was insistent that Ellen not overdo herself during her pregnancy. In fact, he was so insistent that he was clearly on Ellen's last available nerve. Bud could see that, with the harvest in and nothing much to do in the fields, Nick was making a pest of himself in the house and Ellen was liable to let him have it with a skillet upside the head if he wasn't careful. So having just divested himself of a wagon full of good house-building wood at home, Bud asked Nick if he would do him the courtesy of helping him get Annie's little house started while Bud was away at the camp. The next morning Ellen pulled him aside before he got back on the wagon to leave.

"Bud, thanks for asking Nick to help with the house. I swear, if he don't get out of here, I'm liable to kill him," Ellen said, laughing.

"Yeah, I c'n see he's makin' a pest of himself. But you know he's just worried about ya, girl."

"I know. He has a good heart, and he's tryin' to make sure I don't overdo, and I'm grateful for it. But Lord, he's underfoot, and I just about can't take it. I'll ride with him some days; it'll do me good to get out of the house, and Janette will enjoy playing with all the kids."

"Annie and Caroline will appreciate the company, I know it, and they don't git to see you often enough. So you go just as much as you can, and he'll be outta your hair," Bud said, smiling at their scheme. Having Ellen at the house could only be good for Annie and Caroline as well; Bud had steered clear of being in the same room with both of them during his short visit at home, but he thought having Ellen there could only smooth things along that much more in his absence.

The camp itself had been set more or less to rights after the storm, and almost everyone who had taken a short leave to check on his family was back at work and back to the routine. Bud was pleased to see the change hard work and sobriety had made in Frank; his brother's eyes were alert and his wit was quick as it ever was. He and Mark traded barbs with each other all day long. Frank's muscles had grown strong, his beer belly was practically gone, and Bud felt relief in his soul that Frank might finally have come round the bend of adulthood. He hoped the changes he was seeing would stick; this was a much better Frank than the one he had dragged home from town not long ago.

Bud saw a change in Mark too as the days went by, a much subtler change, and he couldn't quite put his finger on what it was that disquieted him. Something seemed to be off, and he didn't know what it was. It seemed like Mark was preoccupied with something. More than once over the last few days Mark was oblivious when Bud called his name or Bud caught him staring off into the distance with a furrowed brow. It was clear something was eating at the man, and while Bud didn't like to pry into a man's business, Mark had become a good friend, and he didn't like to see him in turmoil. Lord knows, I've wrestled with enough in my life to know what it looks like when something's amiss, he thought.

"I'm goin' over to see Mark for a minute," he told Frank late one evening just before bed.

"Can't it wait till mornin'? Ya just saw him at dinner, for Chrissakes," Frank retorted, turning over a red queen in the game of solitaire he was playing. "Dammit, I knew you'd show up, wench," he said to the card.

"I just thought a' somethin', and if I don't tell him now I know I'll forget 'fore morning," Bud lied. "My ole brain ain't what it used to be."

"You old folks can't remember shit, that's true," Frank jibed, and laughed when Bud whacked him on the back of the head.

"Mind your elders, son; don't you disrespect," Bud said, smiling as he left the tent. He made his way in the darkness to Mark's tent and softly called to him. Mark lit a lamp and bid him enter, raising an eyebrow at his night visitor.

"Douse the lamp. It's okay; it's just me," Bud whispered, and Mark blew it out again. Mark's tent was set off a bit from the others so there was little chance they would be overheard, but Bud wanted to be cautious all the same. The hour was late, and the camp was quiet.

"What's wrong?" Mark asked, genuinely curious as to what brought Bud over.

"I don't know. I was kinda hopin' you might tell me," Bud said. "Seems to me somethin's in your craw just now, and I aim to know what it is."

Mark didn't say anything but frowned in the dim light. Bud could just make out his features, and he could see the struggle on his face.

"Look, I don't wanna git in your business, but if it's something I can help with, I wish you'd let me," Bud pressed.

"You ain't gonna like it, Bud," Mark said, finally. "Hell, I don't like it. It's a helluva thing, it is, just a goddamn mess," he lamented.

"Well, just tell me, boy," Bud pried. "What's got ya all tied up in knots?"

Mark had indeed been burdened with a secret ever since he had stolen the ledgers from Dixon's safe and uncovered something he wished he could unsee. At first haltingly, then with greater confidence, he told Bud about Dixon's trip to Brooksville and the lie he had made him tell about the payroll. The money had been made up in the next shipment, but the true nature of the lie hadn't become clear until Mark had had a chance to review the stolen ledgers back in his tent that night. It actually was a relief to tell someone about it, awful though it was, and to have some advice about what to do about it.

He relayed to Bud the events of his harrowing visit to Dixon's safe and his anxiety-ridden theft as he relieved it of its hidden contents. He described the sleepless night reading the ledgers and his dawning horror at what they held and his subsequent trip back to the safe to return the ledgers before Dixon discovered them missing.

"Bud, he's oversold the mileage on the railroad, and he's underreported what we're making on the timber goin' down to the sawmill," Mark confided. "He's got three or four other businesses goin', and the ones that ain't doin' so well, he's sending the payroll to cover. Meanwhile he's skimmin' the sawmill profits and tellin' them investors we're a lot further on than we are and robbin' Peter to pay Paul. Bud, it's an unholy mess, and Dixon's a cheat, plain and simple."

"Christ, Mark," Bud sighed. "I had my suspicions on what kinda' man he was, but I didn't expect this," he said. "What're you gonna do? We've gotta tell somebody. He's gonna run this operation straight inta the ground if it goes on like this."

"I don't know who to tell. What if I send a letter back to one of the investors, and it's someone he's in collusion with? For all I know he's not the only one workin' the scheme. How do I know who to talk to? I'm in a pickle, Bud. I don't know what to do." Mark put his head in his hand.

"I see your point," Bud said. "Let me think on it a minute." Bud was silent as he pondered the problem at hand. Mark was right; it was entirely possible that Dixon wasn't alone in his underhanded dealings, and with the investors back in Atlanta and New York, it was hard to know who could be trusted with this information. Tell the wrong person, and, well, Bud knew what happened to snitches.

Bud pulled his hands through his hair as he thought, and at last he gave it a final tug and lifted his head. "Here now, we've got to see 'em face to face, that's what," he said, pointing a finger at Mark. "Either we get the lot of 'em to come here, or you go there, but you've got to see 'em and spend a little time with 'em to look 'em in the eyes, and you'll be able to tell who's to be trusted. Same as we could see through Dixon, you'll be able to see who we might be able to confide in. But you can't just send a letter and hope it'll get to the right person. No, that won't do atall."

"I can't get them all to come out here. There's no way," Mark lamented. "Besides the fact that it's near impossible to convince them, if Dixon were to get wind of it, and he surely would, he'd shut it down, and I'd be out on my ear. Assumin' he didn't cut it off, that is," Mark said wryly, rubbing one ear with his hand.

"Then you go there. We'll think of an excuse that gets you on a train back to Atlanta, and you go talk to 'em. Take the ledgers with you as proof, and that man'll be strung so high his feet won't remember the ground they walk on."

"Dixon won't like to part with me for long, and what'll he do when he finds those ledgers gone?" Mark asked.

"What can he do? It ain't like he can raise a ruckus. Ain't nobody supposed to know about 'em. Besides, it'll do him good to be all riled up inside and not be able to say anything; might keep him occupied and outta' our business for a change," Bud counseled.

Mark smiled, and the two of them talked a bit more in hushed voices about how exactly they might handle Dixon. It was nearly dawn when Bud finally rolled into his cot to get a few hours of sleep. They had a plan, and tomorrow they would see about setting it in motion.

Robert sat in his rocking chair, smoking his pipe. Ellie and Susan had just left; they had brought him jam and a jar of stewed tomatoes today. There had been no rifling through the old wooden box; Ellie preferred to keep that just between herself and her Papa, and Robert respected that. Not that he wouldn't have enjoyed talking about those things with Susan too, but he understood his little Ellie well and knew she felt a keen ownership of the little wooden box and didn't want to share its contents. That was okay; that was for another day. There had been no talk of Maybelline or of anything else, really, but the current events at the school and the Christmas play that had all the children excited. Parts were being cast and props were being discussed; Susan and Ellie had firm opinions on both and shared them in abundance with their grandfather, who listened with a smirk on his face at the lively chatter on his doorstep. Their little tongues went nonstop through the entirety of the visit, and only after they had left was Robert given the peace of the evening and his thoughts for company.

Maybelline would have loved to see the girls in the play, he thought. She had wanted a girl, and Robert had wished to give her one, but he supposed that wasn't in the stars for them. She would have loved to see the girls learning their lines, would probably have been fascinated at their ability to remember such things, to keep entire conversations in their heads and play them out one against the other in front of an audience. May herself could never have done such a thing, Robert knew. She struggled to remember even the smallest of details; everything had to be written out. She lived by lists. There were bits of paper everywhere in the house, he recalled now with a smile, where she wrote reminders to herself, reminders to him, items to be bought and work to be done.

It was not her fault, this inability to remember even the smallest thing. As a child she had been kicked in the head by a fractious mule and almost given up for dead. She had eventually recovered, and while her body had repaired itself there were areas of her brain that had not. Not only was she saddled with an impaired memory, but she also bore a physical reminder in the form of a little concavity behind her left ear. It wasn't noticeable; her hair covered it, and no one but she and her family ever even knew of it. And she had learned to overcome her memory's shortcomings by living by the written word. She wrote notes to herself daily. Robert had also learned to live by her lists, and he kept those that she had left in a drawer in the bedroom. In the beginning he had not treasured them, but as he got older, they had become dear to him, reminders of the woman who had left him.

He rose now in the evening's twilight and went to the bedroom to lie down and remember May. The chores had been done, his little supper had been eaten, and he was tired. Sleep would eventually come, but until it did, he wanted to remember.

The prospect of another little house that would mean Annie would stay with them permanently absolutely enraptured the children. When Nick first came to see the timber that Bud had brought home, they peppered him relentlessly with questions and begged to be a part of its construction. Where would the foundation go? Would it look just like their house now? How big would it be? Would it have stairs? Please, let it have stairs! Would it have a root cellar? (Robert privately hoped it would not.) How many rooms would there be? How was the roof to be made? Mac especially wanted to know the particulars of the house; he had lately read a book on architecture and was fascinated with construction and design.

Nick was not an architect, but he did know how to raise a simple structure, and he and Bud had talked through an uncomplicated plan that he expected would disappoint Mac. Nonetheless, he endeavored to answer the children's questions as best he could and assured them that they would all play a part in the construction of the house as time allowed, after school and chores were completed. Of course, this wasn't entirely the answer they hoped for, but as it was the best they were likely to get, they eventually allowed him some space to commence the building of the little house. As the month wore on Nick and Ellen became a fixture at the Braxtons'.

This suited Annie and Caroline just fine. Ellen's company took Annie's thoughts away from her grief, and it brightened Caroline's spirits to have Ellen there to help with chores and to talk. Annie did not begrudge Ellen her happy news at all; she knew how long Ellen and Nick had struggled with having children and was elated to find out that she was expecting.

As for the children, they were happy to have yet another among them, and the Bohannons and Braxtons showered Janette with attention. They taught her lessons in the afternoon, as she had not yet begun to go to school, and she blossomed under their care and enjoyed every minute with her playmates. She helped Robert take the cows to pasture and put Bethy down for a nap, she listened as Mac read books to her, and she took rides in the wheelbarrow with Elijah and Levi Bohannon. She and Claire had lively tea parties with their dolls and attempted to have tea parties with the barn kittens. Although the latter were much livelier guests, they did tend to upset the table and teakettle, and they refused to keep their bonnets on despite their hostesses' repeated entreaties. All through the fall, they enjoyed each other's company, the adults and children alike.

One night Annie sat in the moonlight on the porch after everyone had gone to bed and reflected on the day's events. By the time Bud came home again for Thanksgiving, this place would look a lot different than when he had left it, she thought. She did not relish having to tell him that there would be no baby, despite the house going up. It was clear that they did need the extra room, with the Bohannons staying on, so she had no guilt in that regard. She and Caroline had tried repeatedly to extract any kind of information about the children's relatives in Tallahassee. Unfortunately, it appeared that their father had never given them very many details about the aunt who supposedly resided there; if he knew an address or a name he had not divulged it to his children and such information had gone to the grave with him. Caroline had sent a letter to the post office there inquiring about a Bohannon family but she had no idea of the sister's last name or even if the sister knew she had relatives on the way to see her. There just wasn't much to go on. So for the time being, the Bohannons would be staying with them, and the little house would be put to good use even if there was no little baby come spring. God works in mysterious ways His wonders to perform, she thought. Mysterious ways, indeed.

19 A STORM BLOWS

"Shit, shit, shit!" Ruben swore under his breath, as he watched the riders in the distance. He was looking at the south end of two northbound mules, as it were, as he watched Braxton and the Jacobsen kid ride away from camp one early morning. He had heard they were headed toward Brooksville, where he'd been told one of them was catching a train. Why the hell were they catching a train? No one had told him why, only they were going. Cook made all the supply runs, so it couldn't be for that, and no reason for them both to go, anyway. Four times during the past few weeks, Ruben had attempted to get Mark on his own in some small hidden corner, and four times he had been thwarted one way or another, by the Braxton idiot or some other blunt instrument who had come in between him and an opportunity to strangle some information out of the man. Three times he had been thwarted in his attempts to get into the office, with all the comings and goings around the camp house, and he had given up on that pathway. And now here they were riding off. If he still had Casey with him, maybe, but the camp house office was just too busy for one man to do the job alone. And forget creeping in at night; cracking a safe was just not a one-man job—he knew what he was talking about. He was going to find out what the hell was going on.

He went into the camp house and found Dixon sitting at his desk poring over a ledger. The man looked anxious, although what he had to be anxious about Ruben couldn't fathom; every time *he'd* seen him the man was poking his nose where he had no business poking, telling the men to do this or that instead of leaving it to the line bosses, who actually did know what they were doing.

"What do you want, Burroughs? I don't got time for you right now," Dixon barked, looking up and then back at his books. "I heard enough about the stew meat, and I don't care for your opinion either." Ruben had heard some of the men trashing the taste of the meat; apparently they'd been up here giving Dixon an earful and he assumed Ruben was here to do the same.

"I ain't here about that; I'm lookin' for Braxton," Ruben said.

"He ain't here; he an' Jacobsen are up Brooksville. He'll be back tomorrow. What d'you want him for, anyway?" He looked up now. The workmen didn't usually want Braxton for anything; the man was a mouse. He couldn't put two words together, generally.

"Just got a question for him, is all. Nothing big," Ruben said. That answered his question. Braxton was coming back.

Dixon grunted and looked back at his desk. "Then get outta here," he growled.

Ruben took no offense and left without comment. Dixon was a blowhard and nothing to worry about. He had all afternoon to wait, and he thought he'd eat and then find his spot. He had no problem with the taste of the meat; God knows he'd had worse, and sometimes he'd had none at all. He jammed his hat on his head and ambled off to the cook wagon.

Bud sighed heavily and kicked off his boots in the dark tent. He stood still for a minute, rubbing his face. He and Mark had ridden to Brooksville together, mostly to formulate the plan on the way, away from prying ears. Mark had told Dixon that he needed to go back east to see to family, and they'd invented a line about a sick sister to pave the way for the trip. In reality, Mark had no such relation and no intention of even looking in on extended family, save for his specific task. His purpose was straightforward—to take the ledgers to the board of investors who had interest in seeing what Dixon was actually doing on the line, and to formulate a plan for curtailing it. No small task when you didn't actually know any of the investors and had no idea how to find them or whether they were in on any of his schemes. Mark had connections though, and so did his father and uncle, both of whom were well connected in Atlanta's business and social elite. Mark hoped they would be of help to him. It might take time, but he felt it could be done quietly and effectively.

Bud was beat, however, after the long ride to Brooksville and back. So he was not on his guard when Ruben stepped out of the shadows of the small tent and took him from behind, pressing a blade to his throat and gripping him around the neck with the other arm. Bud was pulled off balance, and his hands tugged at the arm in vain as Ruben's vise-like grip dug into his throat. The point of the blade drew a spot of blood.

"Tell me how the payroll comes," Ruben spoke into Bud's ear, in a low voice.

"Comes on the train; everybody knows that," Bud croaked.

The blade dug deeper into Bud's skin. "I ain't a idiot. Which train, what time?"

"Comes on the 12:15 outta Tallahasee," Bud wheezed. "Due Thursday week."

"Who rides with it?"

"Two fellas guard it on the trip and pass it to Jacobsen. Pass it to me while he's gone."

"What do they look like? What's it in?"

"One's got a beard and a bowler, and the other's clean shaven. It's in a carpet bag they keep between them." Bud took in a ragged breath. He knew who this was. It could be only one man.

"You talk about this with anyone, I'll come back and slit your throat for real, do you understand?"

"Yes."

"Lay down on the floor, face down."

Bud did as he was told. He didn't need to look, anyway.

Bud heard Ruben back out of the tent into the darkness and listened as his footsteps faded away. He had known the man was going to be trouble; he just didn't know how or when. He continued to lie there in the darkness and felt gingerly the spot where Ruben—Mustache—had applied the knife. His fingers came away wet, and he wiped them on his shirt as he finally sat up. He could not go to the camp house now; it was too suspicious. But first thing in the morning, he would telegraph Mark to put the payroll on another train. That asshole wasn't going to succeed in his plan, not if Bud had anything to do with it.

The next morning Bud went to the cook wagon and drank his coffee like always, forcing himself to relax and not look as if he wanted to sprint to the camp house. He glanced around occasionally as casually as he could but did not see Mustache. He tried not to appear out of sorts but to be as casual as always, despite the ants crawling under his skin and the whirling in his brain. He nodded to the men at breakfast and took his dishes to the washtub as usual, trying to amble and feeling as though he wanted to run. He made himself walk to the camp house in what he hoped was a nonchalant manner and looked in on Dixon, who was bent double tying his shoes, a difficult task given the girth of the man and the sizeable impediment he was dealing with.

"Cook needs you for a minute, Dixon," he called to him, as he hung his hat on the hook behind Mark's desk.

"What for? Can't he come up here like everybody else?" Dixon barked, slightly out of breath from his exertions.

"Didn't say, only that he wanted ya," Bud said, trying to busy himself at the desk. Of course the cook had said no such thing, but Bud needed Dixon out of there.

"Burroughs was lookin' for *you* yesterday," Dixon said, as he pulled his suspenders over his shoulders. "He find ya?"

"Burroughs?" Bud asked.

"Ruben Burroughs. Guy with the big ol' mustache. Looks like a damned 'leven-foot Mexican."

"Oh, yeah," Bud said. "He found me."

Dixon grunted and stomped out of the camp house without another word to Bud. As soon as he was up and out, Bud scrambled to the telegraph and typed out a message to be sent to Mark to have the payroll sent on another train. He didn't explain why; he knew Mark would do it without having to know the reason. He sent another telegram to the rail office in Tallahassee and advised them of a possible holdup on the 12:15. That one he knew he'd get an answer to, and he did, right away. Dixon was still not back yet, and he rattled off a reply again quickly. He waited anxiously, for Dixon to come storming back into the camp house asking what the hell Bud thought he was up to or for the telegraph to chirp. Slow minutes ticked by with complete silence from all parties, and Bud felt sweat drip down his temples. He wiped his brow with his shirtsleeve and stood in rapt attention, staring at the telegraph, ears pricked for the door.

He looked at his watch. Five minutes now, since he'd sent his reply. Perhaps there would be no more. He started to relax. He blew out a gust of air that sent his hair flying. He turned and had almost reached his desk when the chatter of the telegraph brought him hurrying back. He snatched the telegram up and swiftly read an acknowledgment of his concern and a short message of thanks. He crumpled it in his hand and took it back with him to the desk, where he dropped it into the waste bin. He busied himself at the desk, and just then Dixon slammed back into the camp house.

"Damn Cook—can't find him when ya want him, and he's always around when ya don't," he groused. "If he wants me so bad, he'll have to come find me himself." Dixon threw his weight into the chair behind his desk and resumed his perusal of the papers that littered his desk. "Braxton, throw that canvas up; man, it stinks to high heaven in here."

Bud got up to do as he was told, silently agreeing with Dixon's assessment and knowing full well who made the stink, but he kept his counsel. He'd be out on the line soon enough anyway. And he'd be looking out for Burroughs.

Annie rested in the quiet shade of the trees and watched the children play on the beach. It was a rare afternoon that they got to play like this, and it would probably be the last day at the water for quite some time, as it was going to be getting cold soon. Some fall days in Florida could be beautiful, and they had tried to take advantage of it. She herself had not had much occasion to be still, despite the Ellen's extra help during her frequent visits to the Braxton household while Nick continued to work on the little house. Robert had even come by a few days to help, and that was a surprise. Annie knew the relationship with Robert was strained, but she didn't have all the details and dared not ask, though it seemed to be all right with Bud gone. Bud was due back at Thanksgiving. She missed him terribly, though she tried not to show it. She missed his strong arms and his laugh. She didn't know how exactly they'd all get on when he came back, the three of them together. She tried not to think about it and instead watched the children play together in the water.

There were eighteen of them right now: the eight Braxtons, the five Bohannons, and five Clarks who had come over to visit for the day. Mrs. Clark was in the throes of a galloping case of consumption, and the Clarks had been foisted onto every other family in the town in rotation over the past weeks. Not to stay, of course, for who could absorb a clatter of five children into their midst for the long haul, but mostly to keep them from being underfoot during Mrs. Clark's last days. And they were her last days, surely, for she had been steadily declining over the latter part of the summer and could not be expected to make it to Christmas. It was a pity, too, for Mr. Clark was said to be beside himself and the children inconsolable at school some days. It was the teacher's idea that they be given round to visit other houses during the weekends to give Mr. Clark a break and allow the children to focus on something other than the impending loss of their mother. It had thus far been a successful venture, and each family took the children in turn to take their minds off the coming separation and to show them the care and help that their mother and father could not in their despair. They all knew it was only for a time, and they did their small part willingly.

Ellen splashed with the children in the water, her slightly swollen stomach just starting to show with the wet shift against her skin. Caroline stretched out on a sheet next to Annie, her head pillowed on her hand in the shade. Annie was still and felt herself drifting off, her eyes closed and the breeze gentle on her skin, when suddenly she jumped and sat straight up, eyes wide.

"Caroline!" she gasped, her hand against her stomach.

"What, dear, what?!" Caroline sat up quickly too, her eyes full of concern. "What is it? What's wrong?" She shifted her eyes to the water, sure something had happened to one of the children.

"No, here, here!" She grabbed Caroline's wrist and thrust her hand against her lower belly, shock on her face.

"What? Something bit you?" Caroline's brows furrowed.

"No! Something inside! Something...there! Do you feel it?" Annie sat stock still, her eyes fixed on Caroline's, her hand trapping Caroline's firmly against her belly.

The two sat in silence and rapt attention, wholly focused on Annie's belly, waiting for whatever had alarmed her so. Together they sat, waiting, and finally they were rewarded by a soft, gentle tap, hardly there at all but definite, and the two smiled at each other, tears gleaming in Annie's eyes. "I didn't imagine it!" she whispered, and Caroline shook her head. "It's really in there!" Annie gasped.

They sat in silence, backs erect, waiting expectantly for several more minutes, but the tapping did not come again, and finally Caroline removed her hand from Annie's belly.

"But you felt it, right?" Annie asked breathlessly. "It was there; I know it!"

"Yes, I felt it, very slight, but I know you felt it more," Caroline agreed. There had indeed been a slight tremor that she felt, and she was as elated as Annie at its meaning. "It was definitely there; it was."

A tear ran down each of Annie's cheeks, but she didn't move to wipe them away and instead clasped both hands to her belly. "It's really in there," she whispered. It had felt like a butterfly in a net, like a goldfish in a bowl against the glass, she thought. Gentle and subtle but nonetheless real. She would be a mother after all!

The two settled back in the shade, both alone with their thoughts again, and watched the children play. What a beautiful, beautiful day.

20 NOVEMBER

The fall days marched on with no interruption to the payroll and no sight of Ruben Burroughs. Burroughs had left the camp, presumably right after his late-night visit to Bud, and there had been no sight of him since. No one at the camp had been sorry to see him go, exactly; he wasn't the chatty type and had made few friends during his stay. Most of the men were wary of him, although he hadn't done a thing, save his attack on Bud, which Bud hadn't shared with anyone. Beyond his initial communication to the rail office and to Mark, he'd not said anything about his encounter with Burroughs. He'd done what he could based on what he knew and left it at that. He concentrated on chopping and hauling timber and on Annie. Over the months of separation, she had become dearer to him in his mind, and the hope of a baby filled him with anticipation. He hoped Nick had been able to work on the house while he was gone; he was grateful to him for that, and he looked forward to the day when he could see Annie settled in it.

He and Frank saw each other at intervals, and Bud was pleased with the changes he saw in his brother. The work outdoors had strengthened his muscles, and the lack of drink had cleared his mind and given him a new outlook. He had made good friends in the camp, and Bud was pleased to see him laughing and ribbing the other men with good humor during the down times. Frank even participated in the arm-wrestling competition they'd had, although he'd lost relatively early on in the matches. Bud had lasted a little longer, but he was no match for some of the men in the camp. There was one man, a big Swede named Jorgens, who was nearly seven feet tall and was built like a mountain. He had bested every man, though because of his affable good nature and charm everyone liked him and no one minded losing to him.

It was with anticipation then that Bud looked forward to Thanksgiving

146

and seeing his family again. He'd missed roughhousing with the boys, missed cuddling with Robert and Bethy, and even missed the Bohannons. He wondered how they'd all gotten along without him. Frank was planning on coming with him to stay for the short break that Dixon was giving everyone, and although he wished Mark could join them, he knew he was working hard to see things through with Dixon. He'd only had one short communication from Mark since he'd left—a telegram of only two words: *making progress.* Beyond that Bud could only speculate, but the telegram hadn't brought any suspicion from Dixon, and Bud was able to keep up with the books in Mark's absence. If Dixon had noticed the missing ledgers, he was awfully good at a poker face. Bud hadn't discerned any anxiety in the man, and there had been no disruptions in the payroll, no suspicious trips to Brooksville, and no letters that made Dixon twitch.

Bud's feeling that all was well lasted until he was nearly home and Frank's ceaseless chatter on the trip had finally dwindled to a slow trickle. In the quiet moments Bud thought uneasily about the situation with Caroline and Annie. He realized he didn't know exactly what he was stepping into. He hoped that they had come to a peace; he hadn't really been home very long after the storm came through. Settling the Bohannons in had occupied most of his attention at the time, but things had seemed friendly enough while he was there. Trying to put the anxiety out of his mind, he focused on the road ahead and on Frank's account of the garter snake he and Rand Tolbert had put in Jimmy Stanton's bedroll just before camp broke up for the short vacation. Stanton was an annoying son of a bitch; even Bud thought so, and Bud usually could stand just about anybody.

"So then...so then, after Tolbert put the snake in 'is bed, we all got outta there real quiet, and we was just behind the tent, all jus' waitin' on 'im to come to the tent," Frank relayed, his laughter at the prank nearly overcoming him as he tried to recount the story. "An' Millard, he's just a' snorin' away, he got no idea we'd even been in there, so when Stanton come in, he ain't got no warnin', and Stanton just goes about 'is business, takin' 'is own sweet time gettin' settled. I swear t' God, I thought Tolbert was gonna shit his pants right there, outta the stress a' waitin' for him to get in the bed! But fin'lly he done it, and then..." Frank had to stop for a moment in his story as the giggles overtook him, and Bud laughed at his inability to contain himself. He finally collected himself enough to continue. "An' then, we could hear him a justa' gettin' all comf'rble in the bed, big ol' sighs"—Frank sighed deeply to illustrate—"as he was gettin' himself all cozy, and then this huge, high-pitched *screeeeeech* like you ain't never heard in a man, oh my God, like a banshee straight outta hell he was...*ha, ha, ha, ha*...and he come flyin' out the tent in 'is drawers, Millard right b'hind him, screamin' just the same an' not havin' a fuckin' clue why, and the two of 'em…*ha, ha, ha ha*… the two 'em got so tangled up bumpin' inta each other in the dark that they both fell down in their underdrawers right in the middle of the camp, justa shoutin' like a sinner come t' Jesus!" Frank was overtaken again momentarily by the memory, and Bud had to be patient while he attempted to compose himself.

Finally able to continue, he told Bud how he and his co-conspirators had watched from the shadows as half the camp was awakened by the screams of Millard and Stanton and how the snake was finally found and ejected from the tent. The next morning Stanton was the butt of no end of jokes, and he did not bear his humiliation well; he was teased relentlessly about his late-night visitor and the rather feminine squeals he had emitted in his fright. Even Millard gave him a hard time, despite his own participation in the fracas, and by the end of the day Stanton was out of temper entirely. Bud had missed all the excitement as it had taken place while he and Mark were in Brooksville, although Frank's retelling of the incident made him wish he'd been there to see it. Bud agreed that Stanton was an ass, and even as he had no sympathy for the man being taken down a few notches, he wasn't surprised to hear that Frank had played a part in the man's embarrassment.

"So did he ever suspect that you an' the others were behind it?" he asked when he thought Frank had gotten control over himself enough to provide an answer.

"Naw, he suspected ever'body, and ever'body said they done it, which made it even funnier, because ever'body wished they had!" And he was off again, holding the edge of the wagon with one hand and his stomach with the other, and Bud just had to watch him lose himself in laughter again at the memory.

They finally arrived at Bud's homestead just before suppertime the Tuesday before Thanksgiving, and as Bud and Frank pulled the horses to a halt in the yard by the barn, children literally swarmed out of the house and from all sides. Some of them Bud realized he didn't even recognize, and he hugged and patted and kissed everyone who mobbed him, whether they were his own or not. Frank was not without his own warm welcome, and Nick and Ellen joined them in the yard.

"Good to see ya! Welcome home!" Nick called, as he waded through the children on his way to welcome his brothers. Bud was pleasantly surprised; he had not expected to see Nick and Ellen but was glad of it. In the dimming light he was able to catch sight of a partially formed foundation of a house, and as he clasped Nick into a hug he asked him about it.

"Didja build me a house, brother?"

"Well, I'mma tryin' to, but I ain't doin' the whole thing for you, ya' know," Nick grumbled good-naturedly, as he released Bud from his clutches and raised a hand to Frank. "I 'spect now that you're home for a few days, you'll fin'lly start pullin' your weight around here," he laughed.

"Might even put ol' Frank to work," Bud agreed. "Listen, now, you hooligans, you get these horses unhitched and tended to while I go see to your ma an' Annie," he directed the children, who continued to clamber all over him in their excitement. Frank and Nick wrangled their way around the chattering horde and worked on getting the horses and wagon taken care of, while Bud walked to the house. He had no idea what he was walking into, but he settled his shoulders and prepared himself for whatever lay in store.

He opened the door to find Annie setting the table and Caroline taking a pot from the stove, a warm fire going in the fireplace and lamps lit in a welcoming sight that relieved his anxious heart. Annie smiled and came to him, her belly noticeable but not heavy with the child just yet. He embraced her and smiled at Caroline, who, for a wonder, smiled back as she placed the pot on the table.

"Evenin' ladies, you got anything you could feed a coupla' tired old men tonight?" Bud asked, letting Annie go and holding her out at arm's length. "Lookit you, girl, you're beautiful," he said, smiling at her. She blushed and cradled her belly in her hand. Bud walked over to Caroline, who allowed herself to be hugged and kissed on the cheek. She returned Bud's hug, not precisely warmly but not unkindly, and he found himself pleasantly surprised by her attitude toward him. After being unsure of what he was going to get when he walked in that door, he saw this as a big step forward and felt hopeful.

"It's good to see you, Bud," she said quietly, turning him loose and moving back to the stove. "How was the ride home?"

Bud returned to Annie and kissed her again before he answered. "Uneventful, I guess. Long." He sank into a chair at the table. "I'm just about beat."

"Well, supper's just about ready," Annie said, returning to her table-setting and helping Caroline gather everything for the evening meal.

"Who're all those children out there? I know I got a lot, but some o' them I *know* ain't mine," he chuckled, leaning back in the chair and setting his hat on his knee.

"Those are the Clarks," Caroline answered, as one of the Bohannons came into the house, slamming the door behind him. "Levi Bohannon, do not slam that door, and go out and tell everybody to wash up," she admonished, not a trace of anger in her voice. Bud was glad to see that Caroline did not seem flustered or annoyed at the intrusion, and he raised an eyebrow as he heard a hastily yelled "yes, ma'am!" as the young man went out the door, slamming it again on his way out. Caroline rolled her eyes. "Those Bohannons are gonna be the death of me, they are," she groused, smiling, as Annie laughed.

"They are a mess, I agree," she affirmed. "The Clarks are having a rough time of it just now," she said to Bud, putting plates and forks around him. "Their mama's got the consumption, and their daddy's near delusional with the grief of it," Annie explained. "Everyone in town has been takin' them in, one way or another, while their ma has her last days. We've had 'em for a couple weeks now."

"Well, are they goin' home, ever, or what?" Bud asked. It was none of his business what the women did while he was gone, but if it was mouths to feed, he had an interest.

"Their pa's nearly out of his head, I hear. He ain't been handlin' it well, and Mrs. Lundy says she won't be surprised if he don't throw himself down in the grave with her when it's her time to go," Annie continued. "We're plannin' on keepin' 'em through Christmas, at least."

"Hush now, they're coming in," Caroline cautioned, and Annie ceased. "Here now, you boys, settle down and be still. Girls, make some room, there."

The room was alight with lively chatter and laughter from the children and adults alike, and they had a good time catching up on each other's activities over the long separation. Bud and Frank described their life at the camp as best they could, although Frank did not relate the snake story or his part in it, to Bud's relief. That was all he needed, for those boys to get an idea like that in their heads.

The children, for their part, in between bites of food and pokes to their neighbor or questions to the adults, talked about the excitement of the coming holidays, and in particular the play that was being rehearsed each week in preparation for the big night of local theater that everyone in the school was to take part in, in one way or another. There were so many children in the house that they could not all fit at the table, but some of them sat in the front room and some on the stair steps, some by the fire, and some on the floor. Bud rather marveled at the women's ability to maneuver around and in between them and at their masterful way of handling such a large brood.

As the conversation turned to individual chats among the children, Bud turned to Ellen.

"You're lookin' mighty happy, there, Miz Braxton, with your little belly bump there," he said. "How is the little chap?" he asked, as she beamed in her chair, resting quietly after supper with one hand on her stomach.

"He, or she, is doing just fine, I think," Ellen smiled in reply, looking at Nick. "Turning somersaults most days, jumping jacks the next."

"It's gonna be a boy, I tell ya," Nick said, smiling back at his wife and putting another bite of food in his mouth. "I can tell by the way he moves. Look, you c'n see him even now," and he pointed at Ellen's belly, which was indeed moving ever so slightly as the baby inside turned and stretched.

"You never know, Nick. Could be another girl, and then you'll really be outnumbered," Frank said, pulling Claire Bohannon onto his lap. She leaned against him in pure happiness. It had not taken the children long to discover that Uncle Frank was fun, friendly, and attentive, and after supper he was descended upon in earnest by the eager mob.

"God help me," Nick laughed, and Bud smiled. He loved his children in what he hoped was equal fervor, but he did agree that the girls had him wrapped a little tighter than the boys sometimes. What could he say? He was brought to his knees by the women in his life.

The evening continued with everyone in good spirits, and it was late by the time Nick and Ellen departed and all the children found places to sleep and were tucked in. Nick would be back in the morning, and he and Frank would unload the new timber in the wagon. Then all together they would set about making swift progress on the house. Annie, Ellen, and Caroline would be busy with preparations for their Thanksgiving dinner, and it promised to be a lively and busy holiday.

Caroline blew out the lamp at the table and said goodnight to Annie and Bud, who sat by the fire; she with her sewing and he with his pipe. Caroline did not ask Bud to bed, but did not look perturbed, and Bud did not ask to be admitted. Instead he sat quietly and watched Annie stitch away at whatever item it was that lay in her lap; some white underthing of one of the children's, probably, that he would likely be unable to identify.

"Them children are a sight, they are," Bud remarked amiably.

"They're all good, even though it's loud. I know you didn't expect to come home to even more of them," Annie said, pulling the thread through the fabric in her lap.

"No...how long they gonna be here, anyway?" he asked. "And what about the Bohannons? Were you ever able to find that sister?"

"Just through the holidays," Annie assured him, "and no, we haven't heard back yet. It was too much for their daddy, just now, and we wanted them to be able to have a good break from school without being so downhearted. They're already grieving; we just wanted to help them out a little," she said. "They all get along and help each other, so it's all right. I guess when you've already got thirteen, what's five more," she laughed softly, her eyes shining in the firelight. She knotted the thread and pulled it tight. "There," she said, and laid her sewing in her lap. "You ready to call it a night?"

"More than," he said, standing and tapping out his pipe into the fire. He questioned her about Caroline, his voice low. "She doin' okay, with all the children?"

"Seems to be," Annie answered, putting her sewing away and setting the grate over the fire. "It actually seems to help her, with all the chaos. You'd think it'd overwhelm her, but it's actually having the opposite effect," she said. "Even having the Clarks hasn't ruffled her. She just folded 'em all in, keeps everything goin'. She's been amazing, actually," Annie admitted. "I try to be a help, but sometimes I'm just exhausted."

"Well, I guess you got a few things goin' on yourself, little girl," he said, drawing her to his chest. The fire's glow dimmed as the coals settled. "Listen here, what're you keepin' underneath this dress?" He wrapped his arms around her and kissed her in the fading light.

"A big strong man like you should be able to find out, don't you think?" she asked, draping her arms around his neck and returning his kiss with one of her own, deepening it and causing him to take a deep breath.

"Yes, I b'lieve I'm up to that," he said. "Get along," he whispered, gently patting her on the rear as he pushed her in the direction of the bedroom. There were children everywhere, but they were all asleep, and who cared if they weren't, he thought. He could be quiet. Maybe.

The Thanksgiving holiday dawned clear, cold, and bright, and the children were allowed to play after their morning chores were done. Bud and Frank were working on the house in the morning; Nick would be over any time. They had made good progress, and Nick had given them a good start with what he'd been able to do while Bud and Frank were at the camp. The little house would have a good frame, and there would be a shared kitchen that both women could use for washing, cooking, and boiling clothes. Bud never expected to be wealthy, and what he had was more than he'd ever thought of, but he had been frugal with the money he did have, and he was good with his hands. He was a blessed man, despite his life's difficulties, and he was grateful.

At the big dinner they shared, the Braxton family laughed and joked with each other and shared a time of fellowship and enjoyed the time with the children out of school. The happy time was diminished only by the absence of Robert, who had not been invited. This was felt most keenly by Ellie and Sarah, but there was also an undercurrent of disquiet with Frank, Bud, and Nick and to a lesser extent with Carolyn and Ellen, who had all learned to live with the tenuous relationship they had with Robert. The Braxton men had long been accustomed to his absence, as they had had bouts of it all throughout their formative years and on into adulthood. Although they each had regained some semblance of kinship with their father over the years as they'd aged and become more understanding, and as Robert had become less distraught, none had really developed a close relationship with him. Secretly all felt the deep-seated hollow the lack of relationship left. Bud and Frank, being Bud and Frank, had no idea how to repair the relationship with Robert, and they had not really tried. Nick had made the most effort over the years, but even he didn't have what could be called a close bond with the man. And so Robert was not at the Thanksgiving table and became the object of discussion between Ellie and Bud later that weekend.

"Why can't Papa come to Thanksgiving?" she gently inquired, as Bud sat milking the cows one evening and Ellie forked hay into the horses' stalls. "He was the only one not here."

"Well, I guess he doesn't usually come to things like that, now does he?" Bud answered. He really wasn't sure what the answer was. Because they hadn't made much of an effort to include him, he supposed. Whose fault was it? His, for not being more adamant that his children have a relationship with their grandfather, or Robert's, for not seeking forgiveness for the years of abandonment and strife that they had endured as a family growing up together? Frank or Nick's, for not insisting on it? He didn't know, only that he felt that none of them had really tried enough, and that tugged at him. So he turned it back around. "Would you like to see him more?"

"Yes, I would, and I only get to see him a little bit now that school's back. I invited him to come see our play at Christmas, at the school, but I don't know if he'll come."

Ah yes, the nativity play at school. That had been the topic of much energetic chatter over the holiday, as all the children were looking forward to it. The Bohannons had never done anything like the play before, and though the Clarks were familiar with church plays and skits that had been attempted over the years (there was a notable year where the angel got stuck in the tomb; it turned out that his wingspan was slightly too wide for the entrance, and he had to sing from the cover of darkness of Christ's coming), the play that the school was planning was supposed to be quite the event. He smiled as he finished filling the bucket of milk and pushed the cow off. *An hour and a half of small children forgetting their lines and not being able to hear them talk and probably a sheep would get away at some point,* he thought. He had to hope baby Jesus would be a doll and not someone's actual baby; who knows what would happen if that came to pass…although he thought it would be quite the entertaining performance, either way.

He didn't immediately answer her as he thought for a few minutes. Frank was doing well enough sober that he thought they might all enjoy spending the holiday together. "Well, I guess it would be all right if you invited him to come eat with us on Christmas," he said to Ellie, whose face instantly brightened at the thought of her Papa being there at Christmas with everyone.

"Oh, that would be wonderful! Thank you, Pa! Could I go tell him right now?" she asked, eager to deliver the invitation in person immediately, lest time be wasted.

"Sure, just go tell your ma where you're going," he laughed as she skipped away, glad that he could make her so happy with such an innocuous suggestion and inwardly lightened with the idea that perhaps the relationship between him and his father might be mended somewhat. He knew Caroline and Ellen wouldn't mind the extra mouth to feed, although he thought Frank and Nick might have something to say. Frank didn't dislike his father, exactly, but neither did he have a relationship with him, having been too young to remember May and only knowing the Robert who had abandoned them and been drunk most of his growing years. Nick and Bud had largely had the raising of Frank, and though Robert was present, he had not been *present* most of their teenage and young adult lives.

By the time Christmas rolled around he would have enough timber to finish building the house, and after Christmas he would plan to stay home and finish what Nick had been able to start. And he thought about the blessing of another baby for Nick and Ellen, and his own child coming next spring as well, Lord willing. If Frank could stay sober, and Mark could manage the bookkeeping, things might turn around for everyone. He wondered what was happening in Atlanta. He hadn't heard from Mark, but the last payroll had arrived on a later train, so he knew he'd gotten the message. He wondered if the other train had been robbed or not and if Ruben had made good on his threat. He hoped Mark would be able to get the right people involved and Dixon would get what was coming to him. Bud wasn't a vengeful man, necessarily, but Dixon was just *such* an inglorious combination of ineptitude and criminal transgression, and he hated to see good people suffer for it. He finished at the barn and went to see what the children and women were up to. He hoped it involved pie.

Rube Burroughs had indeed robbed the train—or attempted to, at least. When he left the camp he was able to find a few good men who were willing to take the risk of being shot or captured with the hope of a good payout. There was plenty of cash from the passengers and a few baubles here and there, and his companions were very happy with their bounty from the operation. Ruben, however, was disappointed, as there appeared to be no one on the train with the payroll for the line workers, as Braxton had said there would be. He was quietly livid as he joined his fellow plunderers later around the campfire to celebrate and split the spoils of their endeavor among themselves. He would see that Braxton would pay for misleading him.

All his life people had trodden on him, he thought, as he lay on the ground watching the other men laugh and drink, exchanging cash and trinkets. Everything he had, everything he had eaten or worn or learned had to be taken, and nothing had been given to him his entire life. Even in the orphanage where he had grown up, he had to be on his guard. Other children would steal from you as soon as look at you, and as he grew he found that men, and yes, even the women he'd encountered along the way, would disappoint him in the end. Only Carrie, his best friend at the orphanage, and a few fellow thieves like Gober that he'd run with over the years had been any different. He wondered what had happened to Carrie. He had run away from the orphanage at fourteen, unable to bear the upheaval and commotion of the orphanage any longer. Life would be better on his own, he had thought, and his only regret was that he couldn't go back for her.

He was going to have to lie low for a bit after the train robbery. But he *was* going to see that Braxton paid for his treachery. He remembered running across him in the woods the night he and Casey were together before coming to the camp. He thought he might be able to get back that way, and how many homesteads could there be around that area? Braxton's couldn't be far from where they had met. Somebody would know where he lived, and he would find Braxton and make him pay for leading him astray.

21 CHRISTMAS MIRACLES

After the Thanksgiving holiday, things returned more or less to normal for the Braxton family—or what passed as normal for them. Nick was able to continue working on the house in Bud's absence, and Bud and Frank returned to the timber camp. Bud had decided that he would only work until Christmas, and then whether he had enough timber or not, he would stay at his own homestead and finish the work on Annie's house. Nick had been extraordinarily generous with his time, but Bud felt he could not prevail upon him any longer, especially given that he would be expecting a new arrival of his own. By Christmas, Bud hoped, Mark would have worked out some sort of arrangement regarding Dixon, and he would be back at the camp and ready to move down the line. Bud prayed that this would be so; so many things were depending on him being able to leave them to their own devices so that he could move to pressing matters at home.

His normally easy going, quiet demeanor was becoming more and more fractured as the weeks and days brought Christmas closer, although he tried not to display the inner turmoil he felt to the other men in the camp. He tried to be patient and friendly, when inwardly he was worried and distracted with thoughts of what could possibly be keeping Mark away this long. He had promised Annie and Caroline that he would be home by Christmas Eve, but there had been no word from Mark at all, despite Dixon's repeated telegrams and letters to Atlanta demanding his return.

If Bud could be said to be perturbed by Mark's continued absence, Dixon was nearly apoplectic. It was readily apparent to all within earshot of Dixon that the absence of his primary bookkeeper and right-hand man was wearing terribly on the man, although only Bud had reason to suspect that it had less to do with his dependence on Jacobsen's stellar secretarial capabilities and more to do with Dixon's presumed discovery of the mysterious disappearance of certain incriminating ledgers. Bud believed he could pinpoint the exact moment when Dixon realized that the ledgers were missing; one evening he was sipping his coffee in the relative quiet of the camp house and transcribing receipts in the expenses ledger when a sudden cacophony of sounds erupted from Dixon's office: the riotous discord of chairs being overturned and drawers slamming while papers went flying in all directions like a frightened flock of birds. Shortly thereafter Dixon emerged red faced from his office, calling to Bud over one shoulder as he fled from the camp house, hat in hand, that he was traveling to Brooksville immediately on urgent business and would return the following day. Bud could only stare after him in bewilderment, one eyebrow raised at Dixon's abrupt departure.

Dixon's subsequent return brought no comfort; he was snappish with the men, prone to fits of profanity and profoundly irritable, and seemed to be fixed in a perpetual ill temper. Days of this were wearing on the nerves as well as the ears; Bud took to working in his tent rather than the camp house, to Dixon's further annoyance.

He was thus ensconced with a cup of coffee and a rather confusing jumble of paper before him early one morning, two days before Christmas, when all hell cut loose. He heard a thunder of hoofbeats and the shouting of men, far too many and too loud this early to be just those from the camp. He rushed to the tent entrance and found he was not alone; heads all down the camp line poked out in various stages of wakefulness, and men in their long underwear began to swarm confusedly out of their tents, swearing and asking each other what the Sam Hill was going on. Something big was clearly brewing in the camp house, for a flurry of shouts erupted from it, and Bud could see mounted horsemen flanking its sides. Who these horsemen were he could not have guessed, for they were complete strangers to him, and he was not alone in his confusion. He heard men all around him questioning each other and saw their wild gestures as they tried to make sense of this sudden intrusion into their early morning's sleep. He and others scrambled to dress and get boots on, and en masse they ran to the camp house to see what the commotion was.

Bud arrived in time to see lawmen emerge from the camp house with Dixon among them, hands tied behind him. He appeared to have hastily dressed, and his hair was an untamed profusion of spikes and corkscrews. The two men, whom Bud guessed to be federal Marshals, ushered Dixon to a waiting horse, and others around them steadied the animal and helped Dixon to his seat. He saw them speaking, but in the general confusion of men shouting, could not hear or understand what they were saying to each other. The actions were clear, however; Dixon was being arrested for something, and there was no joke about it. Even now he was being escorted from the camp with no explanation to the burgeoning, questioning group of men outside the camp house watching this event with mixed emotions of confusion and merriment. Order was soon restored, however, as Dixon and the marshals rode off in the direction of Brooksville and a small consortium of suited men, strangers to the camp but very clearly asserting their right to be there, gathered around the meal wagon.

Off to the side of the wagon, where men in close groups were talking and shouting animatedly about what had just befallen the camp, Bud caught sight of Mark Jacobsen talking to one of the men in a suit, who looked stern-faced and authoritative. He quickly made his way through the throng of men and managed to tug on Mark's sleeve .

Mark finished what he was saying to the suited man and turned to Bud. "Bud! I'm glad to see you! Come on, come this way; I've got to talk to you," Mark nodded to the suit and gripped Bud by the elbow, turning him back toward the camp house and relative peace. He said nothing else until they were by themselves in a corner of the camp house.

"Mark, where you been? I ain't talked to you for months, and what the ever-livin' hell is going on?" Bud asked.

"I know, and I'm sorry, but I couldn't risk it. When I got to Atlanta, I talked to my father and my uncle, and they both do business with the board members on the rail line. They set up meetings with them, and it went straight downhill almost immediately, Bud. They've had trouble with Dixon before, they said, and they just needed evidence to put him away. So when I showed up with what I'd seen, they jumped on it. The US Marshals were called, but I couldn't say anything to you, or come back, for fear he'd get wind. So I'm sorry you've been in the dark this whole time, but it's been a circus, I tell you." Mark wiped his forehead. Despite the cold weather, he was sweating. "It took this long to set everything up, but I'll tell you, that man's been over his head for years, from what I've heard. What he's been doin' down here is the least of it."

"Good God," Bud said, relieved that Dixon was taken care of but still concerned about Burroughs. "Well, you got my telegram, though, because we got the payroll," Bud said. "But I didn't hear from you. Boy, I'm glad you're back." Bud clapped Mark on the shoulder, and the tension he'd been under for the last month started to ebb a bit.

"I know; I'm sorry," Mark apologized again. "I was just prayin' everything would go okay with Dixon, and I had to keep my mouth shut; I didn't want to tip anybody about anything. But I guess you didn't have any problem with Burroughs. I guess he's long gone."

"Yeah, I s'pose, although I read in the paper that another train got robbed, and I swear to God it had to be him. That boy's bad news all over. I tol' you he was."

"Yes, I know, but listen, we've got to get back. I just needed to get out of that chaos for a minute, but come on, we've got to go." Mark pushed Bud toward the door, and they both headed back to the wagon to see a much quieter group of men listening to one of the men in suits as he wrapped up his talk.

"...the line, and you men are the heart of it," Bud and Mark caught the tail end of whatever speech the suit had come here to give. *At any rate, it must've gone over well,* Bud thought, because cheers rang out among the men, and as they realized that Mark was among them, they turned to clap him on the back, with shouts of "Congratulations!" and "That's how it oughtta be!" and "Damn straight!" coming from all over. Mark laughed at the confusion on Bud's face.

"All right, all right," Mark said, laughing. "Y'all go on now, and I'll come out and see you in a bit." He raised his hat to the men and turned again with Bud to go to the camp house, the men in suits gathering around him. The line bosses gathered their men together in preparation for breakfast, and Bud still heard whoops and shouts as they walked away.

"What the absolute hell, Mark?" Bud asked in confusion, as they neared the camp house and went in to sit.

Mark grinned as he sat down at a table. The other men sat as well, and one of them lit a pipe.

"I believe you are Mr. Braxton, am I correct?" the pipe smoker asked between puffs to get the tobacco started.

"Yes, sir, Bud Braxton."

"It appears, Mr. Braxton"—the pipe smoker leaned back in his chair and crossed one foot over his knee—"that Mr. Dixon has been perpetrating a fraudulent scheme here on our railroad, and I understand you and Mr. Jacobsen are who we have to thank for bringing it to our attention."

"Well, sir, Mark found the problem. I just kep' the wheels on the cart till he come home." Bud was still standing and didn't move to sit with the businessmen who were gathered around the table.

"Regardless, your actions and Mr. Jacobsen's have allowed us to rescue our railroad from what could have been a very dire situation, and we are in your debt." Bud just held his hat and nodded, then looked to Mark for help. Mark stood and put his arm around Bud's shoulders, which helped him relax just a bit in this group of white-haired, nattily dressed men, and Bud was instantly grateful for his friendship.

"If you'll excuse me, gentlemen, I believe I've got a line to inspect, and I'll just take Mr. Braxton with me," Mark said, turning Bud around. Bud tipped a finger to his head at the gentlemen and walked with Mark out of the camp house.

"You got to tell me what the hell is goin' on, Mark," Bud pleaded. "Who're them, and what the hell you talkin' about, *inspectin'*?"

Mark smiled as he put his hat on and they headed to the cook wagon, which was now mostly deserted as the workers had headed to the timber and the front of the rail line. "Those are the board members of the rail line, or some of them, anyway. They insisted on riding out here and seeing Dixon off. When I told them what was going on, and what we'd seen in the ledgers, they had a lot of questions for me, Bud, about what we do here, and what Dixon does, and how we managed the line and the men. I think I answered all their questions to their satisfaction, and they've promoted me to be Dixon's replacement. They want me to continue to manage the line when it finishes this stretch and moves on." They nodded to the cook, who heaped plates of biscuits and gravy for them and sent them to sit with steaming mugs of coffee.

Bud now understood the workmen's congratulatory wishes earlier, and he was happy for Mark. Mark was a stand-up fella, all right, and he was glad they'd become friends. "That's great, Mark, that's bully, that is," he said, happy that Dixon was gone, happy that Mark would be in charge of things now. Things would certainly be different. That line would go straight on just like it should, and he knew Mark would have things moving fine.

"Are you sure you have to go, Bud? I know you always said you were leaving at Christmas, but does this change your mind at all? I sure could use your help, you know I could," Mark cajoled.

Bud chuckled and stuffed another bite of biscuit and gravy in his mouth before he answered. "No, I'm goin' home to my fam'ly, but this railroad couldn't be in better hands, you know that," Bud said. "I'm real proud a you, Mark, I am."

"Well, you know you had a hand in getting Dixon off this line, and it's appreciated, Bud. The board has given me permission to grant you a severance when you go, if you still feel that you must," Mark said. Bud was astonished. That was more than he'd expected, but damn if he'd turn it down.

"Well, all right, thank you," was all Bud said. He stuffed another bite of gravy and biscuit in his mouth. He really wasn't quite sure what to say.

"I was wondering if you think your brother Frank might be the sort to stay on, though, and help me with the bookkeeping. I remember him saying you taught him well, when you both first came in."

Bud was surprised, and pleasantly so. He hadn't thought of that possibility, but now that Mark had suggested it, he thought that would be a perfect fit for Frank. He was good with numbers too, though he'd need to be taught what to do, and it would be a good move for him. He nodded and swallowed. "That would be won'erful, Mark, if you think it would be all right. Frank would be good at it, and you c'n trust him."

"Then that's what we'll do. I need to go out on the line and talk to the men, and you find Frank and tell him I want to talk to him. We'll work it out. When did you want to go back home?"

"Tomorrow, if that's all right. I can get everything put together pretty quick. You and I can talk tonight about the books I done while you been gone, if you want."

"Sure, sure, that's fine. Here, give me your plate and cup and let's go, what do you say?" Mark took the plates and cups back to the cook, who was closing everything up but had left the barrel of water ready to wash the men's dishes. They left the wagon and walked out to the head of the line, where groups of men were already hard at work, felling trees and hauling logs, setting ties, and laying down rail for the line. It was cold, but the heat of the work had the men in their shirtsleeves, nonetheless.

Bud found Frank soon enough, and as they talked over the events of the morning, Bud felt more and more relieved about leaving the camp. Two days ago he had been a bundle of nerves, but today everything was going to be all right, and he was thankful. *Thank You, God, for small miracles,* he thought, as he, Frank, and Mark turned to go back to the camp several hours later. That evening they put their heads together and worked out a way forward, with Mark in charge and Frank as his bookkeeper. The suits had left that afternoon, and they would send another bookkeeper back on the train at the end of the week with the payroll to help Mark get started off right. "What you gonna' do for Christmas, Mark? You gonna' stay here? Come home with us," he offered, as the three left the camp house that night to go to their tents.

"I'll be here, with the men who don't want to go home on break, but thank you for the invitation, Bud. I promise I'll get up that way to see you in the spring." Mark sounded sure of himself, but Bud wondered if that would actually happen, with all the strains on Mark's time that were coming. He'd love to see his friend again soon, but he wouldn't blame him if he never got free for a visit. Running a railroad was a full-time job he knew that first hand. "Frank'll be going home after you, I guess, right, Frank?"

Frank nodded, and Bud was pleased again to see the change the fall work had wrought in him. Frank was going to be all right, he thought. He'd been worried when they first got to camp, but now he was confident Frank would stay sober and be dependable. He thought Frank had finally found what he was good at and knew Mark would be a good friend and influence on him in his absence.

"Yep, for a couple days, but then I'll be back," Frank assured him. They arrived at Bud and Frank's tent, and the trio said their good nights and parted. Frank had promised Ellie and Sarah that he would be there to see the nativity play at the school, and he would not disappoint them for anything. He had come to treasure his relationship with his nephews and nieces, and he looked forward to the brief holiday. "Long as Bud don't put me to work, I'll be back on time," he laughed.

"Shut up," Bud said, good-naturedly, and gave Frank a shove into the tent, as Mark waved and walked on to his own tent, lantern in hand. The two got ready for bed, and Bud closed his eyes and lay down. *Finally,* he thought, *this is gonna work out.* He drifted off to the sound of Frank's snoring and slept better that night than he had in a month.

The children were thrilled to see Bud when he got back home, and he was glad the stint at the camp was over. It had been good for him all around, but he was glad to be home and back among them. He found Annie in the kitchen, surrounded by children, an apron draped over her round belly, pulling a pan out of the oven and then brushing her hair back from her forehead.

"You got enough for me?" he asked, stomping the dirt off his boots before coming in and closing the door.

"Bud!" Annie exclaimed. "When did you get here? How are you? Come here!" she peppered him, as he made his way over to her through the throng of children hugging his legs and crying, "Pa! Pa!" He hugged and kissed the children, his, theirs, whose, it didn't matter.

"Girl, it's good to see you. How's everything?" he asked, hugging her tightly. He kissed her on the cheek, then held her at arm's length to take her in. Her cheeks were flushed and rosy, and her eyes sparkled. She looked happy to see him, and that warmed him. The ride home had been cold and boring, and he was glad to be back.

When he arrived home he had given Jack over to a boy—one of the Clark boys, who took the horse from him readily, and directed him to be sure to brush the horse thoroughly, feed him, and to hang up the bridle and stow the reins. That night they enjoyed the stories Bud told them about camp; the children regaled him with stories from school, and Caroline and Annie laughed at the way they were both so excited to "be next." With promises that Uncle Frank would be there in time for the play on Christmas evening, they all eventually went to bed, maybe a little later than was normal, and maybe they chatted a little bit more excitedly than usual, but they all did eventually bed down.

Bud stayed in Annie's room, and no mention was made. Caroline seemed perfectly fine to go to her room by herself, and Bud marveled inwardly at the notion as he slid under the quilt next to Annie. This was a different thing, it was, but somehow it was all working out. He wondered how long this would last as he drifted off to sleep.

22 ROBERT'S GIFT

Christmas afternoon the Braxton clan loaded the wagon full to the brim with the Clarks and Bohannons and hitched Jack and Jill for a ride to town. They would be late coming back; they piled quilts and blankets and a basket of Caroline's fig turnovers into the wagon for the trip home. Frank followed the wagon on his poker pony, and the children chattered almost nonstop until they got to town. The party met with no impediments on their journey, and they arrived at the schoolhouse in time for costumes to be arranged and lines to be rehearsed one last time. As the adults found their seats in preparation for the event, Robert made his way to the back of the curtain, and somehow managed to find Ellie among the horde of children.

"Here now, Ellie, I got somethin' for ya," he whispered to her, as he pulled her to the side of the stage, away from the mob of sheep, wise men, and shepherds. Her eyes were stars as she anticipated what he might have for her. That he was here at all was a major event; to think that he might have brought a present for her, for her alone, was too much to be endured.

"What, Papa, what?" she pestered, as he dug into his overall pocket.

"You forgot this at the house t'other time you was over, and I tole' you that you could have it, as a special thing of your Grandma's," he said, and pulled out a ribbon of blue from his pocket. Her eyes sparkled at the remembrance of the token, and she clutched it, smiling. She hugged him hard, and said, "Thank you, thank you!" into his ear as she kissed his bristly cheek. "Go on, now," he said, and she ran off, stuffing the ribbon into her pocket as she went. She knew just what she would do with it when she got home.

Robert made his way into the audience, nodding at Frank and Bud, and then finding Nick and Ellen a few rows back. He nodded at them as well and then sat. He knew he was invited to a small late supper at the Braxtons', but he still wasn't sure he was going to go through with it. Bud and Nick he could talk to okay, but he felt Frank hated him, and he didn't want to go if it was going to make things difficult. He didn't often have opportunities to see his sons, but he also knew what grief he'd brought them, and he was ashamed of it. So he decided not to think about that for now, but just to watch the play. He'd figure out the rest later.

The play was indeed an event, with Joseph forgetting his lines and Mary jabbing him unceremoniously when it was his turn. His cheeks turned red and he stuttered, but he got through it and got a round of applause after one of his monologues. There was no live baby Jesus, to Bud's relief, but Mary cradled the doll who stood for Him as tenderly as if He was a newborn, and the sheep did not stray. The camel fell off the stage at one point, but quickly clambered back up, and was none the worse for wear when it was time to bow to the King. One of the wise men had a hard time telling Joseph of his gift of "franken…frankasis…frankens…" but overall it was a very lovely play, and the schoolhouse fairly shook with the sound of clapping when the final bow was taken.

Ellie ran straight to her Papa, saying, "You're coming for supper, right, you're coming right now, aren't you?" and Robert had no choice but to nod in agreement and acquiesce to her pleadings. Even Ellen, in her late term pregnancy, planned on being there, and Nick held her tenderly by the elbow as he helped her into the wagon. "Well, I wouldn't miss it for all the world," she said, and Nick rolled his eyes but said nothing, merely clicking to the horse and accepting his fate while his daughter laughed with her cousins in the back of the wagon.

Hours later they were gathered in the small house. Robert marveled at the spectacle before him. He could not have imagined such a family as this, many years ago. His heart ached for Maybelline. Oh, how she would have loved to see this many children on such a night! How she would have laughed at the play, and how proud she would have been of the little theater they put on! He was warmed to be part of it, thankful that God had afforded him this blessing. He sat quietly and watched the commotion as Caroline and Annie served out pies they had baked earlier in the morning.

Things had begun to settle down as everyone finished their pie, and Frank, Nick, and Bud sat chatting with the women at the table as the children played with their small presents from the morning. During his time at the timber camp, Bud had whittled wooden horses for the boys and other little animals for the girls. He had known about the bevy of children that he was coming home to, and whittling in the evening hours had made him feel closer to the children, so he kept doing it. Thankfully he had enough to pass around so that everyone had something. The women had been able to get a sweet for each of them in town, and though the Clarks and Bohannons were without their parents this Christmas and missed them, they wanted for nothing else and were grateful to have found a place as welcoming as this brood of Braxtons had turned out to be.

Robert was scraping the last piece of pie off his plate, standing beside the fire, when Ellie came to him. "See, Papa, this is what Tom found for me, this is what I wanted the ribbon for," and she dangled the blue ribbon before him. He placed his plate to the side and grasped the trinket. He smiled down at her.

"What now? Tom give you somethin'?" he said, teasing her. He couldn't imagine what sort of trash Tom had found for her that Ellie deemed a treasure; you never knew with these young folk what they counted as important. Always they had rocks or sticks or something, and each one was a unique and wonderful thing. He prepared himself to gush over a bit of tin or a shiny stone.

Frank and Bud's attention was turned to the firelight, as other children realized that Ellie had given something special to Robert and started to whisper and talk among themselves. Tom knew what it was, and his heart swelled with pride that Ellie treasured the little cross and medallion so; he knew she had kept them tucked away and had not spoken of them before now. At first he had thought she was not impressed at all with his gift, especially since the chain was broken, and it disheartened him; soon he learned that she did indeed find the necklace to be as much of a treasure as he did, and more than once he found her with it in the evening before bedtime, turning it over in her hands and gazing at the engraved M on one side of the metal circle. Together they speculated about what it could mean, but neither one could come up with much, and they allowed it to be a mystery as children are wont to do when some things can't be understood.

"Yes," she said, "Tom found these and give 'em to me, and I strung 'em on the ribbon you gave me, and I mean to wear it on Sunday to church," she said proudly, as she smiled up at him. His eyes turned from hers and his smile faltered as he looked at what he held in his hand.

Slowly his other hand came to his mouth, then to touch the little medallion in his hand, and tears formed at the corners of his eyes. His skin went pale, and his body shuddered; he turned the medallion over and over and continued to shake. Finally he gripped Ellie by the shoulders and demanded of her, "Where did you find this, girl? Tell me! Where did you find it?" His voice was urgent and fragile, and it broke with the emotion that erupted from him as he shook the little girl and repeated again, "Where? Where?"

Her smile turned to fright and concern at the way her papa was handling her; never before had he laid his hands on her this way. His fingertips embedded themselves in her flesh; she would have bruises the next day from the force of his grip. Bud leaped from his seat and grasped his father by the arm in alarm; he would not allow his father to treat one of his children this way.

Tom rushed over from his seat by the door, where he was playing with his siblings; his plate and fork flew onto the floor unheeded, as he sought to calm the trio down. All eyes were turned to the little group by the fire, and quiet fell among them as they watched Robert sink to the floor on his knees, clutching the little necklace in his hands, tears spilling down his cheeks now, looking up at Tom and Ellie.

"Please, please tell me where you found this, Tom," he implored.

"In the cove, up the beach," Tom replied. "I found it and gave to Ellie," he said, confused and scared at this reaction of his grandfather's, and frightened he had done something terribly wrong. Just what, he couldn't say, only that perhaps he had done something awful after all, and surely punishment must come.

Bud rested one hand on Tom's shoulder and the other hand on Robert's. "Here now, Pa, what's the problem? Tom said he found it, and so he must have done, for Tom doesn't lie," he assured him.

"You must take me now to where you found it, right now, Tom," Robert insisted, getting to his feet. Tom looked incredulously at his father and back again at Robert.

"What, sir, now? It's dark outside, and cold!" Tom protested.

Bud stared at his father. "He found that on the beach, he said, Pa. We can't go out to the beach now."

"We must, and we must go now! Right this minute!" Robert gripped Tom by the elbow and dragged him to the door, throwing off Bud's hands and any others that would keep him inside. He thrust open the door, leaving the rest of the family speechless, gawking in disbelief. Bud grabbed his coat and the oil lantern by the door. Nick managed to find his coat, and bid his wife stay put where she was.

"You stay here, and we'll be back," Bud said to a frightened Caroline, as he closed the door behind him. She gathered the children around her in disbelief and tried to comfort Ellie, who stood sobbing with the necklace clutched in her hand, as everyone tried their best to soothe her. She knew only that something was terribly wrong, and she was frightened that it was her fault, although what she couldn't guess why. She peered up at her mother through her tears.

"Where are they going, Mama? What in the world are they doing?" she pleaded.

"I don't know, baby; I don't know, but it's going to be all right. Hush now. Let's get ready for bed; it's late." Things had turned upside down so abruptly that Caroline hardly knew what to think, but thankfully Ellen and Annie were there to help comfort and corral the children. Together the women managed to calm and settle the brood.

Outside, Frank, Nick, and Bud followed behind Robert and Tom, who ran ahead of them, down to the bay.

Despite Robert's age he had been able to follow Tom, and when they finally reached the bay's sandy beaches his frantic demeanor continued unabated. Robert sank to his knees in the sand and tried to catch his breath. Finally, he demanded, "Where, Tom? Where did you find it?"

The brothers had caught up to Robert, and they rested with their hands on their knees. Bud was incredulous. Was his father losing his mind entirely? How long should he let this go on? He turned to his son, ready to tell them all to turn around and go home, when Tom pointed down the beach.

"There, Grandpa; I found it there. You just keep going down that way, and there's a little cove there." They all looked in the direction of his outstretched arm.

A moan emanated from Robert, a deep guttural sound that hardly sounded human, and it wrenched Bud's heart. Nick put his arm around the man, who now knelt in the lapping waves of the beach at Tom's feet. Frank stood apart in shocked silence, seeming unable to do anything but watch the spectacle unfold before him. The cold water ebbed and flowed around their ankles as they watched Robert helplessly.

Suddenly Robert stood up and ran awkwardly toward the cove. The others shared a brief look but then followed, oil lamps held high above the waves, dry clothes be damned. Together they ran down the beach and into the waves, splashing in the water to the entrance of the cove, the light spilling over the rocks as they drew up behind Robert. They stared uncertainly at him, then looked to the back of the cove.

"Tell me now, boy," Robert said to Tom, his voice now gentle instead of frantic. "Where did you find it?"

Tom pointed to the far end of the cove where he'd uncovered the tangle of bones and rags earlier that summer. He was soaked, and water dripped into his eyes. He blinked repeatedly, trying to see clearly. "Right there, sir, there at the end near that big rock."

Robert took the lamp from Bud and waded over to the rock Tom pointed out, while the others came slowly behind him. They looked at each other, but could offer nothing, could say nothing. They could only follow respectfully, hoping this wild tear was nearing its end.

Robert placed the lamp on top of the rock, kneeled, and peered down at the rib cage and skull before him. He began to sob quietly as he reached out and touched the skull with both hands, his fingers caressing the concavity on the left side slightly behind the ear. How many times he had caressed this concavity in life! "Maybelline," he whispered. Robert cradled the skeletal torso into his body, sobbing uncontrollably as the waves lapped around him. His sons could only look on in a mixed state of awe and wonder at his reaction to this discovery.

"She never left me, she never did, she never did," he sobbed. He clutched at Bud and dragged him to his knees next to him in front of the rock. Frank, Nick, and Tom crowded around him in the lamplight, soaked to the skin, watching him as he rocked the skeleton in his arms and cradled the skull to his chest. "She never left me," he whispered over and over to the skull, kissing it, and then looked at Bud with tears in his eyes.

"I was so wrong—all those years. I thought she took off with Macon. But she didn't; she musta' come back and came to our cove after she saw him off, and got caught here in the tide," he said finally. "She was here, all the time."

Tom felt it was time to confess. "I found the necklace by her hand, there between the rocks," he said. "She must have dropped it and got caught, and when the tide came in…." He did not finish the sentence but looked at his father in anguish. "I'm so sorry; I didn't know!" he said, and Bud held him to his chest.

"It's not your fault, now, don't go on so," Bud comforted him and looked at his father, who was now beginning to get hold of himself, even as he still clutched the skeleton.

"No, son, it's not your fault. I'm indebted to you," Robert said, wiping his eyes and gently settling the skeleton back in its place among the rocks. He turned to Nick and Frank, who now knelt with him. "Please forgive me. I took my sorrow out on you, and you paid the price for it. Please. Please forgive me."

Nick and Frank hugged their father in the waves, the three of them cold and shivering. Frank, who never felt he even had a father, thought that he was seeing Robert for the first time, and his emotions were profoundly conflicted. He mourned the loss of the childhood he felt he should have had with a mother and a father who loved him. Years of Robert's belief that Maybelline had deserted him had robbed him of that. But he rejoiced at the father who now clutched him with every muscle fiber in his old body, who ached to atone for the wrong he had brought upon his sons and the years he had lost. Frank decided then that there would be no more time lost, and he gripped his father and his brother together as Bud and Tom looked on in tears. They stayed that way for a few moments more until they let go one at time, and Robert grasped Bud's hand, and then let go.

He looked at the skeleton, now back in its place where Tom first found it. He caressed the skull and whispered, "You sleep well, dear, and I'll come to you by and by. I'm not ready yet, but you'll wait for me, as you have done."

Robert got slowly to his feet, his sons bracing his elbows to ensure he did not fall in the lapping waves. They gathered their lamps and strode out of the cove, holding each other for balance and for comfort, and when they made the beach they wrapped Robert in Bud's coat that he had tossed before trotting into the water. They were a cold, dripping, mess when they got back to the house, and the women set about warming them immediately, offering dry clothes and blankets, coffee and comfort as they settled them near the fire to toast. No one explained anything that night, but all fell asleep together in a heap, and the children found them there the next morning as they wandered about looking for breakfast.

Bud told the story, in some parts in coded phrases for small ears, over a late morning breakfast. All felt something momentous had occurred, although some of the younger children could not have said just what. After breakfast the men, in unprecedented fashion, went back to sleep before the fire, as the women sent the children out to play in the brisk December sunshine. Despite his advanced age and the cold water he had endured during the trip to the cove, Robert did not suffer the consequences of his late night swim, nor did the others in that party who tempted the elements, which any other week would have ensured a cough and fever-- or at least some sniffles. Robert stayed on for a few days before going home, gaining his strength and taking the time to have some long talks with his sons. Frank departed for the rail camp a few days after Christmas, lighter in heart than when he had arrived for his winter break, and somehow feeling grounded and peacefully settled in a way he could not have explained. Nick and Ellen, with Janette, returned home to await the arrival of their new little one, and Bud began work in earnest on Annie's little house, which Nick had begun so well. At the turn of the New Year, things settled into more or less routine, and they stayed that way until February, when all hell broke loose.

23 AN UNEXPECTED VISITOR

As Annie's time of delivery drew nearer, she was uncomfortable and past ready to be done with her pregnancy. She slept little, sat frequently, and had not seen her feet in months. Caroline, for her part, remained well and Bud silently gave thanks each morning that she was so. Verna Dade had come to stay with Ellen when her baby, Mallie Carl, was born, and Verna was expected at the Braxton household any day. Caroline and Susan went to see little Mallie Carl after his birth, and Susan professed him to be the sweetest baby in the world. Little Robert took immediate exception, because for him his sister Bethy was the sweetest baby.

"Well, we're about to have another baby, anyhow, and that will be the sweetest one," Ellie announced, as they rode home from school one afternoon. Tom and Mac hitched the horses to the wagon each morning and unhitched them each afternoon, and all the children went to school each day, rain or shine. Caroline insisted that they go, as much to get them out from underfoot as to enhance their education. The Clarks had stayed on even past the time they were to be moved on to the next house; their mother had indeed passed away, but their father, deep in grief, was not fit to take care of them in his present mental state. In church each Sunday, mother hens clucked about his ability to ever be fit to take care of them appropriately and in their collective wisdom had determined that the Clarks should continue to be passed around the community until such time as their father recovered from his grief. It was intended that they should go the Barnards next, but the two youngest Barnards came down with runny noses and coughs at the last minute, so they remained with the Braxtons. The wagon was full of children, and the school was too, to the teacher's delight.

"Our baby is going to be at least as good as Mallie Carl," Dianna said. "But I think it's going to be a girl."

"We don't need any more girls in this family; we've got enough," Mac teased, and he was thunked on the head for his contribution to the conversation.

When they arrived home they dispersed to tend to chores, and Annie and Caroline busied themselves with packing straw into a mattress in the barn. The little house was nearly finished, and Annie hoped to move into it before her child was born. She prayed that the baby would stay put just a bit longer, until preparations were completed, but knowing how things tended to go awry, she prepared herself for any eventuality.

Later that afternoon Bud took a break from the roof he was nailing and came in to gather his rifle and hunting bag. "I'll be gone till after dusk, later if I get one," he told Caroline, as he left the women in the barn to finish their work. This would probably be his last chance to hunt this year, and he was hoping to make it count. Tom and Mac had gone with him last time, so this was also his last chance for some peace and quiet for a bit. He strode off into the woods alone, not taking even one of the horses with him, intent on spending this one last evening in total peace.

It was up to the rest of the family to finish the chores and get supper on, and secretly Caroline hoped Bud did not shoot a deer this evening, because she was too tired to clean one and despite the meat that it would have brought to the household, she thought she'd rather have a good night's sleep instead of being kept up late putting up venison. After supper she bid the children clean up and sent Robert after the cows.

Ruben had simmered and brewed for weeks after the last job, and the thought of Bud Braxton still niggled at his brain in the evening hours. He had broken with the bigger group of bandits, deciding they were too foolhardy and loud, liable to get him caught if they continued on with their bragging in the saloons and houses of ill repute that they tended to frequent. He had slowly made his way back down around the camp, making sure to stay outside the far edges so that no one might discover him, but close enough to see that they had made quite a bit of headway since he had left the rail's employ. He continued farther on, back to where he remembered coming upon Braxton one night many months before, first making his acquaintance. His homestead could not be far from this place, and he took it upon himself as his winter's work to discern just exactly where that home might lie. He believed he had finally found it, and now lay in the leaves and brush at the edge of the woods, peering at the barn and little houses before him.

This afternoon and evening he had slept, and he was refreshed and ready, for tonight he would make his move. He would look that idiot Braxton full in the face and make sure he knew just exactly what he had cost him, make sure he fully realized the ramifications of his actions in putting that payroll on a different train, and he would look him straight in the eyes as he took his life from him. Ruben had done it before, and he felt no shame in planning to do it again; all his life men had taken advantage of him, had wronged him, had been against him. Nothing he had in this life had been given him; everything he had ever had, he had wrenched from this world. Tonight he would take his revenge against one more assault on his never-ending efforts to wring some peace from this hard life, and he would move on to the next hurdle. He longed for a permanent safe place, a place he could finally rest, but he doubted such a thing existed for the likes of him.

The cows had been brought into the barn and the lamps were lit in the house. Ruben watched from his perch and shivered in the cold. There. There began his chance. He watched as Bud in his coat and hat exited the house with a bucket in one gloved hand, and he slowly and carefully got to his knees. He did not make a move to follow, just yet, and was glad that he had stayed put when the door opened and he saw a woman lean out and call to Braxton. He could not make out their conversation, but he watched it unfold, and the woman presently returned to the safety of the house while he watched Braxton enter the barn and close the door behind him. He could see the light of the lamp under the door, and he got to his feet.

He kept one eye on the house door as he neared the barn, but no one came out, and he turned his full attention to the barn. He carefully slipped inside, quietly, and looked about him. He ducked into the shadows near the door and studied his surroundings from the cover of some bales of hay. He could see Braxton at the far end of the barn, stroking a horse's nose and talking to it. As long as his back remained turned and his focus was on something else, Ruben believed he had a chance at taking Braxton by surprise. He did not unholster his revolver just yet; he planned to do that with Bud's full attention and watch the dawn of comprehension in his eyes as he slowly understood and came to accept his fate. For now it would do just to capture him and disable him, and Ruben knew he could do it.

Closer he crept, as silently as he could go, and watched Bud give water to the horses and toss flakes of hay into their stalls. At one point he almost turned, and Ruben thought for sure he was seen, but Braxton continued to attend to his chores and paid no heed to what was coming steadily up behind him. In the glowing lamplight Ruben saw the familiar coat and hat, and though he could not hear what Braxton said to the horses, he knew that his full attention was on them. All at once he leapt and grabbed Braxton around the waist with both arms, pinning both his arms and making him unable to resist the onslaught. Immediately Ruben sensed something was horribly wrong; his arms wrapped too far around the too-slim body, and the firm muscles he expected to feel underneath his embrace were not there. Instead of a man's shout he heard a high-pitched shriek, and instantly knew he had sorely misjudged his prey. As his victim spun around in his arms, the hat flew off and a tangle of hair whacked him in the face, momentarily blinding him and surprising him even more. Nevertheless, he maintained his grip, and as he finally came face to face with his enemy, he was shocked into stillness and looked into eyes equally as stunned as his own. He could not move, he heard a great intake of breath, and realized he was looking at a dark-haired woman in Braxton's coat.

"Who're you?" he demanded, frustrated that he'd so misjudged the situation and dimly aware that the shriek he had heard might bring someone running.

"I'm... I'm..." was all she could manage, so unhinged was she and so amazed by what she thought she saw before her. This could not be.

He adjusted his grip around her waist to hold her more securely and brought one hand to the side of her face, holding her head with his hand and supporting her weight. She clutched the lapels of his coat and could only nod, when he finally managed to speak again.

"Carrie?" He could not believe what his eyes were seeing.

"Ben!" she returned, and she looked just as amazed as he was. Surely it could not be her that he gripped in his cold hands—his best friend Carrie, whom he had last seen at fourteen when he set the orphanage at his back and swore he would come back to get her when he had made something of himself. He continued to stare at her in shock until the barn door slammed open and a sharp "Hey, hey!" broke his paralysis.

Suddenly a great weight was upon Ruben, knocking him to the floor, and he struggled to regain his footing.

"No, no!" Caroline shouted, and she did her best to pull Bud off Ben, who did not resist Bud's flailing attack but assumed the fetal position on the barn floor, ready to absorb the blows that came. They did come, in rapid succession, but then subsided at the insistence of Caroline, who continued to implore, "No, Bud, no! Stop! Stop!"

Bud looked at her incredulously. Did she not understand what was happening here? This man was an intruder, a criminal!

"It's Ben, Bud, it's Ben!" she insisted, and she kneeled next to Ruben in the dirt of the barn, her arm outstretched against Bud's onslaught. Vapors of breath swirled up from all three of them in the cold air, so short-winded with exertion were they. Bud refrained from further assault upon Burroughs, and Ruben regained his footing. Bud eyed him with suspicion as he brushed himself off, and Caroline stood at the ready, prepared to separate them again should the need arise.

"That's...that's Rube Burroughs," Bud finally managed, and Ruben stood quietly, offering nothing, but searching Carrie with his eyes.

"Yes, Bud, it's Ben, Ben Burroughs. I knew him long ago. We grew up together. He was my only friend for a very long time."

"You know him." This was not a question, merely an attempt to understand the situation on Bud's part, for confusion and suspicion still reigned over his senses, and he was not ready to yield to what he still felt was incomprehensible.

"I do, although"—she turned to look at Ruben—"I don't know why he's here."

Ruben swallowed. A lot would depend on the way he answered, and he would have to be careful. "I worked with Bud at the rail camp. I left a few months ago and was making my way back west. I came upon your homestead, and I thought for sure I recognized Bud as he went into the barn. I thought to surprise him...but you surprised me." He did not know how well this was going to go over, especially with Bud, who knew better, but it was the best he could offer on such short notice. Ruben was not an extraordinarily imaginative man, but he had managed to talk his way out of his fair share of tight spots and hoped his improvisation would not fail him now.

Caroline laughed, a small, nervous laugh, but it broke the tension, and Ruben visibly relaxed a bit.

"I would say so!" she agreed, and though Bud continued to eye them both suspiciously, he did not renew his attack or appear intent upon assaulting Ruben further.

Ruben took a deep breath. "I'm sorry," he said. "It was poor judgment on my part, and I shoulda' known better." He looked at Bud apprehensively and truly was contrite. Seeing Carrie, being this close to her after all these years... it had shaken him to his very core, and he could not trust anything he was feeling just now. In his heart he knew he deserved Bud's wrath, but he felt thoroughly off balance. An hour ago he had been very sure of his thoughts, but now…well, now all bets were off.

"Let's go inside. What do you say?" Caroline ventured, and she turned to pick up her bucket and look around for her hat—Bud's hat. Bud said nothing but stepped aside reluctantly and let Ruben by, then followed Caroline, placing a hand upon the small of her back as she turned and walked to retrieve the lamp, which thankfully had not overturned in the tumult.

In the warmth of the house, they sat at the table, Caroline and Bud on one side and Ruben on the other. Annie came from Caroline's room; she had put some of the younger children to bed and emerged, startled at first to see a visitor, but she composed herself quickly enough. She went to the stove to make coffee.

"Wherever did you come from, Ben, and…well…where have you been?" Caroline reached out and placed one hand upon Ben's and left it there, as if to entreat him to confess.

"Well, I guess I been just about everywhere. When I left you, Carrie, please forgive me for not comin' back. I couldn't. I wanted to, Lord knows I did, but I couldn't risk it. I went on up to Statesville," (at this Caroline nodded) "and I was lookin' for work, just like I said I was gonna do, when I happen to see the Brown Gang." Bud stiffened, for he remembered reading about them in the papers, and they were notorious killers. "I happen to see one o' them kill a man. The sheriff ask me what I saw, and stupid me told 'im. I shoulda' kep' my mouth shut, but I was too young to know any better."

He looked down at Caroline's hand and put his other hand over it, then turned his eyes back to Bud. Bud no longer saw the criminal who had accosted him and held a knife at his throat. This man was markedly different, and Bud could only look back at him in silence.

"They hung the man I told the sheriff about, and the gang knew it was me that squawked. I had t' run, but I couldn't be runnin' home to you, knowin' they was after me and bringin' that upon you. I had t' get as far away as I could, and I did, all the way inta Texas, but they caught up to me." He swallowed hard before he continued. "They beat the sh…the sin outta me when they caught me, but they didn't kill me, though there been times since I wishta God they had." At this Caroline squeezed his hand but said nothing. Annie placed a cup of coffee before him and sat down. He nodded at her, looked at Bud again as if for confirmation to continue, and took a sip before he went on.

"I become one o' them. I had to. I knew they'd kill me if I ran again. I stayed with them a lotta years, longern I should have, but then they become like a fam'ly to me, and I didn't know nothin' else. When we come back around home, you know I came lookin' for you, but by that time everythin' was closed down, and there weren't no one there. I guess you were long gone by then. Too much time'd passed."

"Yes, I left a few years after you, I guess, and I came here to Milton, to teach. I met Bud here," Caroline said. "I didn't know they'd closed down. I never had occasion to go back and see."

Bud knew some of Caroline's past but had never inquired too deeply, as it seemed to pain her to discuss it whenever he brought it up. Eventually he had let it lie and never pressed her about her childhood or how she grew up. Certainly he never knew about anyone named Ben, and he continued to listen in silence to Ruben's story.

Ruben took another sip of the coffee and looked down at his cup as he spoke. His other hand remained covered by Caroline's, and he took a bit of comfort from this. "I did some things I shouldn'a. But I 'ventually broke from 'em, and I stayed a bit in different towns, pickin' up work where I could find it, stealin' when I couldn't. I come up around here, and heard they was hirin' at the camp, and that's where I met Mr. Braxton here." He nodded to Bud, and to his eminent relief, Bud nodded back. He did not elaborate on his assault upon Bud, on the many criminal acts he had perpetrated over the years, or on the recent event of the train robbery in which he had played a very prominent part. He hoped Bud would not feel led to fill in the gaps he had left in his account, for he was not proud of his past and knew there was no excuse for it. He was what he was, but he could not admit to Carrie all that he had done. It was too much.

"Well, it's the good Lord that's led you to us now, and you'll stay here for a bit, won't you?" Caroline pleaded with Bud with her eyes even as she spoke to Ruben. Though Bud had his doubts about the Lord's work in leading a hardened criminal into their midst, he could not disappoint Caroline. She had hung intently on Ruben's every word, a tear running down her cheek when he spoke of running away from her so that she might be kept safe. He merely grunted at Caroline, and she took this for his assent. "You can stay in the barn; it's warm there, and I'll bring you some blankets to bed down with. Are you hungry? Can you eat?" she questioned.

"No, no, I'm fine. This coffee's all I need." He lifted his cup to Annie in thanks, and she nodded. He turned back to Caroline, his Carrie, and looked her full in the face. He gripped her hands in his and said, with a quiver in his voice, "I can't believe it's you, Carrie. I can't believe that it's you, after all this time. I always meant to come back. Please forgive me for leavin' you. I never meant to."

She fairly leaped to hug him, tears in her eyes. "It's okay! It's okay; you're here now, and that's all that matters." Annie and Bud just looked at each other and said nothing, eyes wide, at the spectacle before them. What could they say? This was the most unexpected thing in the world.

Presently Bud stood, and announced, "Let's you and me go make a place for you in the barn. We'll get ya' settled." This had to end, and he was going to discuss a few things privately with Rube Burroughs.

"Yes, yes, you go on," Caroline said, standing and allowing Ruben to rise with her. She wiped her eyes with her hand.

Ruben and Bud took the lamp and some quilts out to the barn, and Bud sent the boys who had bedded down there back to the house. "I don't care where you sleep tonight or if there's room, you go find a place, and tell them I sent you back. You don't come out here again, you hear?" The boys nodded and looked warily at Ruben as they left the barn, and while Ruben endeavored not to look menacing, he was not sure he succeeded. Bud put the lamp down and placed the quilts upon a bale of hay before he addressed Ruben, careful not to turn his back to him.

"I don't know what the hell you're playin' at, but you ain't stayin'," he said to Ruben, who appeared to expect a blow from Bud, if not a lengthy diatribe. "You mighta snowed her, but you ain't foolin' me. I know what you are." He was on the offense, and he wouldn't be taken surprise by Ruben again. He was prepared to fight him if he looked like he might intend to do something rash.

Instead, Ruben just looked down at the floor and then moved to sit on a bale of hay. He placed his hands on his knees and continued to stare at the floor. He said nothing, and Bud was about to speak again when Ruben sighed heavily.

"I come here to kill you, Bud," he said quietly. "I know you switched the payroll on that train, and it cost me more'n you know. But I didn't... I didn't expect to see *her.*" He continued to stare at the floor, and Bud started to relax just a bit. This was not what he was expecting.

"Was any a' that true? What you said in there?"

"It's all true. I lef' that orph'nage at fourteen, and she was my rock. If not for her I wouldna' made it that long. Her and me, we had a plan. I was gonna go get work and get some money, and we were gonna get outta there. I had every intention a' doin' it, too. I meant to do right by her. But...I couldn't risk bringin' 'em down upon her. I couldn't do it."

"Well…well," was all Bud could say. He found no words appropriate just now and was reeling a bit from Ruben's admission. But this man before him, this man was no threat. He stayed silent, and Ruben sat still, continuing to look at the floor.

Finally Bud spoke. "You still wanna kill me?"

Ruben laughed, and looked up. "No, no, not at all. You have every right to turn me in. You know what I am. What I done. You know I ain't no good."

"Hmph," Bud grunted. "You got a mind to change that?"

"I ain't never had a fam'ly like you got, Bud. I ain't never had nobody. Ever'thing I ever got, I had t' take. I don't know what good I am."

Bud sighed. He was taking an enormous risk. But he also didn't relish seeing Caroline's face if he revealed what he knew or made Ruben go. "All right, this is what we'll do. I'm gonna lock my doors tonight, and I got a rifle that shoots straight. I don't guess I'll be sleepin' much. If you don't think you c'n make a go of it, I suggest you just mosey on and leave us be. But if you got a mind t' be a diff'ernt man tomorrow, I guess I c'n help you."

Ruben nodded. He wanted to say, "Thank you," but he didn't trust himself.

Bud walked to the barn door, ever mindful of the chance he was taking here. But…. Hadn't Caroline forgiven him for what he'd done? Didn't the Lord forgive him for every sin he'd committed? He stopped before he closed it. "I guess you better tell me; are you Ben, or are ya Ruben, or are you Rube Burroughs?"

There was no denying it; Rube Burroughs was a wanted man in Texas. And it was entirely possible that his past would catch up with him at any time. But he longed to put it behind him, and he felt he had never been given the chance, had never thought there ever would be a chance. What he was being offered now, what might be possible now, he could only have hoped for. He decided to leap, and if it was to be a leap into a noose, so be it.

"I'm Ben," he answered. "Ben Burroughs."

Bud nodded and closed the barn door. Ruben continued to sit where he was and only moved to make a bed in the hay several minutes later when he thought his legs would hold him.

Bud went back to the house and pulled the latch in. He put his rifle by the door and stared at it. He thought of how differently the night could've gone, had he just put a bullet into Ruben when he first saw them struggling. He had him in his sights and had his finger on the trigger, but in the end there was too much of a chance of hitting Caroline, and he had decided he couldn't risk it. She came out of the bedroom now, her hair in a braid and a quilt around her shoulders.

"Is he out there?" she asked.

He nodded.

"Thank you. Thank you for letting him stay, Bud. I guess we'll find out more about where he's been tomorrow, but I'm grateful to you for letting him be here."

"Mm-hmm. You go on t' bed now and go to sleep. I'll see you in the mornin'." He put another log on the fire and turned back to the door to get his rifle. He did not kick off his boots but pulled the rocker by the fire around to face the door and settled into it. The rifle he placed across his knees, and he tilted his head back. "Go on, now," he repeated, and she finally turned to go back to bed.

He was as good as his word. He did not sleep, only dozed lightly, and kept watch over them all night long. He had no cause to rise, however, for there was no movement from the barn all night, and they did not see Ben again until morning.

Verna Dade arrived the next week, as promised, and inserted herself into the daily lives of the Braxtons with authority and an energy that belied her girth and her advanced years. Bud had just finished the little house, and it had hardly a stick of furniture, when Annie's water broke. Bud and Ben were out hunting with Nick; over the last several nights there had been many deep conversations between the two of them about Ben's change in lifestyle and his intentions to be a man who could be trusted. In Ben's defense, there did seem to be a marked difference about him, and though Bud kept a healthy level of skepticism tucked beneath what he hoped outwardly showed as cautious optimism, he thought there might be the makings of a good man in Ben. Maybe the marshalls would come tomorrow and haul him back to Texas, or maybe they would hang him from the nearest tree. God only knew. But he was strong, and he was eager to be helpful around the little homestead. He frequently remarked on what a "fine family" Bud had in a kind of wistful way, and despite Bud's explanations of how they were not all his by God, Bud had gradually come to accept that they all were his. Even the Clarks had become part of the family, and the children got along about as well as children could be expected to do. Annie and Caroline had come to a peace, and the bizarre situation that had befallen them now seemed perfectly normal. Even Nick remarked on it. "Only you coulda pulled this off, Bud, nobody else."

As Bud and Ben came back near the house in the midafternoon, disappointed about not shooting a deer but looking forward to a short nap, they heard screams from Annie's little house. Bud shot a quick look at Ben, and together they ran toward it, rifles at the ready, unsure what they were about to interrupt. Susan met them at the door with her arms outstretched, saying, "You can't come in here! Annie's having the baby, and you can't come in!"

They held up, lungs heaving and catching their breath, when they heard another scream from within. "Miss Verna's takin' care of everything, Mama says. She says for you to go on in the house."

Bud and Ben looked at each other warily but did as she bid them and walked on to the other house. Ellie was washing dishes in a tub but left it immediately when the men came in, and she went straight to Bud. "The baby's coming, did you know? Mama and Susan went over this mornin' and it could be any time!"

"Yes, I know, babe. We just come from there. Here now, you're drippin' all over me, girl," he said, trying to hold her away from him.

"I know, I know, but can I go see Papa? He'll want to see the baby, and I want him to know the minute it comes!" she pleaded.

"Well, all right, go along, if you gotta go, I guess," Bud said. He didn't know if Caroline would have let her go or not, but he thought it best right now just to allow her to do it. He saw no harm. Bud and Ben hung their rifles, and Ben sat at the table. "I guess we gotta see t' ourselves," Bud said and sought out a loaf of bread. He began to cut slices for himself and Ben, and Ben rummaged until he found a jar of pear preserves.

"We got it," he said. They sat at the table eating bread and pear preserves, listening to Annie scream in the distance, and awaited the time when they might be allowed entrance.

Several hours later, Bud sat at Annie's bedside and held his newborn son in his arms. Annie's cheeks were pale, but she was smiling, and she was all right. Verna and Caroline had seen her through, and she was grateful. Verna was boiling sheets now, and Caroline was tending to children. They were alone for the moment with their new arrival.

"What's his name, now?" Bud asked, as he held the boy up and watched him sleep peacefully.

"I think his name is Lester," Annie said, decidedly.

"Little Lester Leroy!" Bud exclaimed, cradling the child's head in his hand. Lester had nothing to say but merely sucked his hand in his sleep.

"No, no, not Leroy!" Annie protested, laughing. "Not that!" She moved to take the baby and cradled him in her arms. Verna came in and put another pillow behind Annie's back. The little cabin was sparse, but it had been built just in time to welcome its newest member, and Bud was thankful that it was finished. It had been close.

Annie looked down at her baby in the lamplight and then at Bud. "I think his name should be James Lester, but we'll call him Lester," she said.

"Whatever you want," Bud agreed, not having much opinion on the matter. As far as he was concerned, it was up to the women to name the babies and the horses.

"Yes, that's it," she insisted, and watched her new son suck on his fingers in his sleep. He was perfect.

EPILOGUE

He poled the raft downriver and guided it around stumps and logs that threatened to get in his way. His muscles bulged and slackened, bulged and slackened, with the cadence of the swiftly moving water. He was headed downriver to town to get supplies for his family, and there was nothing in his head just now, only peace and watchfulness. It was only a task he had undertaken a million times before and something he would do many more times in the future. Twenty pounds of flour, ten pounds of sugar, and a sack of beans to split between them—besides a list that Caroline had stuffed in his pocket before he left. He surmised it was a long list. Two houses, two wives, and Annie had just delivered triplets. Triplets!

In Mason's General, Bud counted out the money for his purchases.

"How you been, there, Bud? I ain't seen you in a coon's age," Alvin Mason said, writing down Bud's purchases in his log.

Bud grunted. "Good," he said, nothing more.

"I hear tell you got another young'n," Alvin pressed, totaling the purchases. "How many you got now?"

Bud finished counting out the money and slid it over the counter toward Mason. Indeed, his family had burgeoned over the last years, and he was grateful for them. They made his life full, and he counted every one of them as his own. "I have twenty-two," he said and took his receipt from Mason, saying no more before leaving to haul his purchases to the raft for the trip back home. He had a family to feed, after all, and they were counting on his return. Mason merely looked after him in disbelief and watched him exit the store.

ABOUT THE AUTHORS

J.L. Broxson was born in 1936, and he knew many of the people who inspired the characters in this story. His ancestors and relatives have lived in the North Florida area since the mid-1800s, and his memories of the true stories they lived formed the basis of this fictional tale.

D.S. Broxson is his daughter, who spun the tale of Bud and his family from her father's memories and the descriptions of his early life.

THE CHARACTERS

Is this a true story, or is it fictional? The characters, story, and settings in are fictional, but they are based on people who really lived in North Florida in the late 1800s and early 1900s in Santa Rosa and Holmes Counties.

Was the Braxton family real?

Thomas Braxton was born about 1649 in St. Stephen's Parrish, Cecil, Maryland. His son was Thomas Broxson. Thomas and his and wife Ann Jones had a son named John Broxson in 1710. John Broxson married Anna Maria Varn and had a son named George; George married Anna Wilson and had a son named Joseph Robert in 1812.

Did they really own slaves?

Joseph Robert married Matilda Spears and they lived in Holmes County. They owned slaves until the end of the Civil War, when Union soldiers set them free. The family moved to Santa Rosa County, where they cut pines. The slaves followed them and helped them cut the timber.

Was there really a Bud Braxton?

Joseph Robert had a son, Joseph Robert Broxson, Jr., who was born in 1851 and went by the name "Uncle Bud."

Uncle Bud did indeed have 22 children, but they were his own by two wives. He had two houses, and would row 20 miles downriver to buy flour, beans, coffee, and sugar, and row 20 miles back to split the purchases between them.

Was there really a Sharpe?

One of Uncle Bud's sons was named Henry Y., who went by the name "Sharpe."

Did anyone really get hung for desertion?

Joseph Robert Sr.'s son William was hung for desertion in the Confederate Army (in the story the name was Tom).

Was there really a skeleton?

JL (Lester) Broxson's father, Jeff, found a skeleton in a large Indian campground near a bridge over the East River when he was about 10 years old, which would have been about 1920. Instead of showing it to his family, however, he covered it back up and went on his way.

Was Dewey real?

Dewey was one of Uncle Bud's sons. One day Jeff took Lester to see Dewey, and he and Jeff told Lester to get in the pen with the hogs so they could castrate the hogs (not ride them, as in the story). He did, and the hogs chased him and their tusks tore his cuffs while Jeff and Dewey laughed. Humor was different, then, I suppose.

Did they really have whisky stills?

Yes, in fact Mal Barnard ran a still in Santa Rosa County and he sold from the back door of a grocery store. Jeff and Clark Broxson were thrown in jail overnight once for going to the whisky still.

Were they really so poor that they drank right from the cow?

Lester remembers Uncle Bud's son Dewey telling him that they were indeed that poor, so they took turns with one of the calves.

Is the story about Rube Burroughs and Casey lying in wait for Bud true?

Lester's Grandpa Nick was walking back home after selling cattle in Milton and saw a cigarette glowing in the dark. He had put his money in the bank earlier in the day. He suspected that he would be robbed and so he hung his flour sack on a limb and went around them. Later, when he went back to get the sack, he found where some men had smoked several cigarettes laying for him. Rube Burrow was a train-robber in the Southern United States in the 1880s.

Did T.F. Johnson save Bud from drowning?

No, T.F. Parker saved Lester Broxson from drowning. They were swimming in a creek and Lester got in over his head, and panicked. His friend T.F. pulled him closer to shore and saved him from drowning.

Was the story about the load of corn real?

Bud was sent to his Uncle Clark's to attend school as he is in the story, but didn't like it and came back home. On his way back he stole a load of corn and brought it home.

Is the Exchange Hotel a real place?

The Exchange Hotel was built by Charles Sudmall, a Latvian immigrant, in 1914 in Milton, Florida. It was planned to house a rural telephone system. Realizing its further potential, Sudmall leased the building to H. L. Creary, who opened a first class hotel.

Was the part about the cattle ferry real?

The picture on the front cover shows Walter, Grady, Frank, and Nick Broxson (riding) and Willie Broxson (walking) taking cows to town to be sold to a cattle buyer.

Made in the USA
Columbia, SC
25 January 2020